D1304606

BLUES deluxe

a tragicomic
love story

harvey griffin

LONGSTREET PRESS
Atlanta, Georgia

Published by LONGSTREET PRESS, INC.,
a subsidiary of Cox Newspapers,
a division of Cox Enterprises, Inc.
2140 Newmarket Parkway
Suite 118
Marietta, Georgia 30067

Printed in the United States of America

1st printing, 1994

Library of Congress Catalog Number 93-81145

ISBN: 1-56352-131-8

This book was printed by Arcata Graphics, Kingsport, Tennessee.

Jacket and book design by Laura McDonald
Jacket photograph by Bybee Studios, S.F.

Promotional assistance provided by The Lovable Company

A monstrous, ungainly,
triple-sized Thank You to my editor
John Yow.

BLUES
deluxe

The whole thing actually started on *The Chapman Show* about four months after my first *People* cover. That was the cover that counted too, because later, after my name became linked with Honey, my celebrity status became somewhat dubious: a case of gilt by association.

Anyway, I first met Honey backstage, in Chapman's green room, about a minute before it was time for me to go on. I was so wired I was about to explode out the top of my Stetson with stage fright. All my attention was focused on the TV monitor of the band playing out there. Honey snuck in behind me and had probably been there for a couple of minutes before I turned my head and noticed her.

She was sitting there blondly, on one of Donald's little fold-up director's chairs, wearing a black, transparent catsuit, some kind of white, lacy miniskirt that was probably underwear of some sort, a pink bustier with a bikini-top worn over the bustier, apple-red high-heels, and a generous assortment of junk-jewelry. She wasn't actually revealing any flesh that shouldn't be revealed, but the general effect was that her underwear—and there was a lot of it—was all on the outside of her clothes. Her wild hair was pop-from-the-cake blond. Her fingers flipped through a thin hardback book that she held on her lap, and she seemed to be reading intently. But what I remember most was the way her dangerous legs were double-crossed at her thighs and then again at her ankles; and the way her leg muscles rhythmically clenched with a subtle pulsing.

Behind her stood a guy who was obviously her body-guard, a bulldozer in suit & tie. He was looking at me, with his arms crossed, like maybe he thought I was a truth-twisting reporter for the *New York Post* with a hidden camera under my hat.

It's a measure of my self-confidence that my first thought was that I'd been bumped off the show. Honey was not at rehearsal. She was not a scheduled guest. Nobody told me Honey was going to be on the show. Sanity quickly prevailed over my paranoia. I wasn't informed because I wasn't important enough to inform.

The jazz-rock band was winding down, an ending that was taking forever, with Don trying to restart the show, and I was starting to *vibrate* my stage fright was so intense. I was chain-smoking that New York green room into an LA home-away-from-home smog-haven, because it's NO SMOKING out there on *After Midnight with Donald*, and I needed my last-second nicotine fix.

Normally, I would have put out the cigarette right then, automatically. I would have turned away from Honey, and not allowed her or her bodyguard to distract me. I never would have dared to speak to her. But there really was no "normal" in the presence of Honey, and besides, Honey's aggressively non-smoking bodyguard provided introductions.

He said, "*You*, put out the cigarette. You're bothering Honey." He slashed at his throat for me to stop smoking and pointed at a near ashtray.

If there's a hotter entrance for a comedian than being chased out early onto the stage by an angry bodyguard during the host's introduction, I don't know what that might be.

Honey looked up warily as I stepped toward her, and she did some kind of small hand motion that made her bodyguard jerk like someone had yanked back on his leash.

I was very respectful. Slowly, solemnly, I bent over with my hands behind my back, bringing my lips two inches from her left ear, the Camel Filter still smoldering away between two fingers. It was so romantic, too. As I blew smoke in her ear I made it sound like I was blowing up a balloon. (I'm good at sound effects.)

Honey snapped shut her book, twisted her neck around—whisking my lips with a brush of blond—and breathlessly said, "Thanks for the refill, Cool."

The two most famous eyes in the world lazily held my soul hostage.

I put a swagger on my face. I'd been clearing my throat every fifteen seconds for the last five minutes, so my voice came out fine. "When you're ready for a real man, and you've had enough of 'Rolling Stone,' you know where you can come." Wink. My take-no-prisoners smile.

This was during the period when Honey was doing the naughty with mucho-muscled macho-sensation Buck Stone, actor, producer, famous face, all-around-bully.

I started to straighten up, to hurry back to the stage, but Honey wouldn't let me go. She smiled and said, "Mmmmm, Miss May wouldn't like that."

Everyone knew Honey had a heart of Stone, but how many people knew that I kept a Pet?

Don was out there introducing me, and I was bent over, with my hands behind my back like an idiot. Stuck. I absolutely could not move. I was in bondage, and Honey did it just by parting her lips a little, tweaking her eyebrows, and achieving orgasm.

She was looking right at me, and something about her look deciphered the wicked clasping of her thighs, and convinced me that all the time she had been sitting there, she had been secretly masturbating.

It was so outrageous, I instantly went into a hot flash, as if my whole metabolism had been turned up ten times. Still, the idea that Honey would be attracted to me was so inconceivable that I stalled for a few seconds. I mean, I'd just been kidding around, I wasn't really coming on to her.

An instant later Honey apparently thought better of herself, and she silently opened up her book and dismissed me by pretending to read. Her legs distracted me again, as they relaxed and uncrossed, with a whisper of see-through catsuit and a shout of thighs.

I caught a glance of the title on her book. Nietzsche's *Birth of Tragedy*. This was the actress who starred

Worldwide in the movie *Def, Dumb, and Blond*. I
didn't believe that she was reading that stuff, but as I
watched her face, she blushed bright pink.

Thinking back on it, I know now why she blushed.
Honey was birthing tragedy, not cliterbating. Her segue
into simulated masturbatory orgasm was a parody to
amuse me, not arouse me. Honey blushed because I
was so incredibly stupid that I didn't get her joke. What
I got was an erection, and the idiot-idea that Honey was
embarrassed because she made a heavy-duty pass at me,
and I didn't pick up on it.

"You naughty girl," I told her, "you need a spanking."

The cue-boy was on the move then, next to me, walking me away from Honey and toward the stage, pulling
the lint off my coat and the cigarette out of my fingers,
telling me to stand up straight. Standing up straight was
not quite possible, or even taking normal steps, because
some pubic hairs had gotten tangled around my boner,
and it was very painful.

"Cool," Honey's sweet voice called to me, with prom-
ises of pelvic fun, "what I really need is a good *licking*."

They were applauding for *me* out there. I had just hobbled around the corner, two of the bright spots were shining on me, and instead of coming all the way out, I turned
my back on the audience. *I turned my back on the audience*.

I turned back and limped one step inside. Well, the girl
seemed to respond favorably to blow jobs, so I kissed my
fingers and blew Honey a kiss.

Wham! She did a primo pratfall, and knocked her
director's chair over sideways. There she was, sitting, buns

on the hardwood floor, legs slightly spread, stunned, mouth wide open, gaping at me in awe, holding her cheek where my air-kiss walloped her.

What a send-off. I hobbled out, grabbed the microphone, and murdered the audience. Funny? I was more hilarious than orthogenital copulation.

After my stand-up routine, I sat down with Don, and the show went to hell.

We threw some witty whiffle-whaffle back and forth, then Donald held up a magazine for the audience and said, "We have here the latest—well, actually the November *Penthouse*." He flipped through some pages while I cringed. Miss May and I were pictured together in two shots of that issue—but it wasn't a naked spread, honest. Donald said, "There's a big article on you in here about the New Comedy. You and uh, uh . . ." He probably couldn't remember her name.

I gave him some help. "And a lot about yeast infection."

It got a bigger laugh than it deserved (and several hate letters from inflamed feminists), perhaps because at that moment Honey was sneaking around Donald's broken windows from the side that he couldn't see. The audience enthusiasm was a roar. The tiptoe prance in high-heels, the shush finger-to-mouth signal to the studio audience, the wild girlish enthusiasm, the incendiary body, the two playful fingers over and behind Don's head.

Honey patted Donald Chapman on his left shoulder, and traipsed around behind *me*, so that when Don looked over that shoulder, she wasn't there.

"Get with the program, Don," Honey squealed.

Finally seeing her, Don shot the audience his droll self-parodying fourth-wall look. He tossed three cards back behind him, breaking three more imaginary windows.

And Honey sat down, talking a blond streak at Don. "Hi, talk show guy! Here I am! Deal with it!"

After Midnight has two chairs for guests. I was occupying the chair closest to Don, the spotlight-chair. Since my time wasn't up, I was damned if I was going to move.

Honey's instinct for upstaging everyone else was flawless. Being Honey, there was really only one place she could have sat down.

On Don's desk!

So Honey flounced across in front of me, and sat down. On my lap.

·   ·   ·   ·   ·

Let me explain why I immediately cut loose with a boisterously loud Bronx cheer. By shrewdly sputtering my lips at the crucial moment—beginning the raspberry when her splendid buns were in motion, an instant before they actually touched down—I got my best laugh of the show, of the month, of my comic career.

My imitation of Honey's bowel howl was not a sweet sniffle, or a little beanie of feminine flatulence, it was a Royal blast that audibly left her lingerie in torn, gaping shreds. Nobody was upstaging *me*, damn it, not even Honey. That it was in keeping with the theme of "blowing" did not occur to me.

Honey laughed so hard, she would have fallen off, if

my right arm hadn't buckled her securely like a tingling seatbelt. So the first time I touched and held Honey, she was squirming uncontrollably, laughing hysterically, on my lap, on *After Midnight with Donald Chapman.*

Her black catsuit was slippery. She smelled . . . **sweet.** And she felt . . . simpatico.

Eventually, the laughter quieted down enough for speech. Don milked it beautifully by not laughing himself, by just shaking his head, and firing off his tennis ball machine: Talk Show Out Of Control.

"I was just breezing through, Don," Honey said, pausing like a professional for the relaughter to ignite and then quiet down, "and I just had to stop by and say hi." She squirmed on my lap.

"Yeah," Don said. He looked at the audience for help. "You just had to get it out of your system . . . No, no, let's . . . What have you been up to? Tell us what you've been doing lately."

"I just finished my new album," Honey said. "I was in the studio *forever* . . ."

And there I was: demoted to high-chair. For one minute fifty-seven seconds, Chapman and Honey ignored me, conducted her interview like I wasn't even there. I did nothing about it. I silently let it happen. I have no sufficient excuse, I can only plead *Honey On Lap.*

It was the Chapman style: Go with the incongruity.

But eventually, my eight minutes were about up, and I didn't want to overstay my welcome. The first law of talk show comedy is: Get Invited Back. Any second now, Donald will break things up anyway to create a commercial slot, and I absolutely have to beat him to the punch.

I stood up, interrupting everything, holding Honey to me mostly with just my right arm, so that scarcely a high-heel of hers was touching the stage. Honey made a noise of surprise somewhere between a squeal and a whoop.

I said, "I've been a straightman before, but this is ridiculous."

I immediately picked Honey up in both arms, and deposited her where she belonged: on Don's desk. She's a handful, and I'm not the strongest comic in the world, but I managed. Honey smiled, crossed her sexy legs, and made her hips at home there.

My back was to the audience so I turned to give the side TV camera a better angle, and then I pulled the front-row-center gems, that I had saved for someone special, out of my inner coat pocket. The second, third, and fourth laws of talk show comedy are Plug, Plug, and Plug. So I plugged the tickets into her fingers.

"Here, Honey. Here's two tickets."

"Tickets? What do I want with tickets?"

"Choice tickets to the Metropolitan Opera House. Saturday night. Bring along your pal with the pecs, if you feel like it."

"Why would I go to an opera on a prime-time party night?" Blond bombshell cultural appreciation.

I answered, "'Cause that's where I'll be taping my latest HBO Comedy Special. At the Met."

"You gonna sing Verdi or Wagner?" Honey asked.

CHAPTER 2

There's a hundred Country & Western songs about how terrible it is to be linked with the wrong lover when the right lover comes along. That's exactly the way I felt, which means that just having a drop of Honey on my lap put me out of touch with reality. She was the Western World's #1 living goddess, and I was way down the Top-10 list of America's deadbeat buffoons. I had no right to her. I was the roisterous stand-up comedian, high on swagger, low on smarts, dimly recognized by perhaps one in five hundred Americans. Honey was the brilliant businesswoman who had used hard-sell sex-sell soft-sell sing-sell weird-sell & act-sell to foist her sweet & sticky Honey Image into the hearts and minds of anyone with a magazine, videotape, TV, CD player, radio, or movie ticket.

And yet it never occurred to me that I wasn't man enough for Honey, I was just worried about what the media fallout would be if we were seen cavorting together. I was so naive that I thought that her sexual signals had been sent to me personally. I didn't realize that Honey emanated sensuality in the direction of any male automatically—it was her way of dealing with the male sex, and it was largely unconscious, she didn't think about it.

While she was not thinking about me, I couldn't get her out of my mind. I kept thinking about the way Honey had blushed. She seemed REAL, in an industry full of fakes. Honey had been nervous there in the green room because of her upcoming TV appearance. That humanized her, put her in my class. For a moment we had been two fellow entertainers about to go on National Television.

But when the right woman came along, I was with the wrong woman.

·   ·   ·   ·   ·

Miss May and I had a beautifully symbiotic relationship: I introduced her to all of my famous friends, and she introduced me into all of her famous bodily orifices. She thought it was a scream to explain our tenuous bond of union to other party people, in those precise terms, as she held auditions for higher stepping stones. Others usually found her naked ambition to be quite charming. Personally, I was insulted when she would talk about our affair that way; it seemed to be denigrating my masculinity. I like to think that our love took in more territory than that.

Boobs, for instance.

But the point is, I had an ally. I was sure Miss May would sell her soul and the rights to all negatives to see me get involved with Honey, just so long as I cut her in on a piece of the action. (I'm being unfairly flippant here, but really, our "relationship" was a disaster in the final fall-apart stage.)

I honestly explained that she could *not* go with me to the Metropolitan Opera House on Saturday night because Honey was going to be in the front row of the audience, and I planned to ask Honey out after the show.

The Month of May told me to quit fertilizing her. (It's her word for bullshit.) She wanted the fifteen to thirty seconds of on-camera airtime exposure she would get by hanging around before and after my show.

I reiterated the magic word: Honey.

She reiterated the F-word: fertilizer. She refused to believe that I had Honey on my lap.

I told her I had it on videotape.

Fertilizer, she said.

I thanked her for fertilizing my aspirations.

But Miss May yelled Mayday: Saturday night she was going to strip it down for her ex-boyfriend rockstar Tuff, go low-riding around town and go down on the first male she met with solid stuff, then go bar-hopping with some girls from that lesbian bar Muff, seduce a real cutie-bi, spread her out in *my* brass bed, then eat her out until she screams *Enuff!*

Communication problems between me and people with Fallopian tubes are generally outside my area of competence. Perhaps if I ignored the problem it would go away. So I thanked her for being such a kind, understanding young lady, and I promised to introduce her to Honey at a later time.

This was perhaps a presumptuous promise, because

those two front and center seats were conspicuously vacant during the first half of the show. I knew Honey might be late, so I had Robbie Berger, my manager, rope off the two seats with special blue velvet 'reserved' ropes. I even made double sure to set things up so that Honey could enter flamboyantly, upstaging me, if she wished; or unobtrusively, unnoticed by the cameras.

"[Yiddish profanity deleted], McCool!" Robbie had finally shouted at me. "You're on in ten minutes! Don't do this complete neurological-shutdown thing on me. Honey wouldn't come to your show if you juggled chainsaws blindfolded and naked with your putz hangin' out!"

"Just rope off the seats, Robbie, or I'll strangle you with this thing right now."

Let me tell you, I was killer that night. It's on VHS; check it out. I cracked jokes like whips. My resources of wit were inexhaustible. The audience was like Old Faithful, a geyser of laughter every time I opened my mouth.

We had a joy riot out there; and then Buck Stone & Honey cut across the front, and grabbed the two empty front-row seats. They were about the only empty seats in the house. I caught just a glance of the two of them: It was dark out there, and the big lights were in my face, but the 'Rolling Stone' strut was unmistakable; a lithe, feminine shadow was with him that had to be Honey.

She came!

I can't explain it, but I knew at that moment that I was going to take her away from him. When I'm performing, I'm in the middle of this tremendous buzz. Preshow is hell, and the first minute on stage is an adrenalin rush of terror so pure it's almost pleasurable. But once I get that first big laugh, I'm riding a roller coaster, downhill all the way. The danger of it wires me up tight, because the trick is to maintain that fine edge. Go too far and I lose them, don't go far enough and I bore them.

But when Honey sat down, I could do no wrong. I made dainty little humorous touches with my sledgehammer biker language, and got away with it. I couldn't see her, but I was playing just for her. I nuked them. I had to order them to quit laughing so hard, to shut up so I could get on with the show.

I hit them with a machine-gun rapid-fire spate of 17 Iraqi jokes so ghastly and offensive that the groans were almost as loud as the laughter. Kitchen sink of Comedy. I lit up the Met with "how many" light bulb jokes. Nicely matching ribald wit with scholarship, I explained how to judge people by their farting styles. I cited Medical Pejoratives from "Baby Catching" Obstetricians to Three H Enemas (High, Hot, and a Hell of a lot). I exposed them to my pet names for private parts, choice Viet-Speak slang from my tour of Vietnam, and jerked them around with a potpourri of masturbation euphemisms and epithets. I even blooped some bawdy spoonerisms.

I told childhood stories I had never dared to tell before. My first and only *ménage à trois* (happened during the sixth grade, in the back of a station wagon, while the girl's father was driving us home from a frolic on the beach and watching us in the rearview mirror). I had *never* told *anybody* about it before. But it was so screamingly funny that the damn paramedics had to come down the aisles of the Met and rescue, *actually strap down into stretchers*, two of the howlers who had apparently laughed so hard they broke something.

Finally, I cued Robbie, and he got the producer to up the house lights, and we ended the show. Immediately, everyone was on their feet, a roaring, standing ovation. I was exhausted, triumphant, blissed out. I looked down to smile at Honey. There below me, Buck Stone was clapping wildly and then whistling. On his right was a tall, potbellied, bald man. On his left was an incredibly beautiful blond I'd never seen before.

.   .   .   .   .

Dressing rooms are for wimps. Blow in; Chill them; Skate out to my sled: That's my scene. Easier to freeze the words together than to actually do it.

You've seen pictures of my face. God's gift to gigglers, shaded from the sun by a Stetson. Fiercely masculine. Six foot two, eyes of blue. Then I smile, and Jack Nicholson knocks over a whole Lakers' bleacher with envy. (That's the way the Cool McCool Air Conditioning Club describes me, so it must be true, right? Right?)

Anyway, I do get a few groupies who can't find a rockstar or a serious actor to pour their love into. All the little lost groupies were there that night. Robbie's boys were trying to drive a wedge through the violently available hellcats and get me the hell out of there. And two camera crews were muscling their way right along with us, their lights blinding everybody.

I was burnt toast on the ice floe, after that show.

Somehow the messenger faked out the Cool Patrol and stopped me on our way out of the Metropolitan Opera House.

The guy thrust the single, long-stemmed red rose right in front of my face. "Mr. McCool!" he shouted. "Roses are all right; but violets are for Honey; Marlene's Sunday night; seven is the time, so don't get funny."

One of Robbie's boys hit him with a running tackle, breaking the stem of the rose, and mashing and ripping off the petals, as the two of them crashed down onto the walkway. What's he gonna do? Shoot me with a flower? It took about half a minute to get the situation correctly sorted out.

By the time the messenger actually handed me the rose, it was just a busted stem with thorns, and the crowd was walking all over the little red petals.

CHAPTER 3

Marlene's restaurant is right at the core of celebrity central, but it's a poisonously pricey culinary bite in the Big Apple. Do the math on it: Divide customer satisfaction by cost of meal. Of course, if you've already eaten, and are dietetically famous, Marlene's is a hip nightspot to hang out. Right there, all within BB range: Everybody who is anybody.

·   ·   ·   ·   ·

So I show up at six, right?

"Two," I tell her. Peace sign.

"Smoking or non-smoking?"

I'm a fire-breathing dragon in a Stetson, and she asks me this shit?

I do some smoke rings down at her.

"'Smoking' would be past your bedtime, sweets," she tells me. A comedienne.

"No smoking?" I ask.

"I'm sorry, I couldn't possibly seat you there."

"Back off, I was in Nam. Gimme a table, or I'll crack nasty jokes about this place all over Prime Time TV."

She frowns, but then jogs me in near the middle of their waiting list.

That will never do. "Listen," I confide, "screw the food, I just need a table for an hour or so. I'm meeting someone."

"Oh, who are you meeting?"

I wouldn't have answered, except she crosses off my name, and the pencil hovers near the top of the list.

"OK," I say, "I'm here to meet Honey."

The pencil goes way down to the bottom of the list, skips three spaces, and then spells my name wrong: McJerk.

. . . . .

The sound of women fainting and men swearing reverently wakes me up from the fourth quarter of the Pistons-Nuggets basketball game on the bar TV. Either it's the Second Coming Of Christ, or the first arrival of Honey. It's nine o'clock on Trinity Sunday, either way I'm in the wrong place at the wrong time. So I haul buns out of the bar area.

Honey is bodyguardless and serene, playfully disposing of three autograph hounds. She's so cute in her tattered chic jeans and scruffy leather vest. And it's so sexy the way she scratches the inguinal region between her signatures.

"Jimmy!" she shouts, as I haul same buns up to her.

I answer her. It is my name, after all. "Hi, Honey." My capped smile sends reflective beams throughout the restaurant.

.   .   .   .   .

I'm not sure how it happened, but suddenly we were holding hands, and slipping past earth mother Marlene in poly-
ester and beads. It reminded me of the way my ten-year-
old daughter drags me from Disneyland ride to Disneyland ride, when I get her for an occasional weekend. Honey
pulled me along, squealing nano-hellos to her many
acquaintances, pointing excitedly here and there, at
several empty reserved tables, trying to decide.

"Um, we'll have that one!" she suddenly decides.

It's a table for eight, but never mind; Honey wants it,
Honey gets it.

We're smack dab in hostile No Smoking territory.
Honey pats my arm on the table. "Oh, you smoke, don't
you?"

Her arm waves up in the air, clinking with costume jewelry. "Yoo hoo!" Honey sings. "Yoo hoo! Could we get
an ashtray here?"

Two waitresses, a waiter, four Non-Smokers, and a
Marlene rush to oblige.

I feel like I'm having an LSD flashback. I look down at
the row of ashtrays. I look up at Honey. Her smile is
shimmering across her white face, blazing with red lipstick.
I glance around at the other patrons. I'm a little frightened
by all the famous faces watching us, watching her, watching *me*. Child actress/model Chazz Ostrom and an older
woman, probably her mother, have even interrupted
their fierce (family?) argument to gape at us. It's a weird
kind of hush that has just chilled the whole restaurant.

Tom Fury, the most famous failer of Bar Exams, is in the middle of a boisterous argument, but he forgets the refutation. Mediagenic New York novelist Leyla Levy is standing there between tables, wordless, with her little stack of new novel in her arms. Ageless large-nosed singing sensation Angel Underwood has sweet nothing to say to baby-face *Tufguy* Bob Skipper—she sniffs disapproval. Artist Carmen Santana shoves plates and silverware aside, and starts sketching Honey on the white tablecloth.

Honey isn't smiling anymore. She's giving me this wise, sad look. Her eyebrows move a little, and it's like a world-weary shrug at the weight of it all.

And, all at once, I get it. It's a test. Like running the gauntlet. I thought it was insane to meet her here, because everyone would instantly assume that we were sleeping together. But that's exactly why she wanted to do it at a place like this; to see if I could handle it.

So I haul out my pack of smokes. Honey gently takes my lighter out of my fingers and lights my Camel for me. Then, absently, she pockets her new $850 lighter in her vest. It's really quite charming, the way she does it.

The menus are in front of us, and the waiter wants to know if we'd like to start with something to drink, perhaps.

I've been drinking Bud, but I figure something a bit more civilized is called for.

I lean forward and gaze lovingly into Honey's eyes. "I'd like a Long Comfortable Screw Against The Wall."

It's a cocktail, of course, but a woman right behind me at another table shrieks with idiot laughter.

Honey makes with a pert smile. "A Screaming Orgasm please. A double."

. . . . .

We got along famously.

"Where's my violets?"

"Honey, when I feel like giving you flowers, I'll give you flowers."

"A gentleman would take off his hat at the table."

"A lady wouldn't grab her own crotch every twenty minutes."

"It itches," she said with a straight face, and then tossed her blond mane as she glanced around the restaurant.

This silenced me, winning the exchange; not because I didn't have a reply, but because I had so many replies that there was a traffic jam and none of them could get around my Camel Filter and out of my mouth in time. I watched Honey's face light up and mouth a silent hello to someone across Marlene's.

I tried an alternate off-ramp: "So tell me about Stone. Does he still rock your boat?"

Honey iced me with a sharp look.

I continued, "Or are you between a rock . . . and a hard place?" I really wanted to know about Stone. Was I going to get beat up, or what?

After a slow thaw, Honey leaned forward, and softly said: "Tell me about your Penthouse Pet . . . I hear she's a real *animal*."

I stubbed out the smoke on my breadplate, crossed my arms and raised my voice: "Tell me about Stone and Goldilocks . . . going to *my* show, with the tickets I gave *you!*"

Honey leaned even further forward, and dropped her voice even more: "Admit it, Jimmy. I hear she's a terrific suck." There was enough alcohol on Honey's breath to require an explosive atmosphere warning, and we hadn't had our drinks yet. Honey winked, picked up her spoon, and made some wet moves with her lips and tongue on the spoon that did dangerous things to my blood pressure and heartbeat and trouser seams.

Of course it's useless for me to protest that I got involved with Miss May for any reason other than great sex. Everyone knows that a liaison with a Penthouse Pet would be *9-1/2 Weeks* of Anais Nin. Never mind that I was attracted to her because she was quirky & feisty & quixotic & feminine. Never mind that I got serious about the lady before her nude modeling spread was published. Never mind that she never told me about it. Never mind that I now know exactly how the Miss America Pageant people feel about Vanessa Williams. Never mind all that, because Everyone Knows that Penthouse Pets are horny bad girls with high T&A and low IQ who deepthroat at the drop of a garter.

"Oh, she's OK, I guess," I told Honey. "My ears bleed, sometimes the sheet gets caught in my anus."

We enjoyed our Long Comfortable Screw with Screaming Orgasms, until stumpy character actor Michael Robbins came over. He sat down with us as if it were his table, and chatted with us for a few minutes, until our dinner was served. Then he wandered back to his wife and kids.

Seeing Michael so happily married inspired a shift of topic, and a new warmth between us. We talked about the two things dearest to our hearts. Our careers.

·   ·   ·   ·   ·

Then some boozed-up Broadway Bum lurches up from his table, stumbles over, gets down on his knees and presses some play into Honey's hand that he wants to one day direct. He's almost too drunk to hustle, and he has to hang onto the table to keep from falling over, as he blabs away at Honey. I catch a whiff of his week-old sweat.

Honey is bemused, and surprisingly nice to the asshole. I can't get a table in three hours, how does this walking freakshow rate?

Behind him, a line begins to form. Damn it, Michael! Now the whole restaurant wants to come over and socialize.

I tap the asshole on his hemorrhoid and inform him that he has exactly one minute to conclude his expulsion of wind.

"[Vulgar vernacular stinker deleted] you!" he tells me.

"Thank you, I can use that in my next show. Forty-five seconds, and counting."

"Suck [back-talk deleted]!" he says, and breaks some more wind in Honey's direction.

Honey gives me this look. "Borderline intellectual functioning," she tells me.

"Nothing but static in the attic," I agree.

"BlahBlahBlahBlahBlahBlahBlahBlahBlah," Ass-brain says.

My patience is completely gone. "Shop it elsewhere, Pal!" I say, very strong, very hard. A definite warning. I mean, there's a waiting line to see Honey. We have to let others have their turn.

"BlahBlahBlahBlahBlahBlah!" Buster just talks faster.

"Do some of that masculine shit," Honey finally tells me, throwing another test at me.

(Kids, don't try this at home.) I grab Honey's lasagna knife with one hand and his tie with the other hand, and YANK the two together so that the point of the knife stops two inches from his right eye.

I do that bit-part character I did in the movie *Burnt Zombies from Hell*: I'm three parts Nuke-The-Whales and two parts Texas-Chainsaw-Psycho and five parts just plain angry. "Get lost or I'll STAB out your EYEBALLS and PISS on your BRAIN!"

. . . . .

Have you ever noticed that Life is pass/fail?

Broadway Bum is over at his table paying his check and leaving as quickly as possible (he takes his little play with him, and doesn't say a word). He acts completely sober.

There is no line to see Honey.

Marlene is probably dialing 911. Marlene probably hangs up at the first 1, remembering that I'm with Honey.

Famous people everywhere are microscopically examining their eating utensils.

Honey is giving me the silent treatment.

Too masculine? Not masculine enough? I ask myself the question men have been asking since Adam found himself short one rib: What do women want?

She *told* me to get rid of the jerk. Was I too effeminate? That must be it. 'Piss on your brain.' Of course. I can see my mistake now. Any woman can do that. She wanted me to do some 'masculine shit' and I completely wimped out. I knew I should have been more forceful. I won't make *that* mistake again. So, OK. Next time I won't stab out his eyeballs and piss on his brain; I'll stab out his eyes, make him eat them, and then rape his bloody eyesockets.

Jeez, I hope she gives me another chance.

．　　．　　．　　．　　．

But she didn't.

When she got up to add a tittle-tattle Honey-graffito to Marlene's little girl's room, I got an ESP twinge that I'm sure any smoker can relate to. I knew that I had just kissed my best lighter goodbye. If I didn't move fast, I'd never see its little flame again.

"Check please!" I shouted. And I must say, I got it in record time; almost before I'd finished the second syllable.

Three hours to get a table, three minutes to get away. In all fairness to Marlene, the pasghetti was primo pasta, the meatballs were righteous, the sauce was virtuoso tomato puree, and Marlene can Screw Comfortably Against The Wall with the best of them.

Forty dollar tip on the table. Go figure.

I caught up with Honey out on Second Avenue. She was across the street from what I guessed might be her limousine, talking to some guy. My rented limo was on Eighty-eighth Street.

I walked over, amazed at the tubes in this woman.

As I came up behind her, I could see that Honey was practically accosting the guy, pleading with him to do something, but he was shaking his head, *No. No.* The thing was, I had seen him before somewhere, maybe on TV. A few bystanders recognized Honey, but they were acting innocent.

I heard Honey say, "C'mon, Tom, Please!" She grabbed him by his neck and tried to kiss the BASTARD on his cheek. But he pulled away from her.

"Well, isn't this cozy?" I said.

Honey spun around, and pulled me by my sleeve, away from the guy. He was giving me this look, like: Who the hell are you? Which was pretty much the look I was giving him. Anyway, Honey walked me about ten feet away from him, and then crouched down on the sidewalk, pulling on my sleeve. And all the time, she was giving me this total bullshit. "Oh, Jimmy! I'm so glad you're here. I was so worried. But now, you can help me! See, over there? Here, get down, first. Get down, Jimmy. Don't let him see that we're looking at him. Jimmy! Get down!"

"Honey is too sweet for you," I said coldly. "From now on, I'm gonna call you *Witch.*"

"Jimmy, *please*," she said, talking super-fast, "I know I flailed, I'm sorry, I'm sorry I bailed out, but I hate those people, I couldn't stand it any longer, I was going *disco*,

I had to get out of there, I couldn't help myself."

"Tell me another one, *Witch*."

She reached up and YANKED on my arm, pulling me down to crouch with her on the pavement. "Don't be a poohbutt!" she screeched. She peeked up over the BMW parked in front of us. "See the Jaguar over there, behind my limo?"

The guy she was talking to wasn't there anymore. I don't know where he went.

"I've got it figured now. I should have used finger cots before I touched your knife. That's what I did wrong, right?"

She closed her eyes, and her face went absolutely blank for about three seconds. Her body slumped. I used the opportunity to swipe my antique gold lighter out of her vest pocket. Mission accomplished.

The two most famous eyes in the world opened and looked at me. The most famous mouth in the world quietly said, "I didn't bring my bodyguards tonight, and for a driver they send me Barbara Bimbo. Jimmy, please help me ditch this guy. He's psycho. I'm afraid of him. He's under court order to leave me alone, and there he is over there in that Jaguar."

They say that Honey can't act. They're wrong. I said, "What do you want me to do?"

CHAPTER 4

Distract him. There's a celebrity-shooting psycho out there, and I'm supposed to distract him so Honey can get away. No problem. I just wish her messenger had warned me in advance, maybe slipped in an extra rhyme about automatic rifles or Army Surplus hand grenades (you know, *We'll be dining casual and AK-47; a bullet-proof vest would be really heaven*, something like that).

Everything would have been fine. But when I demanded advance payment on the spot, Honey's telephone number, she gave me an 800-number.

. . . . .

The only reason I walked up the sidewalk and crossed the street over to the Jaguar is because if I had stayed crouched down behind the BMW with Honey, I would have strangled the scheming, manipulative little vixen. She ditches me in the restaurant. When I come out, she's kissing some guy I don't know. Then she pretends to be happy to see me, and sends me away on some bullshit errand, Just To Ditch Me Again!

I was really insulted. What does she think? I can't handle a little rejection? I'm a comedian. I spent nine years going from nowhere to nowhere in small towns and mini-clubs with Philistine owners, paying a big piece of next to nothing to a manager who couldn't, performing in front of audiences that weren't. I've had nights when nobody laughed at all. When I left the stage, there was no applause, nobody even noticed I was gone. I've been rejected by professionals! Women are amateurs at rejecting guys. All she has to do is say Get Lost. She can make it as simple or as subtle as she likes. But to bullshit me and send me off on some 'secret mission' so she can scamper into her limo and skedaddle . . .

What really pissed me off was the 800-number. The con would have worked, if not for that. But she has to go and make up a number, and even do a little joke about it. She's gonna get Cool McCool, "the coolest dude alive," to eagerly write down her 800-number and go running off into the night to make a homo*sap* out of himself. What a great laugh to tell the girls about. When I just looked at her, and didn't write it down, she even goes: "Want me to repeat it?"

But McCool does not hurt a honey. I walked away from it. And boy was I pissed. I was so angry I didn't even know what I was going to do. Maybe nothing, maybe just walk.

When I got close to the Jag, parked right behind the long limousine, I could see the guy in there. He was huge. It was hard to see how he fit himself into the V-12 thing.

Look at that thick neck! I bet he does steroids.

As I walked past him on the sidewalk, I could see that he was, indeed, watching intently across the street in the direction of Honey.

Distraction . . . You want a distraction, huh?!

I turned around and stepped up on the trunk of the Jaguar. Me and my Dingo cowboy boots walked all over that Jag. The shocks bounced, the paint scratched, the boots climbed to the roof. I jumped way up and then hit down three times on the roof—BAM, BAM, BAM—for effect and indentation. And to shake the guy up. Maybe I could get him as mad as I was!

I was getting some vocal reaction from inside now. Angry gutter swear-words.

Good!

A gigantic fist shakes out at me. (When his door opens, I'm going to leap off and run like hell until my bad knees lock up!)

I jumped down onto the front hood, and started to walk off the front, but slipped, my butt banging down, denting my pride.

Then, I stood up, between the two cars, inches from the Jaguar's front bumper, readjusted my Stetson, and crossed my arms, my back to Honey's bodyguard in the Jaguar. (Who else can he be, a guy that huge? Honey is putting me on. I've read her bio. I know Honey likes her bodyguards to just fade into the scenery unobtrusively whenever possible.)

Ahh, we're getting down to the vituperative nitty-gritty now. My sexual habits, my genealogy. Genuine he-man pyrotechnic profanity. He said some naughty things about my mommy, too. (When I hear a door open, I'm gone, I'll set a new record for the handicapped 100-meter!)

Honey runs across the street, yells a word or a noise at me, opens the rear door herself, gets in, and the limo takes Honey away from me forever. Good riddance.

All twelve cylinders revving, the front bumper nudging the backs of my legs, the horn hooooooooooooooooonking.

Screw you, Honey. Screw you, bodyguard. I've had my legs broken before.

At that point, I was so pissed and self-destructive that I really didn't care what happened.

The Jaguar backs up, tires squealing, and then accelerates around me, the guy flipping me a bird and a motley assortment of insults.

I had been burning mad, but now my clothes were drenched with sweat, and I was amazed that I had done something so wild. The New York natives were restless: several masculine whistles, some feminine clapping, and a pedestrian shout for an encore. I stepped back up on the curb and walked back to my limousine.

· · · · ·

I'd already had too much to drink. There was nothing on TV. And I was paying too much extra for the cellular phone not to use it at least once. So after a perfect evening of flawless smooth moves, my brain turns to vaporware, and I punch the 800-number.

I have good short-term memory for things like telephone

numbers and breast measurements.

"The Honey Hotline," a female voice says.

I really didn't know what to say. So I didn't.

"The Honey Hotline," the voice says again. "May I direct your call?"

I'm still totally lost. "Direct my call?"

"I'll connect you with information."

I'm put on a kind of hold, where a recording informs me of all the different services I may be connected to with the press of just four additional buttons. There are umpteen different Honey Fan Clubs. There are Honey-talk phone lines. There are phone-order services ready and waiting to sell me Honey T-shirts, Honey Records, Honey Movies, Honey Health Food, or connect me up with Honey-loving pen-pals. There are free autographed pictures, subscriptions to the Honey Newsletter, and the Honey Magazine, tickets to Honey Concerts. Or perhaps I would like to donate to the Honey Charity. The Honey Horoscope. The Honey Love Advisor. The Honey Philosophy. This message repeats, if I have missed any portion . . .

. . . . .

Curiosity almost killed the comedian. I punched the four digits that got me back to the operator. "Gimme Honey," I snarled quietly.

"Beg pardon?"

"Gimme Honey."

"May I ask your name?"

"Cool McCool."

"And the password?"

"Cool McCool."

I was put on hold for about a minute and a half.

"Jimmy!"

"Hello, Witch."

And there we were, through the curse of modern technology, talking to each other on the telephone, while traveling in different directions in different limousines.

"Jimmy, you smart-ass son-of-a-bitch, you were brill! Hulk never knew what hit 'im! Gosh, you're even crazier than he is!"

"Do I hear a thank you? Maybe some sounds of gratitude?"

"Absolutely. You have my eternal, undying gratitude for the next five minutes. I'll even give you my Get Out Of Jail Free card. Say, where ya gonna be next Thursday night? I'm gonna be at Leonard's in Bel Air, wanna come along and ride shotgun? Hey, with a hotwired crazy like you, who needs hired muscle? Whad'a'ya say, Jimmy, it'll be fun!"

"I wouldn't go out with you again if you had the last Get Out Of Jail Free Card in fifty-one states."

She giggled. "I'll tell 'em to expect you."

"I have to work." I said flatly. "Thursday, I'm doing the Garden State Arts Center in Jersey."

"Oh. What . . . about . . . let's see, I'll be parked out there on the West Coast for almost a month, hum . . . Reinfeld's Mansion, Beverly Hills, a week from Saturday?"

"Kenny Johnson's show."

"Oh. You're gonna get overexposure, guy."

"Tushy's in Malibu," I suggest. "Two weeks from next Saturday Night."

"Umm . . . OK! I have to cancel something, but it's no biggie. I'll meet you there, and we'll do something after. Maybe we'll find some Jaguars for you to walk on, huh?"

"Listen, Witch, there's something we have to get straight—"

"What's with this Witch shit!" she screamed in my ear.

"What's with this Jimmy shit?" I calmly replied. "Only dweebs call me Jimmy. The name is Cool."

She was silent, but the connection was noisy.

It was time for some love-stuff; honeys really go for it. I whispered: "Hey, Honey . . ."

"Yeah?" she whispered back, the connection shouting a hiss.

"Honey," I said, softly, "I really enjoyed the Long Comfortable Screw."

She didn't say anything.

I added: "But you're right, I should have taken off my hat during it."

Honey still didn't say anything.

I realized I hadn't said anything either. It's hard as hell to say something important to a woman, when you don't want to put it into words, and you don't want to reveal how important it is to you. "I like talking to you, Honey," I said. The words did not cause the heavens to open and the Lord's fist to smite me. Bravely, I continued. "I really enjoy being with you, too." I winced, expecting angry demons to rend me limb from limb, dismember me, behead me, or at the very least to cause an automobile accident to punish me for revealing Personal Feelings and betraying my male heritage of Emotional Withholding and Psychological Harassment of Women.

Honey was silent in a very noisy way. The word "Jimmy" came gargling up out of the noise, and was immediately strangled.

The telephone started beeping at me, informing me that a cell-net error had taken place.

No shit, Sherlock! Cool McCool turns empathetic and sensitive. *Donnez-moi un* break!

CHAPTER 5

Imagine, if you will, a $6.3 million, tri-level beach house in Malibu. It'll save some extraneous exposition. Fill to capacity with rich & famous people, doing what rich & famous people do best: Completely artificial status race. Put that sun right down on the waves, with a few streaks of orange in the cloudy sky.

At this time, our hero enters into your fantasy. He's thin and tall. You recognize him by the Stetson and the filtered Camel between his fingers. He looks a gray hair over thirty. But you know he's probably close to forty. Handsome devil. (Hey, it's my fantasy too.) If you're a mind reader, and you are, tune in. The man has Honey on his mind. All the other party-dolls are in diestrum. They just don't do it for him.

Put a drink in his hand, requisition a few paragraphs of party dialogue from the latest Jackie or Joan Collins novel, and paraphrase to fit.

OK, now fast-forward through your fantasy to the fun stuff.

No, that's the rewind button. Go the other way. You

don't need to know how I know Tushy. We don't need a flashback.

OK. Get ready . . . three . . . two . . . one . . . PLAY!

.   .   .   .   .

I was talking to a lady with green eyes, green hair, green tattoo, and a bizarre green formal dress like one of Leonardo's flying machines, when:

"There you are, Popsicle-dick. I wanna talk to you!"

A paw with the strength and hair of a bear wrenched me around by my shoulder. It was really quite a trick: My drink splashed out all over the Leonardo flying machine, and my cigarette fell out of my mouth and landed in my empty glass.

Well if it isn't Hulk, Honey's undercover bodyguard.

My spirits flew.

She's here!

Now, I'm slightly taller than Hulk, so I was looking down at him. But he's slightly wider, heavier, and stronger than two of me. So with that one paw, he easily hauled me out of the party and out into the curved drive where his Jaguar was parked. I wondered what it was doing here on the West Coast.

The damage was spectacular, in the light of the sunset. I particularly liked my butt mark on the hood. For a second I could recall the sharp pain when I landed: Whoomp!

I smiled. "Send me a bill, Hulk. I'll pay for it. Don't worry about it."

"You'll buy me a new [verb deleted] Jaguar, you [same verb deleted] [noun deleted]!"

"I'll cover the damage, Buddy. Don't press your luck."

He pressed his luck by grabbing my upper arms in his paws and lifting me about a foot off the ground. He held me there, and yelled up at me. "You'll buy me an [expletive deleted] Jaguar, you skinny prick!"

"No, but I will kick you in the balls."

He tried to twist his body sideways, but then he just gave up on it, growled, and dropped me back down to the sidewalk. The guy was incredibly strong.

I scanned the perimeter quickly, to see if Honey had witnessed this. No. Just some car-jockeys I didn't know, a few after-dark aficionados I could care less about, and Maggie Tiel, my ex-wife. Shit.

"I wanna new Jaguar!" Hulk said, like a spoiled little kid, and he pounded his fist down on the roof of his car. The sheet metal made a banging sound like a firecracker, and there was a new little crater where his fist had hit.

"Well, talk to Honey about it. Not me. I ain't springin' for a new car, dude." I turned my back on him.

He snarled: "Come back here, you pussy!"

I stopped. There were people and ex-wives watching this. Shakespeare said To Be Or Not To Be, and that could very well be the question. The guy was a human tank, and I was skyscraper spindleshanks. I won't tell you my exact weight. It's embarrassing. I turned around. More people drove up in cars and got out to watch.

Hulk grabbed my shirt in his fist, shook me around,

and yelled, "You stay away from Honey, you [obscene term deleted]!"

There was really only one thing I could say in a situation like that. I said the two words. And he hit me in my face with his other fist.

. . . . .

It was like one of Nixon's tapes: Where are the missing minutes? Honey only knows why I was sitting in the front passenger seat of Hulk's battered Jaguar, exceeding the speed limit, while Hulk drove south (well, east, actually) on Highway 1. Hulk was driving while tears streamed down his face. Jeez, Honey must have really bawled him out, maybe she fired him. He was crying almost as much as I was bleeding. The whole front of my shirt was red and sticky.

The left side of my face was an explosion of pounding pain. I felt tentatively around my face, did an inventory of teeth, eyes, noses, chins, Stetsons. Everything seemed to be there, in the right quantity, except the hat. No hat. I started to look around for it. I didn't see it. But I did notice that my blood was doing a hell of a job on his white leather interior.

When Hulk realized I was awake, he stopped crying. "Skinny prick," he told me.

I repeated the two words that had gotten me into this mess, and lit up a bloody Camel.

Hulk was a terrible driver, no wonder Honey didn't want to ride with him. I'm sure it was my imagination, but I thought he said, "The cars are like waves, you just dive right in . . . and the water . . . goes around you . . ." And I'm sure it was my imagination when he crossed over the yellow bumpy divider line, as if to prove his point, going the wrong way on the wrong side of the highway. And I know damn well it had to be my imagination when one pair of headlights crashed up into the dark hillside to avoid us, and another pair of lights squealed across the road and smashed into a condo on the seaside. I knew it was one of my LSD flashbacks. I get them, sometimes—a curse from my teenage drug experiments during the late Sixties. The world starts to melt, and angles seem all funny and distorted and rich with meaning, like a Tom Benton painting, and my skin starts to tingle, and fear grabs me by the neck, as I remember the time I overdosed and was caught in a horrible purple hell that just went on . . . and on . . . and on . . . What I'm trying to say is DON'T DO DRUGS!

This time, though, there was no fear, no gradual melting of the visual landscape, no distortions; just pain, and the rational knowledge that Hulk couldn't possibly be driving on the wrong side of the road. Odd. I didn't think I was imagining it all, though, because Hulk kept calling me a skinny prick.

We didn't stop at a hospital, as I expected; we stopped at another beach house, smaller, less grandiose.

The only thing I could think was: Honey must be here. I wasn't sure I wanted her to see me with blood all over my face and clothes. But then again, with women it's hard to tell, I might get the sympathy vote.

. . . . .

No votes.

No Honey.

My worst nightmare.

I wasn't having an LSD flashback. Hulk was. Or maybe he was on psilocybin. Or crack dusted with PCP & ice.

He was very proud of his beach house, and didn't want me bleeding on it. He said he bought it from Captain Kirk. He claimed it had a force field around it. Nothing could hurt it, not even phasers or photon torpedoes.

"What about anti-matter?" I asked.

"You skinny prick, where you gonna get anti-matter?"

"Same place I got my universal translator. The Starfleet surplus store."

There was almost no furniture in the whole place. Just a TV, a lamp, and a couch in the living room. No rug, no art on the walls, no draperies.

He looked me over and pronounced me fit.

"Nah," Hulk said, "you don't need no doctor."

(Sunday I needed seventeen stitches on my left cheek.)

We talked about Honey.

"Where's Honey?" I asked.

"Wow," Hulk said, "she's just . . . whew! Like . . . super! And just . . . wow, the most . . . wow." Long silence. "And I . . . I just think she's swell. She's just so . . . so . . . so . . . *you* know."

"Absolutely," I said. At least we agreed about something.

He gave me the grand tour of his beach house.

There was nothing at all in any of the other rooms, except for one of the bedrooms, which had one bed, some clothes crumpled on the floor, some First Generation Star Trek memorabilia, and magazine pictures of Honey taped all over the walls.

We discussed interior decoration.

"And this is the den," Hulk said, with obvious pride. "Do you like the Nevelson sculpture? It's called *Midnight Moon*. Books! You like books? I give you books!" His huge hands swept around, pointing. "And check out my choice Felice Rossi! Wanna sit in it? Go ahead!"

I mean, the room was completely bare, just walls and a wood floor. "That's OK, I'll just stand."

We had a philosophical discussion.

"Physical Reality!" Hulk scoffed. "Gravediggers [verb deleted] according to Hoyle. Life is a space warp! [Expletive deleted] Scottie could beam us up any second. Right, skinny prick?"

"Absolutely. No question."

We talked about astronomy.

"You know," Hulk said, his arm arcing slowly through space, his eyes growing wide with wonder and sudden revelation, "the planets . . . *are like grasshoppers!*"

I was silent in the face of this galactic illumination.

The difference between a friend and a fanatic is that with the latter you quickly run out of conversation.

Hulk turned on the TV. Wrestling.

Give me a commercial break.

Then I noticed that Hulk was one of the wrestlers on TV.

Give me a brown out.

I heard the announcer talking about the fight. Mad Hulk, he called the winner.

"Yeah!" Hulk shouted. "I'm drivin' out for a tour of the Eastern States next couple'a weeks. I'm gonna total all those pansy [plural noun deleted]!"

Give me an exit.

Hulk heard me trying to sneak off.

"Where you goin'?!" he shouted at me. "Where's my Jaguar?" He ran to me quick, like an angry crazy-man, grabbed me by my upper arms with both his hands, and yanked and twisted my arms violently.

I roared in agony as something went terribly wrong with my left shoulder. I think he dislocated it. He started pulling me along by the same shoulder, and then dragging me when I fell.

Hulk dragged me to a glass-enclosed patio, left me lying on sand-specked concrete. He switched on bright floodlights. Beyond the glass, between this beach house and the next one, I saw a night volleyball game going on, all lit up by bright lights. A hundred yards down the beach, I saw several small fires and groups of people partying. I managed to sit up, and I found a position to hold my arm that didn't hurt too badly. But there was something very wrong with it. When I tried to move it, it felt like gears grinding. I quickly gave that up. When I looked back at Hulk, he had lost interest in me; he was staring through the glass at the campfires along the beach. I mean, the guy just did not make sense.

I shook out a Camel and lit up. I sat there silently

smoking for three or four minutes, trying to figure out a way to escape from this nut. Hulk just stood there with his back to me, watching the volleyball game. Two teenage girls and a young boy came up to the glass of the patio, and they started talking to Hulk. The glass was about ten feet high, but by shouting they could hear each other. The girls wanted to buy some of his Chocolate Chips. Obviously, not cookies. They could see me too, but apparently, bloody beat-up men sitting and smoking cigarettes on Hulk's patio with their arms sticking out at funny angles were nothing to get excited about. While they were arguing about price—these were some expensive Chocolate Chips—I finally stood up, and tried to silently leave again.

No such luck. Hearing me, Hulk whirled around and came running at me fast. He laughed with sudden, insane glee and picked me up, as he ran, by my underarms. I yelled in sharp agony. He threw me way up in the air, at the glass, almost right at the three people on the other side, and I just knew that I was going to die.

When I hit the glass, the blast of pain was so intense that I passed out.

I woke up, perhaps seconds or minutes later, lying on the hard concrete, within a foot of the transparency. It was not glass, it was some kind of plastic. It had not shattered, as I had feared. Strangely enough, my left arm felt better. I spit sand out of my mouth. Here near the base of the transparent wall, there was about a quarter inch of sand on the concrete. I brushed sand off my bloody face, which was bleeding fresh again, and I got a big piece of sand in my right eye. I don't know why, but getting sand in my eye, after everything else, was funny enough to make me laugh for a few seconds. The three kids who had been outside were gone, and none of the volleyballers seemed to be aware that anything was going wrong on Hulk's patio. I could see a smear of my blood on the plastic.

Hulk was watching me.

Slowly I stood up. I moved my left arm around. It still hurt like a sharp fire, but it seemed to be a lot better now. I put a Camel in my mouth, and lit up.

"Well," I told him, "if you're finished beating on me, I'm going to leave now, OK?"

He shook his head. "Not until you get me a new Jaguar."

"You know, you're starting to piss me off, Hulk!"

He shouted right back at me. "Buy me a new Jaguar, you Skinny Prick!"

I took a deep breath of nicotine, and exhaled. It's hard to be menacing when blood is dripping off your chin, you've lost your hat, you've got sand in your eye, and you hurt like hell. "I'm not buying you any new cars, guy. Let me go now, and I'll go easy on you, Hulk. I won't totally destroy you, and I won't completely ruin your life."

As a comedian, I was a great success. He must have laughed for twenty seconds, while I scowled at him.

I tried to walk into the beach house to leave.

"Hey, Skinny Prick, you ain't goin' nowhere until you get me a new Jaguar."

I told Hulk where he could go and how he could amuse himself while he was getting there.

He came at me again, grabbed hold of me and dragged me by my good arm, this time, through his beach house to one of his bathrooms. He told me, "I'm goin' back to Tushy's." Then he shut the bathroom door and locked me inside.

I tried the door. It wouldn't budge. "You're going to regret this, Hulk!" I yelled at the door. "This is your last chance! Let me out, damn it, or you're in big time trouble!"

They say that you can learn a lot about a person by the personal effects he keeps in his bathroom mirror cabinet. I learned what I needed to know about Hulk. There was nothing inside.

I looked like hell, in the mirror. My left eye was bloated and dark blue. There was a torn, bloody flap of skin hanging on my left cheek. Sand was stuck onto the wounds. My lips were swollen. I washed some more of the crusty blood and sand off my hands and neck and nostrils.

The bathroom had no window. The door was very solid wood. It hurt my knuckles just to knock on it. It was somehow locked from the outside. I could turn the handle, I could see the bolt retract, but something else was holding the door shut. I banged on the walls. They were very solid too.

I thought for a minute, then I broke the float-arm rod off the inside of the toilet, spent about twenty minutes grinding a point on the end of it by scratching it on the inside of the toilet, and then I pried and pushed the pivot pins out of the door hinges. Then I bent my tool into a hook, stuck it under the door and tried to pull the door out of the frame. But it wouldn't budge. Something was holding it from the outside.

I stopped chain-smoking and started rationing my smokes. I thought about destroying the beach house. Flooding it was too pathetic. Burning it down was too suicidal. I sat down on the toilet and waited. Listened to the water rushing down the toilet. Three smokes left. The Roman Numeral scratches dug into the wood of the front wall were not encouraging.

IIIII IIIII III.

A previous occupant? Thirteen days?

So OK, I'm slow. I finally get it. This is not Honey's bodyguard I'm dealing with here. This is a celebrity-shooting psycho with Honey on his mind and Cool in his bathroom.

. . . . .

Hulk made just one mistake. He should have left me a carton of Camels. Like, no way was I going to spend the night in the No Smoking section!

The door was too strong to bust through. I tried to use the heavy toilet tank lid as a battering-ram: no go. This was the door from hell. The walls were heavy hardwood. The floor was forget it.

Ah, but the ceiling was half an inch of acoustic pasteboard. I don't know why I didn't think of it earlier.

I took the toilet tank lid, stood on the toilet seat,

and bashed my way to freedom.

There was all kinds of insulation and wires and supporting beams and stuff up there. But I was excited, and there was no stopping my nicotine craving. I yanked the insulation out and shoved the tank lid up there and climbed into the darkness.

Couldn't see a thing.

I tore my way through the insulation (probably asbestos, damn it), until I figured I was about over the hallway. Then I bashed a nice big hole with the toilet lid.

I was breathing hard now, really excited, as I dropped down. Sounds easy, but it was a hell of a lot of work, especially with a left shoulder that hurt like a sharp knife stab whenever I moved it too far.

And I could see now why I couldn't pull the bathroom door in from the inside. There were four slide bolts in it, one near each corner. I wondered again if Hulk had locked other people in his bathroom, or if he planned to lock up other people in the future. The thirteen scratches were very eerie.

But I didn't really wonder very hard. I had only one thought in my brain, and it was a powerful one.

I walked out the front door, walked up to Highway 1, and walked to the nearest pack of cigarettes.

CHAPTER 6

Attorneys Francis, Lake, Green & Weber have required me to insert a short disclaimer.

I personally know nothing of the following story, other than what has been reprinted herein. I personally have no connection with the following story, other than the short described instance of voluntary cooperation with the Malibu Police. It is understood that my statements to the Malibu Police Department were facetious.

The following is from the *Los Angeles Times*.

BEACH HOUSE DESTROYED BY PHONE CALL

The vacant $2 million beach house in Malibu was flattened in less than one day. It was a competent job performed by the 83-man, 17-woman demolition crew recruited by the California State Employment Agency.

Unfortunately, the owner, professional wrestler "Mad" Hulk Murdock, did not want his beach house destroyed.

Malibu Police stated yesterday that the incident is much more than just a devious prank, that it is a serious case of destruction of property and grand theft. The angry workers, who were all promised $11 an hour, called it a scam. None of them were paid.

A man claiming to be Mr. S.P. Algid, General Manager of Starfleet Construction & Demolition of Long Beach, called the State Employment Development Department on Wednesday to hire 100 wreckers. He said it was a rush job.

"In this economy, we'll take orders for any work that's legal and honest," said agency spokesperson Hallie Morgan. "It's difficult for us to verify every job. Our budget has been cut. We have fewer resources, a shrinking number of available jobs, and a larger clientele."

The work team was hired and the beach house at 12 Seaside Lane was already bashed to bits when the owner's mother, Martha "Maude" Murdock, arrived Friday to house sit. "There was nothing," she said. "It was just wreckage. They even took the TV."

The foreman for the demolition job, Manuel Spreg, said Algid got his phone number from the Employment Department. Algid called him three times, asking the men to bring their own tools and equipment. Algid said there would be a Starfleet Demolition dumpster at the site to dispose of the rubble. Algid claimed that he had already cleared the work with the authorities, obtained the necessary permits, and talked to both of Mr. Murdock's closest neighbors. However, he cautioned Spreg to please make a personal call on the two neighbors to again apologize in advance for any noise or disturbance.

Algid told Spreg that Hulk Murdock wanted to rebuild

from scratch, to erect his dream beach house on the property. A few items of furniture had not been removed from the vacant beach house; these the workers were welcome to distribute among themselves. "Vacant, hell!" Martha "Maude" Murdock was quoted as saying.

The work crew reported for work Friday morning to find the work order taped to the front door of the beach house. Foreman Manuel Spreg took charge and proceeded to organize the destruction. "We didn't know Hulk didn't want his house wrecked," he said. "There's too many scams going on. These people all needed the money. Eleven bucks an hour for homewrecking is good money."

When Mrs. Murdock arrived Friday afternoon, the workers discovered that they would not be paid, and Mrs. Murdock discovered that her son no longer had a beach house, which he had purchased five months previously from actor/novelist William Shatner.

There is no one named Algid in Long Beach. There is no Starfleet Construction & Demolition company.

Malibu Detective/Lieutenant Jennifer Woodlawn said, "It's beyond bizarre. All the guy did was make a few phone calls, and he destroyed a two million dollar beach house. It's just incredible. And we have no real leads. We could get no information from the Employment Development Department. All we have is the fictitious name of a Trekkie. [I have] twenty-one years in the Department, and this [case] tops them all."

"Mad" Hulk was unavailable for comment until Monday. He never flies, and so drove his 1990 Jaguar from Florida, where he was appearing in a Wrestling Match, to

California. Monday morning, he was found wandering around on the wreckage, muttering, "Anti-Matter . . . Anti-Matter . . . Anti-Matter."

By Monday, a juvenile gang had spray-painted obscene pictures of elongated phalli on several large pieces of the demolished beach house.

"Mad" Hulk Murdock, who is himself on probation for drug possession with intent to distribute, and under a court restraining order for repeatedly harassing superstar Honey, attempted to file a criminal complaint against comedian Cool McCool, who, he alleges, "ordered Captain Kirk of the Starship Enterprise to come back in time and destroy [the beach house] by using Anti-Matter. I locked [McCool] in a detention cell, but he must have had a pocket phaser on him, 'cause he blasted a hole in the force field and escaped. [McCool] is an interplanetary spy, I tell ya!"

The Malibu Police were not amused.

Cool McCool and William Shatner both voluntarily agreed to assist with the investigation. Mr. McCool had several stitches on his face, and was in considerable pain due to an automobile accident a few days previously. After listening incredulously to the wild accusations, Mr. McCool replied, with utter seriousness, "Well, it's all in the Enterprise log. Yes, I ordered the Enterprise back in time. Sulu tried to destroy the beach house with phasers, but they were ineffective against the structure's force field. Photon torpedoes were also of no use. Finally, Spock suggested they use Anti-Matter. I also should mention that Scottie has contingency orders. If anything should happen to me, Scottie has orders to come back in time, beam Hulk up, and transport him to Hell Planet in the Romulan Neutral Zone. Hell Planet, as I'm sure Hulk knows, is populated solely by pregnant Tribbles in heat."

The Malibu Police were not amused.

CHAPTER 7

Honey and I cuddled in front of the crackling fireplace. Had I died and gone to heaven? No, these were some very down-to-earth pleasures, and I was achingly alive. We were in my killer solar-heated house above Aspen, Colorado, drinking champagne, lightly petting each other, and engaging in full, frontal mental intercourse without any contraceptive intellectual devices.

I got her to come to me with a single phone call.

Downstairs were some of her friends, and some of my friends, and probably some people who were friends of nobody here (it happens). A little Friday Night get-together. The double-door to my bedroom was open. Honey and I were sitting on pillows between my bed and the fireplace.

Honey was obviously in a very romantic and susceptible mood. She had already started undressing me. She had removed my Stetson.

Ever the man's woman, Honey was pouring my champagne for me, and lighting my cigarettes for me.

She was wearing a green cashmere sweater with nothing

but Honey under it, brown stonewashed jeans, and red furry socks.

My gold, antique Dunhill cigarette lighter/watch was parked in her hip pocket.

I was thinking what any heterosexual red-blooded American male would have been thinking about with the sexiest woman in the world (by popular vote) in his arms. About getting the doors shut, and our clothes off, and a condom on, and my penis inside of her. Not necessarily in this order.

"Jim, be serious," Honey said. "All those homeless people. You cheated 'em. Ripped 'em off. Got 'em to work for nothin'. You slime mold." She ran a sexy finger along where my stitches had been, and kissed my Adam's apple lightly. "I might be inclined to like you, except for that." She started giggling again. I hung on for the ride.

I loved the way she giggled. It started off as a squeaky bird call. Then her whole body shook in that special sensuous way of hers. But she didn't make a sound for the last five seconds or so of the jiggle.

Honey was not giggling over the wanton destruction of a $2 million Malibu beach house. No. Honey would never be so callous. She was laughing at the idea of me locked in the bathroom without cigarettes.

I said, "What homeless people? Hulk?"

"Jim, be serious."

"Have some more champagne."

"I'll hit you over the head with the *bottle* if you don't—"

"They were a hundred people looking for work. They

got plenty of work, according to the story."

"You didn't *pay* them. That's *terrible*! It's immoral! How can you live with yourself?"

J.R. Ewing, on that ancient TV show *Dallas*, was once asked how he could live with himself. He replied, "Once you give up your integrity, the rest is a piece of cake." Now, you know, and my lawyers know, and the Malibu Police Department knows that I didn't destroy Hulk's beach house. Right? Have we got that established? But if Honey wants to believe that I wrecked the place of one of her enemies, in defense of her honor, who am I to disillusion her? At some point in the future, I will, of course, have to tell her everything.

But not just this minute. Honey's body was sprawled all over mine. My hands had staked a pretty solid claim to her peachy tits, and were now exploring her opulent hips for hidden gold.

Never mind that it was my stubborn "integrity" that had caused the whole mess, when I refused to buy Hulk a new car, Ewing's line was just too good to resist repeating: "Honey, once you give up your integrity, the rest is a piece of cake."

Honey went off like Miss Firecracker.

Ten seconds later, I was hugging my groin and wiping her spit out of my right eye. Honey was standing by the fireplace, looking down at me like I had just stuffed a tattooed girl into a Burger King dumpster. She was yelling at me, shaking a condemning finger, and the lady could swear nastier than a team of longshoremen screwing in a lightbulb.

My response to this was a brilliantly masculine demonstration of sensitivity '90s-style: I groaned and hugged my balls. Her feminist sensibilities were apparently offended by this chauvinistic display. She took two steps and stomped on my Stetson.

"Back off," I grunted. "I paid 'em. It was that bastard Spreg. He ripped 'em off."

Honey's wonderful eyebrows narrowed suspiciously. "What do you mean?" Her wonderful fists were on her wonderful hips. Her wonderful stocking feet were on my Stetson.

"Get off my hat! One hundred packets. Check with Jet Deliveries. One hundred packets. Each with four twenties, a five, and three ones in it." I sat up, with effort. "I gave Spreg eighty-eight hundred bucks for the workers, plus a nice big bonus for him. The son of a bitch kept it all. Pour me some champagne, will you?"

"I don't believe you." But she did get off my hat.

I reached and got my own champagne. I tried to laugh a little, but didn't get very far with it; it hurt my left ball too much. That was the one she really clobbered. "You're a kook, Honey." I amended that. "A sexy kook. The willful, unlawful destruction of a two million dollar house on the beach doesn't bother you a bit. But a few out-of-work dudes miss a day's wages and you scream bloody murder and knee me in the balls? What kind of a black widow spider are you? You're supposed to let me come inside of you before you kick me eight times in the balls."

"I believe you," Honey said quietly, after a few moments. She picked up my Stetson, and straightened it. Her mood was mercurial, and suddenly she was very quiet and still. "I'm sorry I hurt you. A little." She stood there by the fireplace, and played with my hat. "What are you going to do about it?"

God, she was sexy. I could hear the party downstairs. It sounded like it was getting pretty wild. I made a long reach, and pulled her down on top of me by her wrist. "I'm going to assuage my guilty conscience by dry-humping a certain semi-famous girl by the name of Honey."

"Semi-famous?!" she objected, interrupting an attempted kiss.

"That is, unless she'd like a nice wet—"

"Jimmy, be serious," she said. She slowly fitted my Stetson back on my head. This was not a good sign. "What are you going to do about it?"

I sighed. "I don't know," I admitted. "I haven't been able to get in touch with Manuel Spreg. I talked to his neighbors. He seems to have used his fresh bundle of cash to take his wife and kid for a vacation in Hawaii. Nobody's home at his house. Of course, I suppose I could make a few phone calls . . ."

"About the workers, Silly. How are you going to pay them?"

"It's too late. I don't know how to get a complete list of the workers without getting myself thrown in jail."

Honey tipped my Stetson off the back of my head, and snuggled her face into my neck. And purred. "Well, you tried. Thanks for getting Hulk off my back."

(The plot had thickened somewhat in the past few days. Hulk was having a hard time of it. Some juvies hotwired his Jaguar and took it for a joyride on Mulholland Drive. It was found at the bottom of "Dead Man's Curve" with a trunkload of controlled experimental psycho-chemicals in and around the wreckage. Hulk was "availing himself of the municipal accommodations.")

I thought I was going to find out if the sexiest stone fox in Aspen was any good at putting on a condom. But the party expanded upstairs and overflowed into my bedroom. Well, I like a little romantic mood music to woo and win a new woman, but this was getting ridiculous.

The Comedian With Two Brains has brought his banjo and single-brained actress-wife who sings. Aspen's Country Western star, Luke Colorado, has his Country Western guitar and his Country Western back-up-singer/lady with him. They sing. But it gets worse. Up comes a loving pair of rockstars in shades with their beatbox. They have to wear shades. It's because their future is so bright.

How did these party crashers get in here? I don't know these people.

Honey squirmed around in my arms, and started singing lead.

There's no justice. One of the men in my bedroom was funnier (by a brain) than I was, another was spacier, and the third was Timbuk-10 times hipper than I'll ever be. And they were all happily involved with wonderful, beautiful, loving women; all having a terrific time singing silly and loud. I can't even get a French kiss out of Honey. And I can't sing.

I needed a sign above my bedroom door restricting the maximum legal occupancy.

The funnier man and his straightlady excuuuuuused themselves, the Country Western couple headed West, and the reluctant rockstars went off for a run in the snow. But one of my Infinity loudspeakers was there by the double-door, and a new cast of characters were drinking and dancing in my bedroom and upstairs hallway.

Before someone else decided to make use of it, I hauled Honey over my shoulders, and flopped her down on my bed. She kicked her sexy legs. I told her to lose some weight. She called me . . . well, Twigs, actually.

We playfully mauled each other. I was doing the mauling. She was doing the playing. W.C. Fields, can't anybody take a hint?

No. But some ace asshole, sitting down for the *National Toilet Enquirer*, started taking pictures of us. Flash! Flash!

I raised my head. "Eject the film pack on the bed, or die!" I snarled.

The asshole, feminine gender, took two more pics,

and whirled around to escape. She bounced off sweet, gentle Timothy, my friend, protector and permanent guest here in Aspen, who happens to be as big as a horse, and who happened to be between her and the double-doorway.

In the most unthreatening way, Timothy suggested, "Please do as Mr. McCool said."

I turned my attentions back to Honey, and mauled away. In a kind of background way, I was vaguely aware of a pack of film dropping on the bed, and of Timothy taking possession of the film pack and the asshole, feminine gender.

After awhile, Honey and I were both doing the mauling. And things were getting, well, pretty exciting. Amend that: painfully exciting. We were both hot and sweaty, and our legs were tangled together, and our lips were tasting and kissing. She wouldn't let me French-kiss her. But Honey's sweaterful of titties were bouncing around, her hard nipples rubbing up against my chest, while my tangled erection was pumping against her thigh, and our arms . . .

Things . . . just . . . stopped.

Honey turned her head a little away from me. The warm, responsive, healthy woman in my arms froze. Ice Age.

Some big guy was crouched down beside the bed, whispering in Honey's ear.

What the hell?

Before I had time to get angry, I recognized him. The second most powerful man in Hollywood was in my Aspen bedroom. Bruce Ranger. Star of the *Nasty Sam* tough detective movies, owner of his own production studio, the guy who refused to play Travis McGee because "Travis is a pussy."

He just kept whispering in Honey's ear. Whispering. I couldn't hear a word, there was too much noise in the room.

He must have whispered to her for about sixty seconds. I just lay there feeling like shit, holding onto a woman gone completely cold. My left ball was hurting like blue blazes, and my erection had shriveled into a tiny little thing about the size of a clitoris.

There's only one thing a man can do in a situation like that, and still be a man. I reached into Honey's hip pocket and retrieved my lighter.

Bruce got up and walked away from her. Out of the corner of my eye, I could see terrified dancers dancing frantically to get out of his way so he wouldn't pull out a hidden .44 Magnum and shoot them dead. But I was watching Honey pick herself out of my arms, untangle our legs, and roll away from me.

. . . . .

I mean, not even a good-bye.

She goes over to the pillows, hunts for her shoes and purse, starts brushing her blond hair, puts on her shoes, springs up, and walks out of my bedroom.

Dancers fall all over themselves trying to get out of her way.

I mean, not even a good-bye look.

I'm still laying there on my side. I don't think I could

have moved, even if my house had been on fire. They'd have had to carry me out, and I'd just be laying there on my side, on the stretcher, staring at where Honey had been.

The dancing and partying goes on. Gets louder. Wilder. Something big breaks downstairs. A lamp going through a storm window? A high-heel going through my fragile heart?

I'm still laying there on my side.

One of my good friends wanders into my bedroom and leers down at me. His name is Marshall. His uncle owns all of Colorado, except for a couple of ski-slopes and a handful of Condos. "Honey just left. And guess who she was with? You'll never [expletive deleted] believe it."

I'm still laying there on my side.

"Wouldja believe Nasty Sam? The Man himself!" And there's a kind of awe in his voice.

I'm still laying there on my side.

"[Sexual metaphor deleted]!" Marshall says. "Hey, Cool, don't feel bad about it. It happens to everyone."

I manage a syllable of conversation. "What?"

Marshall smiles big. "Couldn't get it up, huh?"

"Back off." Two syllables. I sit up on the bed.

"I know what you need, pal," Marshall decides. He winks. "Just you wait a few minutes. I got the cure to all your problems." He disappears through the party.

. . . . .

The energy to get off the bed just wasn't there. I watched the dancers. One of the dancers, feminine gender, was watching me. She was Japanese, or Chinese maybe, wearing a tight Danskin thing, and she wasn't dancing so much as she was doing aerobics. She didn't seem to have a partner. I watched as she hooked her left leg up behind her left shoulder, with absolutely no bend at all in her knee.

Politely, I smiled at her, bowed a little, and looked away.

Marshall yelled at me from the hallway: "Pick up the phone!"

I just looked at him.

"Pick up the damn phone!" he yelled even louder. "It's Honey!"

I looked over at the telephone.

I crawled over the bed and picked up the phone.

I could hear Honey's voice.

"Cool, darling—"

I slammed the phone down.

It was supposed to make me feel good.

It didn't.

Bruce Ranger. The guy was probably older than Honey's father. Groucho, how do I deal with Bruce Ranger? I was going to have to log serious phone time. Monday morning I'd have them put in a WATS line . . .

I spotted the champagne bottle. Someone had taken it out of the ice, and the level had gone down some, but there was still fluid in it. I got off my bed and walked over toward the champagne.

I never got to the champagne. Marshall was suddenly in my way. He pulled me in another direction. "Somebody I want you to meet a relative," he mumbled.

(I know it's not a very good sentence, but that's what
he said.)

.   .   .   .   .

Next thing I know, I'm hog-tied, and dancing with a very
tall blond with the name of Mary Elizabeth McEnroe.
Oh, I get it: one of *my* relatives.

She was pretty and energetic, couldn't have been
much over twenty, and her long Colorado-tangled hair
was going all over my face. Actually, the word *pretty* is
inadequate. The girl was gorgeous. She was wearing
dangerously high black high-heels, black nylon stockings
that went up above her knees, into a strapless black
party-dress that fluffed out about a thousand dollar's
worth. Black gloves. A black midget purse, the strap of
which was tangled around my neck. The *short* strap of
which, which is why her hair was tickling my nose and
mouth and chin as we danced and talked, and she held
me close, and talked fragrant peppermint words at me.

She had seen all my movies. All two of them. And she
proved it by quoting from scripture. But she liked me live
or doing TV better. She referred to some *Friday Night Live*
bits, and one of my monologues on the *Night* show. She
subscribed to the Comedy Channel just to see me, and
had never missed any of my Tuesday Night & Friday Night
'comedy jock' shows (she was taping my show tonight,
she claimed, and planned to watch me after the party).
She mentioned my sixth grade *ménage à trois*.

She thought it was sweet that we had the same last name. (Well, before I had it legally changed, mine used to be McEnroe, too.)

She's smiling, smiling, smiling, and then an anxious look comes to her face. Quickly, she assures me that we aren't really related, or if we are, it's so distant that it's nothing to worry about as far as [sexual slang for copulation deleted] is concerned. There goes her smile, smile, smile again.

She in her high-heels, and me in my slump, put her eyelashes, which she was doing her best to bat at me, just about level with mine. I mean, the girl was climbing over my shoulders and placing her muff in my face in the nicest possible way.

I stopped pretending like I was dancing. I tried to untangle myself from her purse strap.

Her smile, smile, smile turned to pout, pout, pout. The music from my Infinity was booming in my left ear. They had turned the volume up too loud for too long, and burned out the tweeters. There were five people over on the pillows by my fireplace. There were eight or nine other dancers & standers around Mary Elizabeth McEnroe and myself. Sitting over on the edge of my bed were two mixed couples. Standing and talking to the four of them, were two members of the Cool Crew. But when I sadly looked at Mary Elizabeth, it felt almost as if we were the only two people in my bedroom.

.   .   .   .   .

Mary Elizabeth helped untangle me. "Honey left with Nasty Sam," she said. "Marshall told me."

I nodded, and God, I ached.

Mary Elizabeth smiled sadly. A single tear fell down out of her right eye. She smiled brightly, pretending like it didn't happen. Then they started coming out of her other eye too. She held her hand up to cover her face for two seconds, and got herself under control. There were no more tears. Just the streaks that had been tears.

She laughed. A beautiful short little feminine laugh. "I guess I can't compete with Honey, can I?"

I sighed. She was doing a very good job. But she was plain Vanilla, and I was hooked on exotic Rocky Road.

"Well," she said, "I'll let you go, if you'll give me your autograph."

"Sure," I said.

Mary Elizabeth pulled a black magic marker out of her black purse, and gave it to me, all ready to go in my right hand. She gave me a smile that would have warned me if I'd had any brains. Then she adjusted the top of her strapless black dress, and dug her very white left breast out of it. Mary Elizabeth took my left hand and brought it to her so that I was holding the underside of her very white, very warm left breast.

My left hand stayed where she put it.

"Sign my breast," she said. "Please write: All My Love. Cool."

I don't know whether people were watching this or not. I mean, this was not a plain Vanilla boob. [Name of actress deleted] paid $60,000 for two tits not quite this pretty, and my penis was willing to accept Mary Elizabeth's other gift from Mother Nature on faith.

This was a limited edition, imported, French Vanilla boob, very pricey, and this was a very large serving, and of course, everyone in my bedroom was watching this.

I signed her boob.

"I love you," she said, and spoke with a seriousness that stunned me. "I've loved you for seven years, since I was fourteen, and first saw you in Las Vegas. I've written you five thousand letters. I know you're busy, and don't have time to write back personally to every female airbrain with a crush on you. I don't mind, really I don't. I don't expect you to write back. But I've loved you so long, that I know now that I'll love you forever. I'll love you forever. It's my fate, it's my life, it just has to happen that way. You're just the perfect man for me, and I can't help myself. But, of course, I know that I'm just another female airbrain to you."

I started to interrupt, but she wouldn't let me. She forced me to go on holding her warm boob, and I could feel her heart pounding with excitement, and of course my erection was a giant uncontrollable monster thundering in my pants.

"It's not just the funny," Mary Elizabeth said. "That's not even it. It's you. It's . . . you." Tears started flowing out of both her eyes like twin faucets cranked to the max. "Don't you see? We belong together. It's destiny. Our names are the same, like they were always meant to be! Always . . . I've saved myself for you. I'm a virgin. Truly, I am. I'll prove it to you. Right now. We can go anywhere, and I'll prove it to you. Don't you see? I'm for you. I'm for you."

Her French Vanilla boob was coated with her tears-topping. My fingers were getting all wet. And her heart was hammering against my hand. It hurt me to listen to this . . . but I just could not let go.

My poor penis didn't know what to do tonight. It was up and down like a [vulgar simile deleted]. Tears deflate me almost instantly.

"Please," she said, her voice rushing, "I've been in Aspen for eight months, but nobody would let me see you, they said I had to sleep with them first, and then maybe if I was good they would introduce me to you, but I couldn't, don't you see, I'm for you, I'm all for you. I'm for you." And there was an awful desperation in her face and eyes.

I let go of her signed breast, and when panic flared in her eyes, I quickly put my arms around her and held her to me. She hurt so much, it hurt me, and I had to hold her, just to comfort her.

But comforting her was also very comforting to me. And I'm ashamed to admit that I really didn't want to let her go. (My Pet was now installed in my New York apartment, as part of a separation agreement. What I mean is, she owned it now, and I had agreed to provide upkeep for one year, and the two of us were officially out of each other's lives. This was supposed to leave me free to pursue Honey. But I wasn't getting very far in that direction.) Isn't a guy allowed a little R&R once in awhile? "Once you give up your integrity," I told myself, "the rest is a piece of cake."

"Excuse . . . me?" Mary Elizabeth cried into my shoulder.

"I said: I'm going to go take a shower. How would you like to come along and scrub my back? But you have to stop crying first."

She swung back her head and looked at me as if I were Prince Charming with three wishes just for her.

CHAPTER 9

I guess you'd call it conspicuous elimination. I've got bathrooms there in Aspen that I've never used.

It took three members of the Cool Crew to empty the second upstairs bathroom of people.

"Let's shut this party down," I ordered.

The looks of horror and disappointment forced me to qualify that. "Well, at least knock it back to a force-ten gale. I mean, I'm gonna want to go to bed in a few minutes."

All eyes swivel to Mary Elizabeth, who has two black gloved hands locked around my waist.

"You got it," one of the guys said.

"Punch up today's news, get us some clean towels, and let us have some privacy, huh?"

"Uh, which news, Cool?" one of the other Cool Crew asked. (As I understand it, Hugh Hefner has a video team that records even more extensively than my boys do for me . . . and that I don't understand.)

"Which network news do you like?" I asked Mary Elizabeth. "ABC, CBS, NBC? CNN?"

"Oh, *Jennings!*" she answered.

"You got it," one of the guys said, and Mary and I had the bathroom to ourselves.

Mary Elizabeth started undressing. There were some water splashes on the floor, and soggy towels bunched over in one corner. She wiped a clean, dry space on one of the counters, and carefully laid her black dress on it. Then, she took off her black high-heels, and carefully placed them on the counter next to her dress. She had to be careful, because she was so excited that she was trembling.

There was a knock on the door, and a friend there with a stack of clean towels. Through the doorway, he could see Mary Elizabeth and her autographed bosom, carefully moving her black gloves next to her black purse. Through the doorway, I could see big Timothy behind him suggesting that perhaps everyone might like to move the festivities downstairs, and the resulting mass exodus in the direction of stairways & elevator.

I closed the door and took off my clothes. My penis seemed to have forgotten all about the tears.

"Oh, dear," Mary Elizabeth said, when I turned on the temperature-regulated shower spray, and hit the "full-rinse" button. I mean, there's nine different nozzles, and they were coming at me from everywhere.

I winked. "I'll sign the other one after."

Airbrushed young 1990s airheads, like Mary Elizabeth, are a tough group to impress, but my color TV in the shower & remote-control on a rope did it. She was squeaking with astonishment.

Bad nationwide comics, like myself, are also a tough

group to impress, but when Mary Elizabeth pranced into my shower spray, still wearing her black nylon stockings, red lacy panties and red lacy garter belt, and started soaping me up . . . she nailed my nads. Even the left one was feeling no pain.

I had never made love in the shower before. OK, call me inexperienced. But I couldn't think of a more effective way to totally forget about Honey for a few minutes. This was not a plain Vanilla derriere. This was a cherry-topped Hagan Daaz banana-split with fresh strawberries and homemade whipped cream . . . and . . . I had never made love to a girl in a garter belt. OK, call me inexperienced.

Even everyone's favorite Penthouse Pet (she was eventually voted Pet of the Year) laughed at me when I bought a couple of skimpy little garters for her (for my birthday). She refused to put them on.

She called them retrogressively sexist devices for the enslavement of women—patriarchic, hysterical and paranoidal perversities—brutally repulsive, chronically ill violations of femininity, revealing my goose-stepping hatred of pudendum, ridiculing her spirituality, and it proved that I was a misogynist for my debauched and depraved desire to reduce her to the lowest stage of humiliation.

I silently put the sassy underthings back in the box. (I do not attempt to delve into the nude-model mind. Three famous orifices are enough, thank you.)

Which reminds me: Mary Elizabeth kept thanking me. As she shampooed my hair, she thanked me. As she washed behind my ears, she thanked me. As she soaped my neck, she thanked me. As she squished her perfect boobs against my back, she thanked me.

I hit "full-rinse" and she screamed happily.

It was a neat equation of revenge: Honey had run off with a superstud about twice her age, she was probably screwing him right now; Mary was a wet dream about half my age, just dripping for it.

It was no use. Some simpering shred of integrity was still festering away deep down somewhere inside my soul. It didn't matter how hard my penis was. I just could not screw the girl. She was not Honey.

I turned on the news.

"Thank you, Cool, ever so much, yes, thank you," Mary Elizabeth said, hugging my soapy tummy and back.

I turned on the sound.

Perhaps I should mention that the color TV was mounted into one wall, safely behind a shower-proof glass panel.

"Where does the sound come from?" Mary Elizabeth wanted to know.

"Hey, I just live here," I told her.

Peter Jennings was in the middle of telling us how it wasn't even safe to take the train anymore. The big news was the latest transportation disaster involving an Amtrak locomotive . . . a DC-10 fell on it.

But Mary Elizabeth was thanking and cleaning almost every part of me. And leaving no part untouched.

I firmly controlled myself, before Mary Elizabeth firmly controlled me.

I hit the rewind button, and put Mary Elizabeth in front

of me, at a safe distance, and we watched some TV.
From the beginning. (I never watch anything in real time.)

"Jennings has pretty good TV-Q," I told her. "He
needs it. There's a technical name for this type of screen
image, which is the most boring way to shoot TV. It's called
a 'Talking Head.' Now, watch, and see if you notice
anything." I killed the sound, and double-checked with
my water-resistant wristwatch. Yup. Same old, same old.
Jennings kept better time than my quartz crystal.

She didn't get it for almost a minute, and then she suddenly kindled into incendiary giggles. "He's stuck!" she
shrieked. So OK, I was wrong. I apologize. She wasn't an
airbrushed airhead. A waterlogged vidkid would be more
accurate.

I hit "full-rinse" and Mary Elizabeth shrieked again,
slapping me in the neck, twice, with her Colorado-
whitewater-drenched hair.

"Every six seconds Jennings goes through that little rit-
ual. Over and over. It doesn't matter whether he's talking about the national debt or cocaine babies. He bobs
his head, tips it a little sideways, he blinks, he nods
again, he looks down, his head slides right a little, then
jukes left. Every six seconds."

"He's stuck!"

"OK, let's see if I can find a shoulder shake."

I fast-forwarded, and Mary Elizabeth lost it. Watching
Jennings do his robot routine at high speed turned Mary
Elizabeth into a hysterical & horizontal woman. Both her
slippery hands were on both of my slippery feet, and
her wet head was poking between my wet knees.

So OK. Call me kinky. Mary Elizabeth's sleekly wet black nylon legs. Mary Elizabeth's bright red soggy panties. Mary Elizabeth's bright red gender-gap-reducing garter belt. Cool McCool's gravity-defying penis.

I hauled her back up and turned her around. "You missed it. There, I'll go back. Once in awhile, he'll slip in a shoulder-shake to break up the monotony. When he fits a shoulder-shake into his routine, it takes nine seconds."

Mary Elizabeth turned her head just enough to say, "Thank You, Cool."

"Ah-oh, here comes a commercial. Whenever he does that, a commercial is about to pop." Sure enough, seconds later they were paying bills. I fast-forwarded to two other commercials. Both other times, just before the commercial, Jennings made a surreptitious little glance down, then guiltily looked quickly up again, and his eyes slid out reverently to the right.

But Mary Elizabeth was suddenly turbulent. She twisted her whole body around. "That's genius! Cool, you've got to do this one! Please work this into a skit or something! Or maybe talk over it? You've got to! It's genius!" Her eyes were big and wide and utterly serious. "It's really funny!"

. . . . .

I put on my clothes while Mary Elizabeth got naked. She unlatched her wet stockings, slinked them off, laid them on the counter. Her hands were on her translucent panties, tugging them downward. My penis was limply fitting easily into my underwear.

We had watched some TV and had a few laughs, but Honey was back in my mind.

"Thank you," Mary Elizabeth said, as I watched her sweet blond muff. Didn't do a thing for me. She added, "It just wouldn't have been right." Her garter belt was on the counter now.

"Please stop thanking me," I told her.

"Oh, but I have to! I could see how much you wanted to! I know I'm just an airbrain, but really, it wouldn't have been right! I'm for you . . . but . . . it just wouldn't have been right! I was so worried, but you're such a gentleman, Thank You. Really. Thank you."

I buttoned my shirt and looked at her.

Her impish face. Her indecent bush.

My inhibited penis.

And she squeaked the next words out in a frisky way: "To lose my virginity in the shower! No, no, it just wouldn't be right. That's why I had to keep my panties on. I didn't dare take them off!"

I was completely dressed now, and Mary Elizabeth was completely undressed.

For a moment all I could think about was her virginity washing uselessly down the drain. "Full-rinse."

I didn't get away fast enough. She took one uneasy step toward me, and then almost ran to me. Mary Elizabeth put her arms around me. "Please take me into your bed." Her eyes were so bright, her lips were so juicy. "Please make me into a woman." Her arms were so eager. "Please make me into your woman." She was trembling with excitement.

I shook my head, sadly. "I can't."

Her trembling stopped. She was awed. "You love her."

I nodded.

We were both silent for a long, long time. Mary Elizabeth untouched me. She put on her black dress, her black highest-heels, her black gloves. Her wet little lacies and stockings remained on the counter.

"I'm going to leave now," I said.

"No you're not!" she said, sharply. "You're going to feel me first. You don't believe I'm a virgin, do you? You think I'm just another airbrain who would say anything to go to bed with you. I'll let you go, but you have to feel me first."

I cleared my throat. "I'd rather sign your other breast, if you don't mind."

"But I do mind. Come over here." She sat down on the bathroom chair, spread her legs widest. "Come here."

I stood there by the bathroom door. It would be so easy to turn my back on her, and walk out. Actually, it would have been the hardest thing in the world to do.

A single tear fell out of Mary Elizabeth's right eye. "Please?" She was trembling again.

Actually, it would have been impossible for me to turn my back on her.

So I got down on one knee, there between her legs. She scooched forward. She lifted up her dress.

"Feel," she said.

"Mary—"

With her teeth, she held the hem of her dress up, and

with her two gloved hands, she gently took my right hand and pulled it to her. When my hand didn't want to move, she pulled harder.

And sure enough, there was a little something there, just inside, that I'd never felt before. OK, call me inexperienced.

And call me semi-hard . . .

Fully-hard . . .

Painfully-hard . . .

She let go of her dress, with her teeth, and it fluffed down. But her hands held my hand tight, and weren't about to let me go just yet.

"Remember, I'm for you. No matter where you go, or what you do, I'm for you. I'll always be your virgin girl, until you make me a woman. I'm for you. I'll always be your girl."

"That's not healthy," I said.

"No. I am healthy. You can be sure of that."

She told me her telephone number. And I knew it would be a long, long time before I'd be able to forget that number. Her gloved hands gripped me so tight, it hurt.

"I'm for you," Mary Elizabeth said, over and over, like a mantra, as her hot, slippery fluids gushed over my fingers and dripped down my palm. "I'm for you."

CHAPTER 10

It would have been undiplomatic to wash, so I had *Eau de Mary Elizabeth* all over my right hand.

Timothy and the Cool Crew had everything under control, downstairs. The drug usage was appropriately covert (forty or fifty of the partiers were all under a bright green and white parachute, heads bobbing around as some of them danced). My 100,000 dollar stereo system was only being used 30,000 dollars' worth. The party damage was taken care of in advance: Timothy showed me a blank check he had apologetically acquired. I looked at the signature on it. Yup, the damage was taken care of.

"Listen," I told Timothy, "can I sleep in your room tonight? I need some serious privacy. You can stay in one of my bedrooms upstairs, OK?"

"It's not locked," the big man said.

"There's a girl upstairs. Her name is Mary Elizabeth McEnroe. Be nice to her. But make sure she's out of here before morning. And, Tim . . . I don't want to see her again."

On my way out to the separate guest house, I passed

some more famous party crashers. They were bundled up against the cold. I wasn't. I started to go over to shake hands, but prudently decided on a fast furtive frozen wave.

.　　.　　.　　.

Timothy had a little pillbox on his dresser with three compartments in it. Up-arrows. Down-arrows. Squiggly lines.

I swallowed one of his pink "down-arrows" and splashed down, dead to the world, in his waterbed.

Despite the "down-arrow," I awoke very up-arrow. The bed was sloshing all over the place, and there was something alive on top of me. The room was completely dark. I couldn't see anything. Whatever was on top of me was very furry, like a big animal. But it was human, and it was female. It was doing female things, and I could smell some perfumey female smells. My pants were open, and female fingers were digging in there . . . very *cold* fingers, I might add.

In my dream, I had been making love with Honey. Words can't describe how wonderful she was. I'd need a new language. I was immediately pissed as hell that Mary Elizabeth would chase me down here and wake me up from heaven, from absolute nirvana. But maybe it was Honey, on top of me, back from her quickie with Bruce Ranger. So my intense anger went away just as quickly. I know it sounds strange, but I was waiting to see if I was angry or not.

"Dritchell, get off my dick!" I shoved her off me. "God damn it!"

I was angry. I swam over toward a light switch. God, I hate waterbeds. This was not a waveless waterbed. After a few seconds of floundering around, I found the switch.

Amanda Dritchell said, "[Colloquial naughty deleted], Cool. I thought Honey [verb deleted] you into the ground, and that you were hiding out down here, all limp and exhausted and [taboo expression deleted]!"

"Back off, Dritchell."

Forget what you read in any of the garter-strewn pages of Bob Guccione's publications, her real name is Amanda Dritchell (and if you eyeball her photo-shoots carefully, you will find no courtesan's teasers, no Puritan-pleasing half-cup bras, no misogynistic crotchless panties, or sex-trivializing garter-belts).

Blue jeans, cowboy boots, T-shirt & faux mink coat. "Hot in here," she said. She took off the simulated mink like a sexual challenge. It was said that a *Penthouse* scout discovered her while she was wearing just blue jeans and T-shirt.

I had given her the McCool T-shirt. I had given her the Dingo boots. I had given her the full-length phony mink, which actually cost more than the coats made from dead animals. Her watch, her bracelet, every piece of jewelry she was wearing, I think, were things that I had given her. Even the turquoise belt. I really didn't know what to make of it. When I would buy her clothes or jewelry, she'd always thank me like crazy, but then she'd never wear them.

"So when you gonna introduce me, huh? Y'know that

whore left her soppy stinky undies all over my bathroom. Skimpy pervy little icky yucks. You'd think Honey
would have some smarts. Say! Were you two [double-
entendre deleted] in *my shower?*"

"Back off, Dritchell. What the hell are you doing in
Aspen?"

"And Honey wrote masochistic crap all over my mirror with lipstick!" She growled like a lioness defending
her veldt. "Oh, I could tear out her bottled hair and
strangle her with it!" Her voice mimicked a nasty child's
voice: "I'll love you forever. I'm for you. I'm all for you.
I'm your virgin girl. Love, ME." Her voice resumed its normal bossy princess timbre. "Were you two playing dirty
sex games? You know I hear Honey's really into bondage.
I hear she can't come unless she's all tied up. What'd you
do? Tie her up and whip her with her own garters? In my
shower! And what's that 'virgin girl' crap? Virgin my
[female bodily part deleted]!"

"Dritchell . . ." I mean, where do I start?

"So when you gonna introduce me, huh? You promised."

This is about the way our conversations usually go.
Over the edge of the flat Earth. Usually my rebuttal is to
remove her clothes and kiss her into silence. However,
in this instance of integrity, my tool of debate was not up
to the task. My brain was bewitched by Honey.

"Cool." She waved her hand in front of my face.
"When are you going to introduce me to Honey?"

"After *I* get introduced into Honey."

"Don't fertilize me, you liar! I can smell her all over you!"

I forgot that my right hand was still fragrant with Mary Elizabeth's bodily liquor.

"Dritchell, you and I are history. Let's stick to the agreement. You can have the apartment in Manhattan, OK? But you don't have any bathrooms here in Aspen. This is my place."

That silenced her. For about two seconds.

After boasting that she could seduce Honey away from me, if she wanted to, Amanda launched into a long, feminist analysis of what had gone wrong with our relationship.

This was going to take awhile, so I lit up a Camel. It hurt my heart. God, I missed Honey. Where would I find another woman to light my cigarettes for me?

I listened. And honest, I listened. I smoked. And honest, I smoked.

Amanda couldn't hold still while she talked, so she was making all kinds of waves that were very distracting. I mean, I practically needed a surfboard to stay on top of this conversation.

I grunted. (A woman wants a man to make some noise occasionally, while she's talking to him.) I said, "Yeah." (A woman does not regard these "listening sounds" as agreement or endorsement, but rather as permission to continue speaking, as a signal of emotional involvement and continued understanding.) "Mmmhm," I said. (A woman, after all, does not want to feel as though she is speaking to a wall.) "Hmm."

"Are you listening to me?" Amanda Dritchell suddenly asked, in a sharply hostile tone of voice. (Oops, I sometimes forget the most important conversational stratagem. A woman is a vain creature. A woman wants a man to watch her while she is talking to him.) "Cool! Do you have even the faintest IDEA what I'm saying?"

"I'm a condescending bully on a one-up trip," I repeated back to her. "The only life-script I have shared with you is the I'm-smarter-than-you script. I never listen to you. I'm not interested in you. All I want is hot- and cold-running pussy." Pause. "My turn to talk?"

I reminded her that I had once asked her to marry me, to settle down and grow some kids; and if that wasn't *interested in her*, what was?

She shook her head, furiously. She opened her mouth, but I plunged ahead, before she could get words out at me.

I reminded her that I had asked her to go on the road with me, to be with me all the time, that I wanted to listen to her all the time. I swore on the muse Thalia that I always listened to her. But I admitted that most of the time, I couldn't understand her. I quickly added that I didn't mind, though, because I found her very inspirational.

She looked daggers at me for that one, and climbed over on my legs, but I kept talking, *fast*.

I reminded her that she was the one who had given me the long lecture on personal space in a relationship. That I had always wanted more closeness, affection, romance and intimacy between us. That I was just trying to play the game by her rules.

I pointed out that she was the one who thought up the famous-friends/famous-orifices analogy and repeatedly applied it to our relationship.

I tried to mention that I found it insulting that my girl-friend would go around offering her orifices, up for stabs, to anyone with more famous connections.

But no, no, *No*, didn't I ever *Listen*? (Amanda slapped my thighs and shouted me into silence.) This was what everyone automatically thought about our relationship, so she had to re-educate them. The way to deal with prejudice is head-on. By actually saying what was in the back of everyone's minds, in the most straightforward, brutal way, she was forcing people to take her seriously as an intelligent woman. Didn't I ever listen to what she said? Was I so caught up in my own macho trip that I was completely deaf to any kind of verbal subtlety? And what about Honey? Was I going to introduce her, or not?

Her hands were on my thighs now. And they were doing female things.

Well, screw it. I'd had enough with integrity. I was getting horny again, and this gal knew it. For the first time, I noticed that Amanda had even dyed her hair that faint tinge of red that I really like.

I smiled. And she smiled. We both knew what we were both thinking. We had had some absolutely fantastic sexual bouts just after fierce arguments.

I didn't love the girl anymore, but I did like her; there was still real affection. So I told her the truth. She deserved to know. I told her all about how Honey had left the party with Bruce Ranger. And I told her all about Mary Elizabeth, the superfan that Marshall had apparently been saving for me. I explained how we had taken a shower together, but that nothing had happened. I told her how the girl had insisted that she was a virgin, and how she had forced me to feel her so that I would believe her. Then I got off on a tangent about how I didn't like the Cool Crew promising fans of mine introductions to me in return for sex. I was going to put a stop to that fast.

Amanda was very quiet as she listened to all this. The surface of the waterbed was eerily still.

When I was finished, Amanda gently spread my legs very wide.

She snuggled down very close, between my legs, and she gave me this smile that I'll never forget.

And she hit me with her little fist.

I went into my brilliantly masculine demonstration of sensitivity '90s-style.

"Don't fertilize me!" she screamed.

The waterbed was sloshing all over the place.

She gathered up her mink coat and stomped out into the snow, leaving the front door wide open.

"Aaaaaaaagh," I said. The same damn left ball.

CHAPTER 11

My left testicle had swollen to almost the size of a tennis ball. I had my pants and boxers down, and I was standing, staring at it in the mirror, when Timothy closed his front door and then came into his bedroom.

"Oh," he said.

I just looked at him. It hurt like hell with every heartbeat, but what was really frightening was the SIZE of the thing. "You think Michael Jackson will want to buy this left ball?" I asked.

Timothy didn't say anything.

"Elephant-man balls," I said. "Never mind, it's not very funny."

Timothy said, "Uh, there's a phone call for you. It's Honey. She's waiting."

I didn't know what time it was, but it wasn't light yet. "Give her a message for me, will you? Take the phone, and slam it down hard enough to break the phone. That's the message."

The man as big as a horse said, "Now, Cool, you know you wanna talk to this woman."

It took about four minutes for me to hobble through the

snow back to my house. (I've got a cordless telephone, but nobody seemed to know where it was.) The thing I like about Timothy is that he never once offered to carry me.

"Shut up," I told everyone in my living room, as they watched me hobble like a cripple over to a telephone with some privacy. There were only about twenty people left. The party was pretty much over. A few horizontal bodies writhed under the bright green and white parachute.

On the way, I dug a fresh Stetson out of a closet.

I lit up a fresh Camel. I tilted the Stetson over to a jaunty angle, nicotined my lungs with a nice big suck, and then picked up the phone in the library. I could hear someone breathing on the other end. Actually, I could hear two people breathing.

"Hi, Honey."

The other extension at my house in Aspen hung up.

"Mmmmmmmmmmmmmmmmmmmmmmmmmmmmm," Honey said, "go in and get a sex test, will ya? I'm gettin' one, Monday. Like, it's life in the Nineties, right? An' we'll . . . get together. And compare notes."

I smoked into the telephone.

Honey breathed into the telephone.

I was exhausted. And my heart hurt even more than my balls. I just could not think of anything appropriate to say. "My left ball hurts."

"Good!" she snapped. "I should have kneed you twice as hard!"

I was so outraged that I held the telephone receiver out at arm's length and stared at it. What kind of a woman was this?

Faintly, I could hear Honey's voice come out of the receiver, and it had a sniffy, self-righteous tone and quality to it. "How was tall blond Miss Sweetmeat in the black dress?"

Then I remembered that some of Honey's friends (Spies!) had come to the party, and obviously reported back to her my antics in the second upstairs bathroom.

Automatically, I said, "Hey. Nothing happened. Honest." I immediately squinched my eyes tightly shut and cursed myself for being a terminal wimp.

"Jimmy, I didn't do anything . . . I can't talk about it, but I didn't do anything."

I smoked into the telephone.

Honey breathed into the telephone.

"Don't be a poohbutt, Jimmy! I didn't do anything! I'm not any good at good-byes! I had to go with him, so I went. But I didn't do anything."

They say that Honey can't act. They're wrong. I believed every word. She even made me feel guilty.

"OK," I admitted, "I felt up her vagina. We took a shower together, we watched some TV, and I felt up her vagina." Pause. "She wanted to prove to me that she was a virgin." Pause. "She's still a virgin."

"I'll accept that. It explains the nylons."

"What?"

"Carrie said, 'Black nylons, before; bare legs, after.'"

"Boy, your spies really come across with the info, don't they!"

"My spies are the best."

CHAPTER 12

I'd like to write a few words about our mental relationship. For a long time there wasn't any.

I fell in love with Honey when she blushed. She sat on my lap on *Donald Chapman*. But could I get her wonderful buns into an opera house? We Screwed Comfortably against Marlene's wall. But I so much as touch her dinner knife, and she skips off with my cigarette lighter, leaving me with the check. I even walked across a V-12 Jaguar for her. What did it get me? An 800-number. When I whispered love-stuff in her ear, fate handed me a cell-net error.

For the love of Honey, I was locked in a psycho's bathroom. You know what that got me. A left testicle the size of a tennis ball.

Just when I think I'm about to score Big Time, and we're on my bed cuddling like crazy, the first male to come along takes her out of my arms with a few well-placed words whispered into her ear.

Does this discourage me? Hell no. For the love of Honey, I throw ex-girlfriends off my stiff dick. For the love of Honey, my penis defies a French Vanilla boob with my name on it and a natural blond virgin vagina in a garterbelt.

This is a mental relationship? This is not standard seduction procedure, as far as McCool is concerned. If you were to tell any of my ex-ladies any of these Honey-related facts, they would have pointedly questioned the feminism of the woman in question. "What? Cool walked on a Jaguar for a woman, and they never once talked about The Meaning of Life? That's funny." (That's how comedians and the ex-women of comedians laugh at a joke.) "You mean he has a testicle big as a tennis ball, and he and Honey never stayed up all night discussing Metaphysical Desert Islands, the McCool Philosophy, The Natural Superiority of Women, Fifteen-Minute Fame, Sex As a Form of Insanity, Fascist Father-hood, The Death of Dreams, The Divine Purpose of God, or The Myth of the Female Orgasm? That's funny."

I met Maggie Tiel (Magdalene Hersch, in those days) at a MENSA meeting. So OK, I walked in the wrong hotel conference room by mistake, big deal. I was smart enough to con my way inside and up next to the sexi-est angelface at the meeting.

I met Dritchell on Trump's yacht, in pre-Pet post-pose nights. She was hiding from a megamillionaire she didn't want to talk to, hiding out with me, inside a canvas-topped gas-powered lifeboat. We were using the emergency light, snacking on the emergency food, drinking emer-gency distilled water, and we were discussing emergency sex (Date Rape, actually) from opposite sides of the law (the lifeboat). I didn't know who or what she was. She didn't know who or what I was. I remember giving Amanda Dritchell a chaste kiss on her forehead, and kidding her, because of our provocative conversation. "You win. Your body damn near talked me into it, but your mind definitely talked me out of it. I'll just have to go buy a *Playboy* and play with myself." And I remember the look she gave me. She didn't say anything, but her look sure wasn't silent. I remember that I had to say something, so I said, "No, really, it's so nice to meet a woman who's smarter than I am, and confident enough of herself that she doesn't feel that she has to take off her clothes to attract a guy. I mean . . ." But she started shrieking with uncontrollable laughter that gave away our hiding place. The megamillionaire found her. But suddenly Amanda became very possessive of me. She started holding my arm with both of her hands, and she told the megamillionaire that he was a megajerk. I remember, as we were walking off the yacht, Dritchell told me, "I'm glad I met you tonight. I've got a feeling about us, y'know? My last boyfriend was a real clown."

· · · · ·

Honey and I first made love on television.

I met Honey secretly, at night, at a honeymoon resort place. I won't tell which one, but I will give a hint. The grounds were in the shape of a gigantic heart. Each bungalow was built in the shape of a heart. It had a heart-shaped bed, a heart-shaped Jacuzzi, little heart-shaped plates on a heart-shaped table in the dining room. The fireplace was heart-shaped. Right, that place.

Honey and I exchanged sexual histories. These were not heart-shaped.

We discussed AIDS and former Surgeon General C. Everett Koop. Honey thought he was really sexy, with those big sideburns. I wondered out loud if they chafed his wife's thighs.

I said what every heterosexually active male says these days: That my penis was a virgin as far as the anus was concerned; that it had never been inside an anus, but that *if* it had, it would have only been inside nice clean virgin girl-anuses, and only then while sheathed in laboratory-tested spermicide-drenched double-strength condoms, five condoms thick, and *if that*, well, my penis would have refused to ejaculate, and immediately dunked itself in full-strength Clorox bleach within seconds of withdrawal. Ouch!

She gave me a wonderfully skeptical Honey Look.

The television swiveled its hips (well, it rotated about fifty or sixty degrees back and forth by remote control, so no matter where we were in the room, we could make the TV look at us).

And because it was her favorite show, we sat down on one of the couches, rotated the TV toward us, and watched a rerun of *Twin Peaks*. Honey had the remote control.

Honey lit up a cigarette for me, by starting it in her own painted lips, and put my ancient gold Zippo in her blouse pocket for safekeeping.

And there I was, in a honeymoon resort, with the sexiest, the most famous woman in the world, watching television. Here we were, and we had hardly touched each other. Not even a hello-kiss. The only time our fingers had touched was in handing sex-test reports back and forth.

Honey's softly tousled platinum-blond hair, Honey's gleaming diva lips, Honey's seductive show of thighs, cleavage, arms . . . Cool's Stetson, Cool's Camel Filters, Cool's dangerously bright smile . . .

During commercials, I became intimately acquainted with her mind.

"Would you like a drink?"

"No, Jim. Thank you."

"Would you like a cuddle?"

"Not during *TP*, Jim. Please."

"Would you like some more potato chips?"

"Shhh, the show's back."

During another commercial I told her that Robbie was nervous about me seeing her. He couldn't say why, he just said that he didn't like it. Honey mentioned that her main manager, Claude Boxer, dismissed me as a has-been.

"A has-been?"

"He said you're the clown who still does Hinckley jokes."

"Everybody does Hinckley jokes! Especially since they caught Jodie Foster going down there again, visiting him in that institution."

"[Expletive of disbelief deleted]."

"I swear to Jimmy Durante! She's been visiting him once a month, and giving him blowjobs. But she won't swallow. How do you like that? The guy shoots the President for her, and she won't swallow."

"That's sick," she said, but she laughed a little as she said it. "And that's bullshit."

"You're right, it's bullshit, but it makes good copy. All they really know is that she visits him once a month, and that after she leaves, there's sperm on the floor. Nobody really knows, for sure, whether she blows him, or pulls on his pole, or just watches him yank on himself. Maybe she strips for him, to get him excited . . ."

"Shhh, it's back."

But she had insulted my pride, and I wasn't going to let her get off that easily.

Next commercial, I whispered into Honey's ear: "Personally, I think Hinckley is grandstanding. I think he jerks off in his padded cell, puts it in a baggie, and then smears it on the visiting room floor as Jodie leaves."

"You're a perv, Jimmy." But she was giggling. That silent giggle that jiggles her whole body. "That is so dumb. Do people laugh at shit like that?" She giggled some more. She was getting silly now, I almost had her. (The whole art of comedy is really just conning them into a silly mood, when they'll laugh at anything, and then keeping them there for a few minutes. I can't really explain it any better than that, and I don't really understand how I do it.)

"On a good night, people laugh. Is this a good night?"

She wouldn't say. She had stopped giggling, and just looked at me.

I said, totally serious now, sad, and even a little tired, "Jodie *really* visits him, strictly for the publicity, to keep her name in the news, so people will keep talking about her, and her name will keep coming up for new parts—

you think they let just any female direct?"

That got her half the way. Loud cackling Laughter. She was just silly enough. I had her now. A professional psychologist could have analyzed her whole set of secret motivations, just on the basis of her laughter caused by those precise words said just the way I said them. But I was a professional comedian. I made her tinkle.

Riding hard on the theme, I said, "She may win another Oscar, just 'cause of the Hinckley visits. She'll get the crazy vote."

Honey's laughter was simmering now.

I added, disillusioned and depressed at the whole world, "And nobody's really done a lab test on the sperm. Foster probably brings it in herself, in a little baggie, and smears it on the floor when Hinckley's not looking."

She exploded in violent laughter. And it warmed my insides. I may have even smiled just a little one, for a second, I'm not sure.

"[Fast blitz of five outrageously offensive Hinckley jokes deleted]," I said.

"Oh NO!" Honey shrieked, completely out of control now, and she started clutching her crotch through her black leather skirt and crossing her legs. "Stop! You're gonna make me pee, you bastard!" she squeaked, convulsing so intensely that she fell down off the couch, and started writhing on the floor, wheezing with laughter, looking probably about how I looked after she kneed me in the balls. "Show's back," I told her, stone-faced.

•   •   •   •   •

All good television shows must come to an end.

Honey left the television on, but she gave me all her attention. "Where would Jimmy McCool like to have Honey?"

I really didn't know how to respond to that. None of my normal smooth-moves were working worth a damn with this woman.

"The bedroom?" she asked. "Or would you rather have Honey down on the hard floor of that kitchenette? Tell me. Would you like to have Honey, romantically, in front of the fireplace?"

I grabbed Honey and hauled her into my arms and carried her there. I set her down on it.

The two most famous eyes in the world sparkled at me. "How career-oriented!" she said.

.   .   .   .   .

In her next *Rolling Stone* interview, Honey was asked where her favorite place to have sex was. She replied without hesitation: "On television!" The interviewer was slightly startled by this. "I wasn't aware that . . ." "Oh, yes," Honey said. "It was a Toshiba. Thirty-two inch. Killer!"

.   .   .   .   .

So OK, you want to know, how was Honey on television? Did the fox know how to put on a condom? Was she any good in bed? (We eventually did get there.) I'm the guy with hands-on experience, you figure, and you bought this book to find out this one fact! While I'm at it, you want to know what her FQ (Fellatio Quotient) was. You want to know if all the S&M rumors are true. And just what the hell is the Honey Position anyway?

That awesome Hollywood lover, Philip Channing, in his autobiography, lists Honey 4th. (There are 473 women listed and ranked in his autobiography.) Well, it's obvious to me that the man either can't count or is really into tongue-baths, since I've had the star-screwer he lists 2nd, and all she wanted to do was lick my buns, suck on my toes, and have me come all over her ankles. Frankly, I was more bored than excited, and lost my erection several times during the, quote, sex act, unquote. Honey told me she's never had any kind of sex with Philip, unless I counted phone-sex (one time when Philip Channing was trying to talk her into meeting him at his suite at the Carlyle). Honey said he sounded so horny that she thought he came into the mouthpiece. If the only sex Honey had with Phil Channing was phone-sex, this would explain how she could fall to fourth place.

Danny Sonnenfeld was desperately in love with Honey during the filming of *The Robbery* (the movie she did for his production company), and for about a year afterward. Some brave interviewer asked Sonnenfeld if Honey was any good in the sack. Rather than punching the guy out, Danny's face slowly lit up into a glowing grin. Honey told me she thought Danny's butterfly tattoos were cute.

Buck Stone's mother has said that although Honey and her boy made the perfect social couple, she wasn't sure they were properly matched in bed, because Honey didn't seem to be considerate of Bucky's need to wear ammunition belts, spare Uzi cartridges, and ketchup stains on his guerrilla nighties. Honey told me that wasn't it at all; she has nothing against guns in bed, but Bucky kept pulling out the wrong caliber.

About the time I was enjoying Honey on television, the *National Toilet Enquirer* had a pair of front-page pics of Bruce Ranger and Honey. Ranger was quoted as saying, "No Comment." You have to admire the man's style. I asked Honey one more time about her and Ranger, and she repeated, "Don't be a Poohbutt!"

And so, finally, the words you've been waiting to read, my in-depth sexual analysis of Honey:

I'd need a new language.

CHAPTER 13

Robbie Berger is the greatest. He's one of my all-time favorite guys, and just about the meanest son of a bitch in the business.

How mean is he? We're there at the Polo Lounge taking a meeting. It's the bar in the Beverly Hills Hotel. Every table has a phone, right?

Wrong. Our table has three phones, and a FAX machine. It also has a gigantic Cartier juice blender and a tiny gold Gucci microwave oven on it. Two tables close to ours have no phones on them, and glaring, dissatisfied diners. Nothing is too much trouble for Mr. Berger.

It's a side table with a view of everyone entering or leaving. I am hiding behind sunglasses & lowered Stetson & puffed Camel smoke.

My photograph is matched with Honey's on the cover of about a third of all the tabloid shit-sheets in the supermarkets. I don't know what I'm worried about. Honey's picture is this huge eye-catching glob of color. My pic is a tiny little black & white insert on most of them. The headlines vary. But the theme is clear: COCKROACH CRAWLS UP LEG OF GODDESS.

Oh, but I didn't tell you how mean Robbie is. This guy orders a New York Steak and he puts it in his gold and silver super-blender, and then drinks it. He has three Espresso coffees on the edge of his side of the table. Robbie is screaming into two of the telephones like a Jewish maniac on methamphetamine. When he needs more energy, he puts one of the Espressos in the microwave, heats it until it is boiling over, hauls it out (it's 212 degrees, and bubbling over onto the white tablecloth), and then tosses it back like a shot of whiskey.

(He's an ex-ex New Yorker, he's got the all-over winter tan, the outdoor Jacuzzi in Beverly Hills; the guy just does not look back.)

Pentagon Pictures is faxing us a proposed contract. Five pages have already burped out of the machine.

Robbie's beeper starts going off. I mean, we're in *2001: A Space-Cake Odyssey*. Robbie's got three telephones there; one on the table, faxing like mad, while his mouth jump-cuts between the two phones in his hands. And off goes his beeper. I don't know if this is *film noir* or *cinéma vérité* or just an SP-FX gag.

Robbie cradles one phone between his neck and shoulder, and awkwardly reaches inside his white California suit. He tosses this little black beeper out on the table at me. "Get it, will ya?" he says. It's making enough noise, now that it's out on the table, to further disturb nearby diners, so I make a grab for it.

I don't know much about beepers. But I figure I can probably make it shut up without hurting it. Or hurting myself.

Wrong. I push one of the buttons, and it pops open like a Jack-in-the-box. It's not making noise anymore, but I can't believe what I'm looking at, so I don't do anything.

"Excuse me," Robbie says into his right receiver.

"Excuse me," Robbie says into his left receiver.

"Baby," Robbie says to his best client, "talk to it."

"Huh?"

"Answer the phone, Stupid!"

Excuse me. *2010: A Space-Cake Odyssey.* "You're talkin' to the coolest dude alive," I say into the itty-bitty cellular phone. Immodesty becomes me. "Oh, hi Honey. Say, I told you not to call me here . . ."

Honey's Hotline Ladies are really operating double-time to scope me out here in the Polo Lounge on Berger's cellular phone.

It's Honey's birthday. She's all depressed because it looks like they're not going to shut down the set to throw a surprise Birthday Party for her. So she wants to be sure I show up and "surprise" her.

"I don't know, Honey, I'm awful busy."

"Please?" she asks ultra-sweetly. "Everybody's just tromboning." (Screwing around, in Honey-talk.) "I need some attention. Just stop by and give me something."

"Nix," I tell her. "I gotta do some fiscal stuff with Berger."

"Come on, Cool," she pleads, and I know she's desperate when she doesn't call me Jimmy. "Wrap it up real pretty, with a nice big bow, will ya?"

I blow a silent smoke ring that hangs and hangs and hangs, but does not hang up.

A silent Honey-pout. My face grimaces. I have to grit my teeth.

"It's my birthday," she cries. Are those real tears I hear on the telephone? Maybe just one. One lonely glistening tear making its way down the pink and flushed cheek of the most famous face on four continents. "Just give me some violets then. Something."

She's right. She needs some attention. After all, she's Honey. I should run right over to her, hold her hand, fill the shooting stage with flowers.

I firmly tilt down my Stetson, and take a cruel suck on my Camel Filter. "Honey," I say, hard like Humphrey Bogart, "I wouldn't give you the sweat off my balls." I hang up, and blow out a hefty cloud of cigarette smoke. At least, I assume that folding the thing and snapping it shut hangs it up.

Robbie says, "[Indecent expression deleted]," and hangs up the phone in his right hand. "Eight million's as high as they'll go."

Fiscal . . . fiscal . . . "For both pictures?" I ask.

"Yeah." He suddenly looks at the left receiver like he's going to dump it in his blender and eat it. "Don't shit me, Sid!" he yells into it. "You dig him outta that meeting if you have to [foul Yiddish language & nonstandard Goyische behavior deleted]!!" Robbie winks at me. "I'm on hold," he tells me.

I reallocate a portion of my brain to business, so that only 90% of my mind is daydreaming of Honey. "It's bull-shit," I tell him. "I'm a genius. I want genius wages." A genius is someone whose last picture made a lot of money. My last one made $45 million, for which I was paid $200,000 plus one and a half points. I wrote it, I starred in it, and I got diddley: $875,000.

"Cool, Baby, you don't get turnaround on this. They can lock this up in the courts for five years. You want to be between projects for five years?"

"Robbie, we do it my way, or we don't do it."

"Cool, Baby, we'll be celebrating New Year's 1999 before these pictures come out!"

"Robbie. Baby. We do it my way, or we don't do it. You just remind them that I have final cut on *Ice Cubes*. I'll kill it, I swear to God, I'll kill it, if they get tough with me! You tell Pentagon I'll leave the $12 million it cost them to make *Ice 99* on the cutting room floor! I own all the out-takes, and I'll *out-take both pictures to death*, by God, if they try to push me around! I'll have every kid watch-ing the Comedy Channel bad-mouthing these movies!" This is sound and fury, signifying nothing. I have given birth to these movies. They are my babies. I could no more harm them, than I could stop breathing. I do not have the heart to dull the sharpness of even the most minor whimsical moment of either of these pictures.

There may be someone meaner than Robbie Berger at that: Mark Rosenthal, chairman of Pentagon.

The SOB has me by the left testicle.

I have two finished pictures, ready for release. But

there's this little problem. My fee.

The first picture I starred in disappeared from the theaters after just breaking even, but it's still hot in the video rentals.

So Pentagon Pictures went after me.

I signed a two-picture contract. (Never again.)

My second picture, and first picture for Pentagon, *Paying Dues*, is a HUGE box office success, surprises everyone.

So I'm the new genius. Flavor of the month is more like it. Pentagon wants the second McCool picture yesterday, if not last week. No problem.

I wrote it, I starred in it, we used their money to make it. *Ice 99*, we called it. I'm only going to make peanuts, but the picture is the funniest thing I've ever done.

But there was a whole subplot in the work print of *Ice 99* that never made it to the final cut. Pentagon was not interested in making any more Cool McCool pictures, and had no use for the out-takes, so I acquired the rights to them, and I financed a fourth picture, *Ice Cubes*. Most of *Ice Cubes* we had to completely re-shoot, because the out-takes weren't as solid as I thought they were.

Anyway, Robbie drove an awesome distribution deal for *Ice Cubes*, giving me 11 points of the income. So now I'm going to make the big bucks!

Wrong. Pentagon misses the release date for *Ice 99*, and they suddenly claim that *Ice Cubes* is not an independent picture at all, but just the second half of *Ice 99*, and that therefore my payment is going to be one and a half points.

So Pentagon has a year of my work in the cans, and it's the best work I've ever done, and they're going to bury it until I agree to their terms. There's a lot more to the actual suit, but the bottom line is that they're trying to save themselves ten, twenty, maybe even thirty million dollars.

The telephone glued to Robbie's left ear comes alive. Robbie says, "Mark, this is Robbie." There is a pause. "Bullshit, Mark. Now, I want you to listen very carefully." Robbie can be very rational when he wants to.

This wasn't one of the times. Robbie buried Rosenthal in bullshit. McCool, sign an exclusive five-picture deal for $9 million per picture plus profit sharing? McCool, destroy his own best humor, kill his best jokes? McCool, throw $8 million down the toilet?

Or maybe Robbie was burying me in bullshit, talking to a dead phone, who knows?

After he hung up, he drank some more of his steak. Amazing. We've got four phones, and a FAX machine, and none of them are being used.

Robbie Berger gives me this look: Well, I invited you here, I may as well talk to you a little. But he doesn't talk. Instead he zaps and slugs down two boiling Espressos, one right after the other. "McCool," he finally says. "Take a pass on this one."

I didn't dignify this with a comment. It was an ironic way to phrase it.

"McCool . . . you two are the wrong package."

"The penetration is good." Hell, if he's going to throw around insider's lingo, I can do it too.

"McCool, man to man, stay away from this woman. She's nothing but trouble."

"Berger, man to man, back off."

"Baby, it isn't you. Trust me on this, I've seen it happen: you'll be bankable for a few months, but two, three years down the Coast and the spin on this could kill your career. It's just not cool."

"Drink your steak, before it gets cold."

And there we sat. Silently. Four telephones, a FAX machine, and two people with Honey in their heads, completely uncommunicative.

CHAPTER 14

It was a closed set on the Ursa Major lot, but they had a golden golf cart and a professional golf-cart driver to speed Yours Coolly to the secret shooting stage where Honey was making her latest movie.

The Black driver gaped at my raincoat, and then up at the sunny Southern California winter skies. "Where's the rain, Jack?"

I pointed a fingergun at him. "'Just Drive She Said.'"

Forty-three disgusted people became even more disgusted when I arrived. We're talking screenwriters, actors, stunt women, starlets, a PA, a couple of ADs, publicists, a gaffer and some gofers, extras, an art director, some set construction people, technicians, wardrobe people, a best boy and sundry walk-ons, cinematographer, cameraman, second cameramen, day players, unit production managers, stand-ins, the producer, the director, and twenty other people whose functions and titles I could only guess at—and they all look at me and go, "Oh, it's the cockroach."

The forty-fourth person got all excited and ran over to

me like I was his best friend and he hadn't seen me in two years. I have never been able to figure out George Thicke's exact position within the Honey Hierarchy, but I have copped a few fast facts. He's powerful. He's always nearby. He's queer. He's got a crush on me.

"She made one phone call," George Thicke told me, "and came back with PMS!"

I looked over at Honey's trailer. "Well, I know it's not PMS."

"You should know, Pally. But she started screaming totally crazy stuff and then ran into her trailer. Won't come out. That was more than an hour ago. Say, it's not going to rain, is it?" He touched the fabric of my raincoat.

I ignored that, and probed for information. "What time is the Surprise Birthday Party?"

"Oh shit, oh shit, oh *shit!*" he squeaked. "Who told you?" His heterosexual act was blasted to hell by two octaves.

"A piece of advice, George. Next time you guys organize a secret party for her, leak the info to her somehow, so she can act suitably surprised. Instead of unsuitably pissed-off that everyone's forgotten about her, and nobody loves her. What time is the thing?"

"Nine o'clock tonight."

I gave him a bleak look.

"Cool, go talk to her, will ya?" Finally, he took his hand off my raincoat.

"I'd bump up the party time a little, if I were you."

This is the New Hollywood. Honey's trailer is the same size as everyone else's.

But this is the New Hollywood. Honey's trailer is

inside the set. Everyone else who rates a trailer of their own has to go off the set to get to their trailer.

Now, when I go out and shoot a picture, I bring along the Cool Crew. But Honey had the whole Honey Brigade: accountants, lawyers, agents, financial advisers, boyfriend.

At the moment, the whole Honey Brigade (less boyfriend) was dug-in around the Honey trailer. Two advance scouts were up the stairs, tapping on the door and trying to sweet-talk the living legend back down to earth. They gave up, and walked down the stairs.

This little temper tantrum of Honey's was probably costing Ursa Major Studios upwards of $750 a minute, just in below-the-line costs.

So the boyfriend went over.

Here comes the cockroach, I could see all of Honey's Barnacles thinking, as they hung on tight around her trailer.

I indicated the raincoat I was wearing. "Raid-proof," I told them.

Well, at that precise moment, Honey's trailer door flies open, and a fresh, exuberant Honey starts prancing down the stairs. She's a pro, and she's had her little pout, but now it's back to business. But when she sees me, Honey jerks to a halt, and almost falls off the next to the last step. I stopped walking about six or seven feet away from her.

The way she was looking down at me, WHOA! We don't need Star Wars, one Honey in orbit would do it.

Honey doesn't say anything. Except with her eyes.

I don't say anything. Even with my eyes.

The forty-some other people don't say much, although there is some whispering as they watch us.

I haul out the little black box from inside my raincoat.

Do I say Happy Birthday? Nah, I just throw the little black box at her. Underhand toss.

She catches it.

Is it wrapped, all pretty, with a big bow? Nah. It's just a tiny black box.

"What's this?" Honey asks. "The sweat off your balls?"

My take-no-prisoners smile. "Yeah." What a woman. God, I love this woman.

Well, Honey opens the box. Her anger turns to amazement. I have never seen her mouth open so wide, before or after, on screen or off, in bed or out. "Who do you [Honey-invective deleted] think you are? Richard Burton? Who do you [same Honey-invective deleted] think I am? Elizabeth Taylor??"

My take-no-prisoners smile. "Well?"

It's 15.25 carats. It has a name. The Noah Diamond. It's got a certificate of authenticity from De Beers. Flawless, semi-famous blue-white circular diamond, provisionally mounted on a band of gold for her ring finger because I didn't much like the other settings.

She looks at the diamond. And then she looks at me.

And then she looks at the diamond. And then she looks at me.

And then this funny kind of half-smile comes to her face, like I just suggested a pervy sexual act to her, but that the more she thinks about it, the more she wants to try it anyway.

"Yeah," she says. "Yeah. Yeah!" She jumps down off the last two stairs, and whizzes into my arms. She gives me the biggest kiss imaginable, and a huge one-armed hug. She releases me and starts jumping up and down. "Hey, everybody!" she shouts. "Everybody!" She runs up to the steps of her trailer, and goes up two steps. She proudly displays her diamond. She's so excited, she's jumping up and down on the step. "Hey, everybody! Isn't this a KILLER diamond? WE'RE ENGAGED!!"

.   .   .   .   .

This was as much a shock to me as it was to everyone else on the set. When I said, 'Well?' I was asking for a simple Thank You for a Birthday Gift. I never dared to presume to ask her hand in marriage.

To my credit, I didn't actually faint. (It's about the only credit I've got left after buying that hunk of ice.)

Someone started to clap. Someone else clapped too. And then everyone was applauding.

I sort of blanked on what was happening. The next thing I knew, Honey had her arm around me again, and all these photographers were taking our picture. We were outside in the bright winter sun. I don't know how we got outside.

It was a goddamn press conference. Reporters and cameramen and all kinds of people. They had me put the ring on her finger, and then I had to take it off and put it on again several times so everybody could get a good picture.

I tried to get my mind in gear. I dug my pack of smokes out of my raincoat, and stuck one in my mouth. Honey was talking to one of the reporters, but she was automatically reaching inside my raincoat to get at my shirt pocket where I always keep my lighter.

Then I remembered. Our love affair had progressed to the point where Honey had nine of my lighters. And I have a thing about lighters. Mine are all expensive oldies. Were all expensive oldies, because Honey now had some of my best lighters.

I stopped the reach of her hand, by grasping her wrist. It surprised Honey enough so that she stopped talking mid-sentence. I opened the raincoat for her to see the insides.

There, stuck with Velcro all up and down the sides, were 47 different kinds of cigarette lighters. "I thought I'd better stock up," I explained.

Honey giggled, her whole body shaking, and she gave me the purest look of love I've ever gotten from her. "Isn't he the greatest?" she asked everyone else. "That's my Jimmy."

She selected a lighter, and lit my Camel with her left hand, and that's the picture that made the cover of *US*.

CHAPTER 15

The savage thundering roar of a Cizeta-Moroder V16T supercar screaming up the rude curves of Sunset Boulevard at 2:30am Tuesday morning in 2nd gear at 88mph, with the 560hp engine revs way into the red at 9500rpms, is the sound of pure terror.

That's a lie. The Cizeta tach has no redline marked on it.

"Aren't we going a little fast?" I shouted at Honey. "What's the redline on this thing?" I was huddled into a tight clutch of seat-belted fear. You understand, the speed didn't bother me a bit, it was the fact that she wouldn't let me smoke in her pearl-white perfect exoticar that was making me nervous.

She took her eyes off the twisting boulevard for a full three seconds, and looked at me with Honey's biggest smile. She yelled at me, her eyes glazed with thrill. "If it breaks, it means I went too fast!"

She laughed and made a wild happy yell. While she looked at me we streaked right through a red light.

As an afterthought, Honey slammed on the breaks.

We skidded to a yowling, yammering stop, way out of true. I opened my eyes. She blows 430,000 bucks on this buggy, and she can't get anti-lock breaking? We're almost perpendicular to Sunset, on the wrong side of the road.

Honey was swearing in a very unladylike way, trying to find reverse. "This clutch sucks!"

The engine sounded just as formidable at idle as it did with the tachometer needle over at 10,000. I saw it: we must have been going about a hundred. 16 cylinders. 64 valves. 8 camshafts. Normally aspirated fear.

Honey let a car go by, going our way, and then burned rubber in reverse to get out of the way of two oncoming cars. She straightened us out, only now we were parked in the fast lane of a blind spot around the curve in a 35mph zone.

"Fun, huh?" she said. "Better'n doin' a concert!"

I was fumbling with my seatbelt, and my door. I got the seatbelt off, but couldn't figure out the door in time.

"Time me," Honey said. She saw me trying to get out. "Jimmy, we're not there yet."

"I'm there!" I assured her. Damn this door.

"Jimmy, don't play games. Time me. Zero to sixty, come on!"

Don't play games? "It's OK, I didn't really want to meet Dave The Axe tonight. I'll just get out here, and walk back to the beach."

"Oh Jimmy, lengthen your leash. Come on!"

Headlights came around behind us. Honey dropped the clutch and stomped on the throttle, and did a simulation of an astronaut's blast-off acceleration. She burned two seconds of rubber and zoomed over out of the way to park in the No Parking slow lane.

"Time me. Zero to sixty."

I put my seatbelt on, and then counted her down by the blips on my chronometer. "Ready . . . Set . . . Go!"

The acceleration just about knocked the watch off my wrist, and I had to lean way over against Honey to read the speedo.

OK, I was impressed. This Italian monster was more than a full second faster than the best I'd ever done in my German 911 Carrera 4. "Four-point-two-six seconds," I shouted at her. She was still accelerating, the tach moving dangerously into the upper thousands while in second gear.

"Shit!" She slammed on the breaks again.

When I opened my eyes we were at a full stop in a 40mph zone. Another ten feet and we'd have made it up to the red light.

"I wasn't ready," Honey said. "One more." She patted the dashboard. "Come on, baby, you can do it. Three-nine. Three-nine, you can do it." She looked at me, her face all flushed with excitement. "You can wait till the light turns green. No hurry."

"How considerate of you."

Well, there weren't very many cars on the road this time of the night.

The light turned green, and she made another shot at the zero-to-sixty record.

We were driving from Honey's beach house in Malibu (everyone's got one there except me and Hulk) to her old man's townhouse high above Beverly Hills. For 'old man' read *Dad*. Father. Progenitor. Dave The Axe.

Honey only knew two forward gears. 1st & 2nd.

Honey only knew two throttle positions. Idle & foot-to-floor.

I don't mean to say that Honey was a bad driver. She was an excellent driver. She just had a very cavalier attitude about engine revolutions and posted speed limits and the color of traffic signal lights and the level of nicotine in my bloodstream.

Nighttime speeding was just a thrill-seeking hobby with Honey, but she attacked the hobby with the same ferocity and ruthless energy that she poured into her career. She (the Honey Brigade) had empirically determined the deadest hours of the week for zooming and sneaking around LA's backroads. Tuesday mornings were the deadest of the dead. The Cizeta-Moroder V16T was wearing a legal-in-most-States "Stealth Bra" which absorbed police radar rather than reflecting it. It was also fitted with an illegal-in-all-States K and X and Ka Band radar broadcaster that broadcast speed frequencies at 75% of the actual speed of the Cizeta. So, if Honey was bombing down the road, say, at a loafing hundred and ten miles an hour, the cop behind the radar gun would read off an only slightly naughty 82 on his machine (and think that he shouldn't have eaten that extra jelly-filled donut).

Honey brought the Cizeta to a carefully controlled stop and parked it legally. "Good baby," she said, patting the dashboard. She turned to me, and she was still breathing fast and excitedly. "It's not safe for me to drive on this stretch of Sunset. They all know this car, and I don't have a driver's license." Sweet Honey smile. "Your turn!" She slipped off her driving shoes, threw them back of the driver's seat, and pulled her go-go boots back on.

We both got out and exchanged places.

My clothes were drenched with sweat. It was running off of me in rivers. Alkaline, salty perspiration. We were in California: I'd have to fill out an environmental impact report on it eventually.

Once again, I want you to understand that the fast driving didn't bother me at all. It was the prospect of meeting Dave The Axe that had me in this cold sweat.

I don't know what I was worried about. I was sure we'd get along fine. He was one of the few people who had ingested even more LSD than I had.

CHAPTER 16

Honey likes to fritz up her hair. She'll put bizarre crimps in it. Maybe curl it sexy-slow and sprinkle it with gold-goddess stick'em-sparkles. Or she'll tie & tease it so it's spilling out at weird angles from a ponytail in the wrong place. Or she'll kink it into a bimbo's version of dread-locks, and hide behind aviator sunglasses. And everyone knows what she does for clothes: She eats the Paris fash-ions raw, and vomits up a mess that somehow manages to be even hotter.

But tonight, her blond hair was freshly peroxed, and it was the straightest, longest, most natural-looking fine-tooth-combed hair in Southern California. Her clothes reminded me of granola, love, peace, 1967. Madras shirt & mini-skirt, pink patterned stockings and black go-go boots. (Just looking at her made me want a joint, badly.)

And big, bulky jewelry: the idiot piece of costume jew-elry masquerading as an engagement ring.

I'm sorry, but 15.25 carats of genuine diamond looks like cheapo zircon bullshit on Honey's finger.

Is she trying to tell me something, as she keeps

scratching my arm with it, while I am driving and trying to concentrate on the tricky curves of Benedict
Canyon?

I drive Honey's Italian supercar into a well-lit Spanish courtyard that is anything but imposing. The other
cars include Rolls-Royces & BMWs & other snazzy stuff,
but the heavy white plaster walls of the courtyard mean-
der magically. Behind them, I can see glimpses of the low,
sloping mission tile roof of the home beyond the trees.
It's a few acres of Santa Fe, New Mexico, teleported to
the LA back hills.

I shut off all sixteen cylinders.

It created a peaceful silence that any words would
have ruined.

Honey and I get out. She gets the keys. Toss.

Crickets.

Water sounds, beyond the courtyard.

Honey has my lighter.

"I need a joint," I wish out loud, just as she brings a joint
out of her '60s flag/purse, and lights it with my lighter,
and passes it to me.

What a woman. God, I love this woman. I love her so
much my eyes mist up.

The moon is a beautiful chunk of white, with a big bite
taken out of it.

She's in no hurry. I'm in no hurry. We both look at the
moon, and pass the joint back and forth. It is absolutely
killer weed. I haven't smoked grass in years, but tonight
the mood just seems right.

We smoke the whole joint, including the roach, without saying a word, just standing together, my arms around her, looking at the moon and feeling the night.

The silence between us: perfect and loving.

Honey holds her left hand up in the moonlight. The gem is sparkling brilliantly, as she turns her hand, and we both watch it from different angles.

Honey squirms out of my arms.

"I don't love you, Jimmy." And there was a long pause. Painfully long. "I'll never love you." The water sounds seemed abnormally loud to me. Honey turned and looked up at me, straight on. "But I respect you. You're honest. I respect that. So I want us to talk true-blue for a minute."

The crickets were a piercing screech.

"I'll never marry you, Jimmy."

"Honey—"

"Shut up. I won't candy-coat it for you, Jimmy. I'm using you to keep my name out there. We're a mismatch. We're so dissonant that we're news. You and me, we're controversy. You're sick and perverted, and that appeals to me, because it's really screwing with people. It's—"

"Honey—"

"Shut *up*, Jimmy! You're a good lay, and that's all you'll ever be to me. A good lay, and good publicity. And if you want out of the whole thing, you can have your diamond back right now." She took it off her finger. "You can't afford to give me this. Admit it, Jimmy."

Words came out of my mouth. "True-blue. You want true-blue. OK, I'll give you true-blue." I was very proud of myself. I was still vertical. I was still conscious. "True-blue." Obviously, I'm stalling. I mean, there is nothing to say. My heart has collapsed into a runny pool of serious pain. "True-blue."

Sometimes, when I'm stoned, I say completely wild things, that don't even make sense. But before I say the completely wild things, I usually think they're pretty sharp, so first I make with my take-no-prisoners smile.

"Chicken," I said.

Take-no-prisoners smile.

"What a coward!" I told her. "You're afraid to go in there. Here we are. We've been out here for forty-five minutes, in the driveway. We're just standing out here. 'Cause you're afraid to go in there. Why? Why did you even want to bring me here? You're making such a big thing out of this. Introduce me to your father? At three o'clock in the morning? You just about total your race car trying to get arrested, so you can avoid having to see the old son of a bitch. But, no, that doesn't work, so we get here, and you mess around out here for almost an hour, and suddenly shove the ice back in my face, just to avoid having to go in there? I happen to know you haven't seen your father in more than two years. Robbie told me. There you are, all dressed up like a flower child, and you've dragged me up here, and now you throw all this crap about love at me. LOVE?? Just who the hell said anything about love? And who the hell said anything about marriage? You did. Think about it."

Well, she's trying to be cool, too. She's tossing the hunk of ice up and down in her hand, while I'm talking.

"Honey. I gave you a *Birthday* present. Not an engagement ring. If you wanna think we're engaged, that's *your* problem, that's not my problem. I was just going along with the gag."

Honey tilts down her granny moon-glasses, and looks up at me over the rims.

Am I out of words? No way. "Honey, I couldn't buy that kind of publicity."

Honey is looking at me so intensely and so silently that her whole body is shrieking at me, but I haven't the faintest idea what it's saying.

I added: "And you don't know shit about my finances."

Well, her eyes, her face, her body are all shrieking at me. What, I don't know. Her mouth says not a thing.

I put a cigarette in my mouth. "Gimme a light."

Is one of the two most famous hands in the world going to slap my face? And what about one of those knees, that are definitely not like a virgin's, is one of them on its way toward my groin? This woman supposedly studied karate for two years. Will she leave me lying on cobblestone, broken-boned & broken-hearted?

Honey is wide-eyed as she looks at me over her grannys, and her head is tilted at a psychedelic angle. Her lips, the most silent and natural and famous female lips in the Western Hemisphere, are open just enough for me to see a hint of teeth.

The voice, small and insistent, issues from that mouth: "You're fulla shit, Jimmy."

"I'm gonna pay to see your hole card, Honey. If you want to stay in the game, you have to call or raise." I tilt my Stetson to a brand new SuperCool angle. "Gimme a light."

Ah-oh, I'm in trouble now. Honey pushes her granny glasses back up her nose. She clenches her ice in her little fist.

So fast, I never could have blocked it, she whisks the cigarette from my lips and throws it over her shoulder near the edge of the courtyard.

"I want you to make a good impression," she explains, as she hooks my arm in hers and walks me toward the Santa Fe style townhouse.

"Right," I agree. "McCool, the litterbug."

Honey fits her phony-looking jewelry back on her famous finger.

As we approach the front door, a final bout of nervousness overtakes her. She stops, opens her big '60s flag/purse, hauls out another pre-rolled doobie. We're there, right in front of the damn front door, and she lights it, takes a big '60s-suck.

I give her a word of encouragement: "Chicken."

Honey takes a second '60s-suck, reaches forward, and pulls on this silver mechanism that makes a chime go off gently inside somewhere.

Honey has time to take a third '60s-suck.

The door begins to make opening sounds.

Honey grabs me by the neck with cold famous fingers and sticks the joint in my mouth with the cold famous fingers on her other hand.

The door is opening now.

Honey whispers a sweet endearment to me: "Raise."

CHAPTER 17

Ever see a barefoot butler wearing blue jeans and Banana Republic? I was looking at one.

"Promoted to graveyard, huh, Larry?" Honey says, while dragging me by the arm into the foyer.

I didn't say anything because I had just taken a massive inhale. The woman had given me a Thai stick. It had been a long night. It was going to be an even longer morning.

There is some laid-back jazz playing in the background.

This guy in blue jeans and Banana Republic is either more wasted than we are, or he's gone through Butler's School, because his face is devoid of expression. His toes don't even curl. Honey at the front door, and no reaction. He says, "Hello, Ivy. Your father is in the amphitheater. This is a pleasant surprise." He turns to look at me. "You must be Mr. McCool. Welcome."

"Right on, bro," I say, with a minimal exhale.

· · · · ·

"My mother had just died," Honey told me. "And all the kids were making fun of me. They used to chant 'Poison Ivy, Poison Ivy.' They were just dorks. First grade stuff. It sounds silly now, but it really hurt then. So I changed my name. Oh, I was Jennifer for awhile, and Helga for a week."

"Helga?" I asked.

A good, shy, little Honey smile. "I had a friend, and her name was Helga. Good thing I didn't stick with Helga, huh? Anyway, my teacher humored me. You know. 'And who are you today, little girl?'"

Honey was silent for a few moments as we walked through the mellow, spacious Spanish & Indian home.

"Axe always called my mom 'honey.' I decided I wanted to be Honey. The teachers and the kids thought I'd grow out of it. But I didn't. I made everyone call me 'Honey.' In eighth or ninth grade, Axe changed it legally. There's a little form you fill out, that says that you made a mistake, and that the name is *supposed* to be . . . . And I grew into it. And now I'm Honey."

"Helga?"

·   ·   ·   ·   ·

The laid-back jazz playing in the background is Dave The Axe and a few friends. As Honey and I enter the amphitheater, the music changes character. It is not laid-back. It is not jazz. There is nothing 'background' about it. It is 'In Yo Face!' And it is not friendly.

The guy has a goddamn amphitheater built into his home. Retractable roof. Of course, it's a modest amphitheater, I don't think it could seat more than four hundred.

After Honey and I sat down, it sat four. The other boy/girl couple sat way down front, worshipfully. Two young kids, 160 degrees around the amphitheater. They looked like teenagers. And they both went into a raw freak when they saw Honey. Gapes. Points. Squirms. Honey and I had our butts to the back circular white plaster wall. If it is possible for a woman to sit on tiptoe, Honey was doing it.

Me? I was tranqed.

Dave The Axe? No Prob. Lemme at 'im.

Blue jeans & Banana Republic whispered into my left ear: "May I serve you a drink, sir?"

I turned my neck so slow it probably took seven seconds to swivel my forward-eyes to look at him. I slowly-slowly exhaled a lungful of Thai stick into his face. We locked eyes: I like to think that we understood each other. It seemed to take weeks for the exhale to complete itself. The barefoot butler did not blink or flinch or react in any way, and at the end of my exhale he straightened his back and walked away.

．　　．　　．　　．　　．

The things women lug around in their purses. Honey opens hers enough to start the DAT recorder inside.

Dave The Axe is down front, on guitar. He has a drummer doing it with him. And a bass player. It's all he needs.

The guy has the chops of God. Dave was at Monterey when Hendrix burned his guitar. Dave played his guitar.

Dave was at Woodstock when the wet crowd chanted for the rain to stop. When Dave picked up his guitar, plugged in, and played, the rain stopped. Dave was at Altamont, when bikers killed a kid and Keith Richards shouted to "Stop That Man There!" But Dave had already said as much with his fingers.

I don't know why the world has heard nothing from Dave The Axe in ten years. Clapton would hock his guitar for cocaine if he could hear this guy. Beck would go back in the garage and stay there. Gatton, trying to keep up, would ski his fingers up the frets and just Fender-Bender his Telecaster into a thirty-second-note pile-up of frustration.

This man is hot tonight. Dave is firestorming.

The butler in blue jeans is back. He has a large Mendocino water for Honey, which she starts drinking from the bottle. Blue Jeans has something for me too. He sets this carved wood tray in front of me. It has three kitchen matches on it. And two Thai sticks.

The butler didn't understand me at all. Only wimps ask for an extra match.

·   ·   ·   ·   ·

The set is over, and here comes Dave The Axe. He is an old lion. Fifty-eight. A grim, masculine force with immense dignity. Long salt & pepper hair. Longer than mine ever was.

The male youth across the amphitheater belongs to the male drummer. Down on stage, they are copping feels and kissing. It is really disgusting . . . the way they are pointing and gaping up at Honey as they gossip about us. The female youth belongs to Dave The Axe. She is scampering up the steps of the aisle, hanging onto Dave's arm for dear life.

"Quick," Honey says. "Hide this." She puts something in my right palm. It's the DAT cassette. I watch her drop the tiny recorder to the carpeted floor and kick it sideways and down out of sight under the seats in front of us.

I stand up.

Honey stands up. She kicks my ankle with her go-go boot, and gives me a fast, furious look. It's a secret message of some kind. But all I can decipher is the pain.

And there we are, the four of us.

Man of few words, that's Dave The Axe. "Hi, Honey."

"Hi, Axe," she says.

Then comes the silence.

I'm too stoned to initiate conversation. The female youth is hiding behind Dave; huge, silent eyes, peeking around his shoulder. Honey attacks my ankle again with another secret message.

Dave has only seen his daughter in magazines and movies for the past two years. He expresses his pleasure at seeing her in person by grabbing her flag/purse and rummaging through it. He gives her the purse back.

"Where is it?" Dave asks Honey.

"Where is what?" Honey snaps.

Blue jeans and Banana Republic walks along our back row from the other side, gets down on his hands and knees and baretoes, and then stands up with the tiny portable DAT recorder in his hand. He brings it over to Dave. Dave opens it. No cassette.

"Where is it?" Dave asks again.

"Where is what?" Honey snaps back, doing an astonishingly lousy acting job for an actress of her reputation.

I start to throw in my two bits.

Dave The Axe gives me one second of brutal eye contact. "Shut up, shithead."

Dave looks back at Honey, and the tiniest smile edges into the side of his face.

Don't ask me to explain it, but suddenly Honey isn't nervous anymore.

"So," Dave The Axe says grimly to Honey. But he isn't really grim, because this smile is trying to edge its way into his face.

"So!" Honey says right back at him. Perky. There is about the biggest smile that she can do without showing her teeth, and it's all over Honey's face. Slowly, slowly, slowly, the teeth of Honey's wonderful smile appear, and it just melts that old man's heart.

The next second, Honey and Dave are hugging each other tight, while the young girl is trying to hang onto the clump of father and daughter by one male sleeve. The young girl looks to be about fifteen, but I could be overestimating her age by a couple of years. This young brunette girl with Axe is dangerously desirable, and so tender it would break a man's heart—if mine wasn't already broken.

Dave The Axe looks over Honey's head at me, and it's a gentle look, as he asks her, "Are you really gonna marry this shithead?"

"I'm really gonna marry him," Honey growls. "Mmmm, I've missed you so." Honey is purring with contentment.

She never purred in my arms like that.

"Welcome to the family, McCool," Dave The Axe says, holding out his right hand to me for a shake.

Finally, I decode the pain in my ankle. It's the DAT cassette. I'm still holding it in my right hand.

"Here's the tape, sir." I give him the damn DAT.

.   .   .   .   .

As a comedian, I was a great success. We never did shake hands.

Then Axe unhugged Honey and introduced the girl. Katherine. His wife.

"C'mon," Dave said. "I'll fix us all breakfast." Dave yelled, "That's It!" to his band, and he and Katherine turned away from Honey and me.

As they walked out of the amphitheater, Honey whispered to me, "He married her. Gosh, I used to babysit Kathy!" She squealed with nearly silent laughter, and then bit her lip. "What luck! He likes you."

He likes me? "Who said anything about marriage?" I feebly objected. "I wouldn't marry you, if—"

"Oh, shut up, poohbutt," Honey fondly said, and smacked me three fast kisses. My chin. My cheek. My nose. "Let's go eat."

.   .   .   .   .

Huevos Rancheros. Hot? My eyes were watering. My nose was running. My mouth was a second-degree burn. My throat was a bleeding, scalded wound. My tongue may have burned completely off . . . I wasn't sure.

Dave The Axe was cooking. Was he trying to show off? Was he trying to kill me?

Honey scarfed her food and demanded seconds. Her hair wasn't on fire. She wasn't even smoking. She and her father got into a big argument about the DAT cassette. She wanted to play it for her producer. Honey told him that he really, really, really should put out an album, even if he didn't want to play live anymore. Dave told her to go to hell. She tried to tell him how good he was, but The Axe just chopped her right off.

"Shithead," he told her. It seemed, at the time, to be his all-purpose term of contempt.

Katherine may have been barely out of Junior High (for all I knew, she was still in Junior High), but she was a hell of a conversationalist. "Mr. Honey?" she asked me, scrunching her face into grotesque disbelief.

What I mean is, she stalled all conversation for at least thirty seconds.

I finally called to Dave The Axe. "Uh, sir, do you have a degau—"

"That's Sir Shithead to you," Dave said.

"Uh, Sir Shithead, do you have a degausser? One of those big magnetic bulk-eraser things? As a special favor, would you bulk-erase the DAT cassette I gave you, and then give it back to me? I'd like to use it to get some recordings of Honey's sports car."

He looked at me as if I were crazy. Honey looked at me as if I were crazy. Katherine was more discreet, and merely mumbled, "Mr. Honey," under her breath, with a giggle.

Dave shrugged, stirred his Huevos Rancheros, and then walked out of the kitchen with the DAT cassette.

We did not scald our tongues in total silence, thanks to Katherine's remarkable capacity for small talk. "Mr. Honey, you may have noticed Ivy's whims of steel? When you say, 'I do,' that's the last decision she'll ever let you make." The Mrs. Axe smiled sweetly, while the Rancheros sizzled away, and Honey's eyes narrowed to lethal laser slits. After a moment, Dave came back and gave me the DAT cassette. He served himself and sat down with us. I hid the DAT very carefully this time.

Dave was eating.

I was making a good impression (dying for a tobacco cigarette).

The sun was starting to paint a sunrise on the clouds outside the kitchen window and beyond the Spanish courtyard.

The women were casting silent witchcraft spells at each other.

Katherine pointed to her wedding ring. Some kind of secret message. Well, it wasn't intended for me, so I didn't worry about it.

Abruptly Honey stood up. Totally frosted. "Let's go, Jimmy."

I pushed my chair back a little, and pulled Honey by her wrist down onto my lap. "We can't go, Honey. We have to do one thing first."

"What?" Honey snapped.

"I've never made love in an amphitheater at dawn. Dave, we're going to go make some beautiful music."

I stood up and dumped Honey off my lap and pushed her toward the amphitheater.

Dave The Axe didn't even look up from his Rancheros. "The shithead has met her match," he said.

CHAPTER 18

I had to jump-start Honey, but, as concert-goers can attest, Honey is every bit as entertaining in an amphitheater as on television.

Perhaps I should mention the source of the family strife for the five of you who haven't heard.

Dave The Axe thinks that Honey has sold out. Honey has humiliated him by what she has done and become: a professional naughty teenager.

Honey postcoitally countered that Dave was just pissed because she shredded his rep. He wasn't Dave The Axe anymore. He was Honey's Father.

Dave said he didn't give two droogy grooves for his reputation. He was a Guitarist. He was a Musician. Honey was just a sexy spudismo, a little transcendental vegetation for the Couch Potato Crowd. Then Dave got really insulting. He called Honey an Entertainer.

But Honey could toss the mud pies too. She called Dave The Axe a well-known has-been.

Dave said he was tired of being victimized by [unmentionable Axiom on hypemakers deleted] dedicated to a snappy phrase, and puppet masters who market you for twenty percent and then sell you like soap. Genius is meant to peak and pull out, or be wiped out permanently.

Honey said, well, you've been wiped out permanently. (Honey said that to Dave The Axe!)

The Axe said, gently, that success was a shot of heroin. Just as thrilling and just as self-destructive. That it was really gonna be up to her. She had to decide whether she wanted to go on putting the needle in her arm.

There was an odd emphasis to the way he said it.

Honey was silent. I didn't know whether the needle had penetrated her thick skin, or if she just had nothing to say.

Dave told her that he's been there. That when it's happenin', you lose control over what's real. You're a trolley, skiddin' down tracks that other guys laid down for you, and there's the wire above you, zappin' you fulla juice, and keepin' you buzzed and blind, and you're just roarin' down the tracks, pickin' up speed, gettin' locked into it. Until . . . (Dave hit his fist into his other palm.)

But Honey was silent. And Dave asked her if she really wanted to go through the rest of her life changing her phone number every thirty days.

Honey said yeah.

And there was a long silence that just burned a terrible crease of pain on that old guy's face.

Even though she's hurting Axe, Honey loves him. And I can see that no matter what happens, that she'll never feel for me the way I see her feeling for him.

.   .   .   .   .

Honey let me drive her Cizeta without argument. And
this is one hell of a beautiful hunk of automobile in the
daylight. I strap myself in behind the wheel and start up.
The speedometer goes up to 220mph, and this speedometer is not kidding. Honey is right about the clutch,
though. It sucks. It belongs in an 18-wheeler.

"I'm worried about him," Honey says quietly. "Larry says
he hasn't been out of that house in three years."

I digested this. It was easier to digest than breakfast.
"It's a nice house. I could live there for three years with
Katherine. Yeah, I could do it."

Honey just sits sad and seatbelted.

I try to cheer her up. "That marriage is gonna have problems, though. In a couple more years, she's gonna get zits."

.   .   .   .   .   .

The Cizeta has a car stereo that costs more than most people's cars. I plug the cassette into the DAT player, and
fiddle with knobs a little while I drive.

The sizzlingly subversive wail of Dave The Axe blasts
out at us from all sides.

Honey turns down the sound. "I thought he erased it."

"He thought he erased it too," I tell her. "I read owner's
& operator's manuals. You can't bulk-erase a DAT. It
has something to do with the density of the particles on
the tape."

I was very proud of myself. I had tricked the old son of

a bitch. After completely blowing it, I had retrieved the situation.

Does Honey thank me? No. She just shuts off the car stereo.

Honey is in one of her moods. She needs to talk. And she needs for me to listen and make listening noises. I'm even looking at her as much as I can while driving down the hills.

Me? I'm not in anything as limp-wristed as a *mood*. I'm balls-up heartbroken. I'm passionately in love, dangerously in love. We are talking *unrequited* here.

I am over the edge with a woman who really doesn't care a whit for me. All I am to Honey is a way to put a little more spin on her publicity. McCool the curve ball.

Honey is explaining to me how I have joined a very exclusive club, and she launches into this long story, by way of explanation.

I mean, I really want to know about this, right? But I'm making with listening noises all over the place, and enough eye contact to just about run us off the road.

· · · · ·

It seems that when Honey was about eleven or twelve years old, she and Dave went river rafting on the American River with some other people. A father-daughter trip. Dave did not advertise who he was, and he pretty much just wanted to sit in the middle of the raft and take pictures of the awesome whitewater, with his water-proof camera, as the raft crashed through the Class IV rapids and the waves washed over the people in the raft. The guide had other ideas. The guide wanted Dave to put down his camera and paddle.

The guide also refused to take the young girl through the roughest sections of the river. He pulled the raft over before the tough rapids so the girl could get out. Dave The Axe, being a real man on a father-daughter trip, got out without complaint and walked with Honey around the rocks of the rapids.

Honey, of course, being Honey, was beet-red mad. Dave The Axe was not nearly as good with an oar as he was with a guitar. Twice, as he was trying to take photographs, his oar slipped out of the raft and floated away. Dave and the guide had words.

And the guide called Dave The Axe a shithead.

Well, this is the man who once grabbed big, rowdy Lou Carney and shoved him so hard he slid completely across a table of catered food, crashed through the window behind it, and splashed down into a canal in Venice, Italy. This is the man who beat up Keith Moon and Keith Moon's driver and Roger Daltry's bodyguard in a pub brawl.

But this was a man on a father-daughter vacation.

Dave formed the shithead club. Since Honey was only eleven or twelve at the time, she couldn't remember exactly how he did it, but Dave completely reversed the psychology, and made being a shithead something desirable. They were the intrepid shitheads. The brave shitheads. Whenever young Honey would rap on the rubber raft twice with her oar, everyone on the raft (except the guide in the rear) would raise their oars together to touch in the center. They would shout, "Shitheads!" A second oar touch. "Uug!" A third oar touch. Then they would each rub the rubber raft in a sexy circular motion, and say, "Aaaaaaaah."

The two guys near the rear started "accidentally" dumping the guide in the river, for fun, since he obviously wasn't shithead material. And when they would approach gnarly whitewater, and the guide would start shouting paddling instructions, Honey would rap twice on the raft, and the crew would mutiny by instead going into their routine.

Honey remembers that by the end of the run, as a result of the crew virtually ignoring the guide's instructions, the raft overturned once, dumping everyone in the icy water, and wrapped around a big rock once, again spilling everyone. But everyone had a great, if cold, time. And no one was hurt.

And the name "shithead" stuck in her family as an endearment, a standard of perverse excellence.

Honey said that none of her boyfriends had ever been nominated to shithead status before. I was the first.

"That's . . . really exciting."

CHAPTER 19

The heartless and the brokenhearted bombed down the boulevard and up the highway bypass to Honey's Lodge.

My fiancee's basic complaint concerned what she considered insufficient velocity. Seventy miles an hour in a fifty-five zone was insulting the integrity of her Cizeta.

Anyway, we're on one of those spur-of-the-moment type adventures. We're both stoned-over on a Sunday morning. We've both got work to do. Honey has her upcoming World Tour to prep for. I've got a *Night* show to do. We both need rest more than romance.

But Honey's in one of her moods. She suddenly wants to drive up the coast and "trombone" at Honey's Lodge. It's this quaint little place in Big Sur. The lodge is not named after her; it's been there a long time. Reservations are required months in advance; for some of the special rooms, years in advance. Honey figures she'll just show up, and have her pick of the rooms.

With the exception of booze, I had been pretty much drug free for more than a decade, so I was still buzzed from the marijuana. Also I was wondering what the hell

I was doing.

Usually, when I do the *Night* show, I write jokes for a week, then take my routine into a comedy club to try them out live and polish them up. Here I was, the day before the main event (and every *Night* show is the main event), and I had written nothing, rehearsed nothing. And here I was, ridiculously in love, driving up the coast in a ridiculously expensive car, with a ridiculously famous woman who allowed me to hang around her only because her fans thought it was ridiculous.

We got as far as Oxnard.

"This is ridiculous," I said. I stopped the car.

A parked Cizeta-Moroder in Oxnard on a Sunday morning draws only slightly less attention than a grounded UFO. Thank Harpo for the tinted windows that are up, hiding Honey.

I don't know what I was going to say. I love you? I love you, but you're no good for me, so I'm going to turn the car around and get back to work? Keep the ice, but goodbye?

It's times like this that make me wonder if I have any free will at all.

"This is ridiculous," I said. I started driving North again.

．　．　．　．　．

We go one stop light.

"Jimmy, stop the car." Honey's voice is small but insistent.

We are waiting for the people belonging to the pickup ahead of us to get back in the pickup and drive. The light turns green. The car behind us honks. The three people standing in the road stop staring at our car, they get back in the pickup and go. We go.

"Jim, stop the car." Her voice is even smaller, even more insistent.

We go another stop light. The light turns red, and we stop.

"Cool, stop the car, please." Her voice is just plain sad.

I pull into this place. Big sign. EAT. Next to it, another big sign. GOOD FOOD. It has to be fate, because there's this third big sign. Neon. Flashing. HUEVOS RANCHEROS.

Honey says, "Stop the engine. But leave your seatbelt on."

Done.

"True-blue time, Jimmy."

"OK, Ivy."

I'm looking at Honey.

Honey is looking at me.

God, I need a smoke. I even wish I could wear my Stetson, but this car is so low that there's not enough headroom for a six-foot-two-inch guy like me.

"Jimmy, you can smoke, if you want to."

"I don't want to, Honey. You can open the window, if you get too hot."

"I'm not hot. Jimmy, I know you want to smoke. Smoke." She gets out my gold lighter and lights it up. The flame is so lonely.

"Honey, I know you want to open the window. Open it."

Mexican standoff. She puts away the lighter, and for the time being, I stop bugging her about the window.

Very tenderly she places her engagement hand over mine. "You wanna know how I know that you're in love with me?" Honey asks.

So much for the Mexican standoff.

Honey looks wistful as her eyes search into mine. Her voice is melancholy, and she lingers slowly over each phrase. "Because after we make love, your eyes water, and you almost cry. You're not crying because you're happy. You're crying because you're sad. You're sad because you think that you're miles and miles away from me. You think you can't really touch me. You're crying because your arms are around me, but you're hurting because you're thinking that you can never really get ahold of me."

.   .   .   .   .

I couldn't even talk at first. After a moment, I said, "This is so embarrassing. You shouldn't have to know about this. I tried to keep it a secret. I didn't want to have to confess this, but my allergist says that I'm allergic to your pussy. I know my eyes get all runny, and it looks like I'm going to sneeze, but honest, I'm on special medication now and—"

"Jimmy, be serious."

"Honey, what are you trying to do to me?" I'm sure I must have sounded hurt, because I wanted to wail that she was tearing me up inside.

"What are you trying to do to me, Jimmy?" She push-es my hand away from her hand, and then she turns her whole body around there in her seat, so she's mostly facing her tinted window. I can only see the edge of the left of Honey's face.

"You can roll down the window, if you'd like," I told her.

I guess there were things she could tell her window that she couldn't tell me. "Jimmy, you know, when you first came onto me, I thought you were gay. Straight guys just don't come on like that. And you acted so immature. You were like this tall, scrawny kid . . . grown bold on beer."

She sort of laughed to herself.

"And what a mouth," Honey said to her window. "You've got a bullshit line for everything, Jimmy. You talk like a rip-and-skip artist. I only met you at Marlene's on a dare. You were just a way to fill up an empty evening. Karla Lightfoot told me you were acute eroticism, and to go. I didn't get it. All I saw was a fast mouth and your nice blue eyes. But then . . ."

And it's funny the way two people can remember an early shared event in their lives so differently.

". . . we were waiting for the food, and you were giv-ing me those weird looks, and I finally said, why are you looking at me like that. And you said, I'm flirting. It just . . . it was like putting color on a black-&-white TV.

"And then when that burnout came over with his play, and you grabbed my knife . . . he . . . really . . . thought . . . that you were going to stab out his eyes. It was just so outrageous . . . I don't know, suddenly you weren't a big kid anymore. Suddenly . . . I don't know . . . your big blue eyes with your long dark lashes still looked kind of feminine, but . . . they looked like the kind of blue that I could drown in. And you weren't skinny anymore, you were . . . slender. And I didn't want lasagna anymore, I wanted you, right there on the table, and I didn't care who watched. I got so hot it scared me. So I ran away."

She stopped talking. What? Isn't the window listening carefully enough? Window! Get with it. Listen!

"You're such a bastard," Honey told her window. "You're gonna make me say it first, aren't you?"

.   .   .   .   .

Honey brings both her hands up to her mouth, and she's huddled there, curved against her side of the car, biting on her engagement thumb. She looks like she's hurting. Maybe hurting as much as I am. I mean, my heart is gone. My macho self-image is gone. Scrawny? Feminine? Gay?? My balls have slipped out of my scrotum. They're down on the floorboard somewhere. I have to be careful where I put my feet.

What's left?

The truth?

.   .   .   .   .

"Nothing breaks you down, does it?" Honey told her window. "I keep thinking I'm going to get through to you.

But nothing gets through."

"I love you," I told Honey's window. It sounded so lame. I'm a comedian, not a poet. It even sounded to my ears like I was joking. "Honey . . . really, I do." I stopped talking. That just made it sound phonier.

She doesn't believe me. She's just shaking her head, slowly. "I thought I was using you, but you're really using me, aren't you, Jimmy? I thought I had you under control, but you're the one pushing the buttons, aren't you? Well, here it is. I hope you can handle it . . ."

She loves me? She loves me?! She loves me!

Honey tells her window the three sweet syllables that some men long to hear, ache to hear; the three syllables that other men dread and fear.

". . . I'm pregnant."

The truth is, mostly I was just confused.

Honey could do safe sex commercials. She is the original No Condom, No Copulation female. Every time we have made love, she has insisted upon a condom. Every time. There have been no spills, no condom rips or tears, no condom slip-offs. Never mind her satisfaction, Honey demands a prompt withdrawal after I ejaculate (and never mind my satisfaction—that's the last thing I want to do). Honey puts the condom on. Honey takes the condom off. Honey unrolls the condom, stretches it, and ties it off after with a knot (why, I don't know, that's just what she does).

Don't get me wrong. She was very loving about it. More than very loving. Honey did it with the sweet adoration of a Priscilla for her Elvis.

But now here Honey is, pregnant, and my sperm have not been, at any time, intimate with her eggs.

"I'm going to have the baby," Honey told her window, stubbornly.

"So, who's the father?" I mean, I don't consider this an unreasonable question, under the circumstances.

Honey turned around in her seat and looked at me. And she was really looking at me this time.

She took a wild swing and slapped my face.

"You really don't get it, do you, Jimmy? You just don't get it at all. You're the father."

She's right. I don't get it at all.

"I stole your sperm." She sounds guilty.

"You stole my sperm." I guess I was repeating the words to try and figure out what they meant.

"When you went to the bathroom," she said. She sounded furtive. Quickly, she added, "When you were in the bathroom, I nipped open the condoms with my finger-nail file and smushed them up inside me." There goes the Honey blush. Her eyes looked away, but then they looked back defiantly, straight on at me.

I mean, it's so unbelievable, it has to be true. Nobody would make up a story like that.

"Well, if I'm the father . . ." I took a controlled left-handed swing, and slapped the face of the most famous woman in Oxnard. Hard.

Her famous eyes flared. She was a silent but very deadly female. Hell hath no fury like a slapped Honey.

But I was angry too. And I was shouting. "You're smoking Thai sticks!? You're pregnant, and you're smoking Thai sticks!? Do you know what THC can do to a fetus? Are you [Coolism deleted] CRAZY??"

The anger was gone from her, so quickly, it was as if I had ripped it right out of her. She was so still, I didn't know what she was going to do. "But . . ." she said. It was a tiny little strangled objection.

And then she groaned; and I hope to never hear another groan like that from anyone.

Both her hands hugged her womb. "I'm so sorry," Honey's tortured voice said. "I'm so sorry. I'm so sorry."

Honey was not talking to me.

And then the actress who does not know how to cry, cried.

. . . . .

Honey was right about Honey's Lodge. We get her usual room. It has a waterfall in the living room. The walls are boulders. There is a lily pond in the bedroom.

We check in without luggage. It's MO for me, but it must be a new one for Honey.

Big Sur is a pretty cool region. No one has asked for Honey's autograph. Quietly, the word spreads through the forests and hills.

"Honey and Cool McCool are here!"

"Honey and who?"

. . . . .

We were both so tired that we headed for the foot of the

bed. Under the fur, it feels to my butt like a plain old bed, thank Fanny Brice. There we sat, holding each other, leaning against each other, too tired to undress, too tired to lie down.

I was too tired to smoke a cigarette, that's how tired I was.

How tired was Honey? Here's how tired Honey was. She said, "Jimmy, I lied. I'd love to marry you. I don't care what they print. I don't care if anyone knows. Or if everyone knows. I don't care. I love you. Please don't ever leave me. God, Jimmy, it hurts, thinking that I might lose you."

It was a tender moment between us. I had to clear my throat, just to talk.

"Honey. What I said before, about being in love with you. I mean, you know I was just joking, right?" I couldn't quite keep a straight face.

She was almost too tired to smile. But she smiled. "That's funny."

CHAPTER 20

My sister is a character. Let me give you one clue. She went to St. John's College in Santa Fe, New Mexico. Great Books Program. She dropped out two weeks before the end of her Senior year. Grades are not reported to the students, but the more than mildly upset dean shouted a 3.4 GPA argument at her to please stay. Second clue: With 2,500 years of Western Philosophers to choose among, Toni's favorite philosopher is Diogenes of Sinope. Toni told the dean that one day Diogenes was seen sitting in a public square most of the afternoon gluing shut the pages of a book. Toni handed the dean the college catalog, and walked off campus. The catalog was glued together. I was just finishing high school, and about to go into the Army when these awe-inspiring facts were related to me about my heroine. Third, and final clue: My older sister has been slowly gaining weight most of her life. Last I saw her (she lives on a yacht in Newport Beach), she must have been about a hundred and eighty pounds. But every time I'm in LA, she puts me off, on one pretext or another. We're talking six or seven months now.

She just doesn't want to see me. What about Honey? Don't you want to meet Honey? Come on, I've told Honey all about you, she's dying to meet you. Toni assures me that it has nothing to do with me. Or Honey. She just isn't ready. She wants to surprise me. End of clues.

. . . . .

Now, when I hit the road, I carry one thin traveling bag. We're talking 1 jacket, 1 tie, 2 pairs of pants. When I need clothes, I buy 'em. When my clothes get dirty, I toss 'em.

When I hit the hotel in a city I haven't played before, I pop one of the boys with a fifty for him and a fistful for shirts, shoes, socks, underwear *et cetera* (Braun, Mennen Speed Stick, fingernail clippers, aspirin, caprice).

I'd rather buy new things and lose them, than lug them around. Jackets are a bitch to get a good fit on, without a tailor. Pants are impossible. My tie is lucky.

But usually, my clothes are there already waiting for me. I'm a little like W.C. Fields, in that I've got stashes all over the world, little secret stockpiles. Mine aren't money in banks. They're clothes in closet-Cool-groupies' closets.

Some sailors have a woman in every port, I'm told. Well, I'm telling you, this comedian has a closet in damn near every big city. Hey, this is the age of AIDS, the post-feminist decade, the time of house-husbands and Frosty Paws and penicillin-resistant STDs: Let the groupies be the ones well-hung. And hey, they're so *grateful.* For four tickets, two kisses, a couple jokes, and ten minutes of talk, *they bring the clothes to me*, and they're always buying me extra stuff. I don't know how they do it, but it almost always fits, and I can't remember the last time I encountered a wrinkle. Some of the girls come to me with a fleet of bellboys rolling a damn wardrobe.

So McCool travels light.

My dream is to evolve until I carry NOTHING. Just me, my Stetson, and I (Camels).

The scribbles in my pocket pad while on the plane are 20% of the evening's show.

Now, when I hit the stage, and I can do it ten seconds before the curtain, I've got just two questions.

Where's the microphone? Where's the water?

I prefer ElectroVoice and Perrier, but I'm not picky. I can go on with Radio Shack and backstage toilet tank.

Sheri followed me at the Sands one night. I remember, because I checked my bag, and it got sent to Mexico City. Anyway, I happen to arrive early, and I'm standing there backstage during this brutal sunset, lugging all my luggage, which is one lit Camel cigarette with filter, and I'm watching this long caravan of huge tractor-trailer rigs unloading Sheri's enormous set. I mean, I understand the concept of "show business," but Sheri is one of those major stars that people come just to see her and what she's wearing—or not wearing. Props, or even an act, really aren't necessary.

Showtime: When I got there that night—Sheri's set took up the whole stage—there was just about five or six feet of side-stage for me. I did a killer show in a groupie Tux with two 4-packs of Perrier and a can opener for props.

(Back in '89 when Perrier went to twist-offs they caught me by surprise, on stage. I didn't believe they were for real. I thought Keven Feldman had rebottled them as a put-on. I was there with my can opener out, going, what's wrong with this picture?)

Now, when *Honey* hit the road, she didn't believe in preferential treatment. She wanted to be treated just like the rest of the little people. Not!

It took three Boeings and a road-full of limousines to spearhead the Honey Brigade. Like *Satyricon* by Fellini.

Honey's brand of entertainment required *three* sets. They were gigantic $1.2 million monsters that couldn't keep pace with Honey's jets, so her stages had to sort of leapfrog over each other on the ground. *Three sets!*

And when the Honey Brigade hit a town, they HIT That Town. The Establishment didn't stand a chance, because as every kid knew—and perhaps this was Dave's real objection—Honey was The Establishment.

.   .   .   .   .

My, my, let's do a missive on money for a moment. Movies are glamorous, TV is America's favorite entertainment, but the really big bucks are in Rock & Roll.

Honey's always been popularly acclaimed (and critically lambasted) for her movies and TV roles. But it wasn't until Honey turned her formidable energy to Pop Singing that she became a super-rich living legend, and started zapping up there on the *Forbes* Top-40 Entertainers List every year. This was no airhead on the airwaves.

What Honey wanted, Honey got. But you really had to see the lady in her bifocals, sludging through a gut-busting stack of distribution contracts, to really appreciate her business acumen. This was no boardroom-bimbo.

Sure, she was backed by suits with smarts, but I was there when Honey switched to Maxwell Records, and she had the Japs' middleman, Lewis Rudner, drooling with admiration. She's there with the pen in her hand, and the reporters are right outside, and suddenly she changes her mind.

So, OK, Honey's spies are the best, and she knows precisely what Michael Jackson's royalty per record is. She names his actual royalty rate, which is the highest royalty for any artist in the history of CDs. "Wouldn't it be sweet if the bustier made one penny per more than the glove?" Honey says.

The ballpoint is clutched in the most famous painted fingers in the world.

Big silence in the boardroom. You could hear a pen drop.

In fact, that's what we heard.

Nobody gets it. They all look at me: Have I been teaching Honey a sense of humor? But she's standing up now, and her suits are closing up their briefcases.

There are other record companies, right?

Well, Lewis pulls the scene together (keeps his job as record chief of Maxwell Records), gets Honey to sit back down. No problem. The contracts, of course, will have to be changed. This will cause some delay . . . One of Honey's suits hauls out a new set of contracts, all typed up in triplicate, with the new highest-in-history royalty rate.

Impressed? I was too, but that's nothing.

After she signed, there were some fringe areas that still needed hammering out.

Honey did her hammering with her red littlest finger, pointing across the table.

Honey & Rudner were arguing over foreign royalty rates. They were batting numbers back and forth across the table like ping-pong balls. Lewis Rudner was on his side of the table, hammering his fingers on a calculator, and feverishly consulting his royalty guide. Honey was on my side of the table, figuring out the French royalty rate, doing the conversion and taking off the VAT tax, in her head!

Impressed? I mean, I have to use my fingers to do thirteen minus five.

I've never made the *Forbes* Top-40 List. That year, I made $3.25 million on public appearances. Not too shabby. $2.1 million the year before. Diddley-squat millions on movies for the two years, but a whopping multi-multi-jumbo oodles-of-millions-of-dollars secret salary as the Comedy Channel's most popular jock, head writer, and senior vice president. (Take a wild guess, triple the guess, add a lion's share, and that's pretty close.) They wanted me real bad, and Robbie made them pay for it.

So I wasn't just any grubby cockroach crawling up the leg of America's goddess. I was a cockroach with cash.

Just wanted you to know.

So, OK. Maybe Honey did make a little more money than I did.

At least, I don't need 33 tons of $4 million cargo and

a minimum crew of 107 just to put on a show, Goddamnit! All I need is my Frequent Flyer pass and a couple extra pair of pants. Maybe an extra jacket. And hey, I can make my own luck, if necessary.

Considering that, I was doing pretty damn good, thank you.

CHAPTER 21

Roughest crowd I ever played, was opening for Honey at Sir Morgan's Cove. It's this little 300-seat tavern in a blue-collar town near Boston. Worcester. Honey wanted to wade into her World Tour, try out her act live in front of a small group before taking it into the big stadiums.

Big secret, right? Nobody's supposed to know, right?

When The Honey Brigade pulled in front of the club on Green Street, there were 7,000 fans, on cars, on rooftops; solid sidewalks and streets of flesh.

. . . . .

Everyone is screaming, "HONEY! HONEY! HONEY!"

Honey is loving every second of it. The goddess is really coming alive. I mean, it takes about twenty cops to get us safely into the club. What a thrill. Seven thousand mouths, all yelling for her!

Backstage, Honey gives me a word of encouragement: "Hah!" Isn't she cute?

A guy tries to introduce me. But it's impossible.

They won't shut up. They want Honey.

I go out anyway.

Three hundred beers pounding, three hundred mouths shouting, "HONEY!"

Hecklers don't bother me. I love 'em. I eat 'em. They're like all-you-can-eat shrimp. I mean, they're not like real food, they're like appetizers. They just make you hungry for more. I crunch one and go, "All right, who's next? I know there's more of ya out there. C'mon! C'mon!"

But this is something else. This is like I'm sitting there at the table and I order shrimp, and this dumptruck backs up to my table, and the thing buries me in shrimp. Then a cement-mixer backs up and slops on the secret sauce.

"HONEY! HONEY! HONEY!"

I mean, they don't even know I'm there. They don't need a warm-up. You couldn't get a hotter crowd. If they don't get Honey on stage in two minutes, we're going to need the fire hoses and the tear gas and the billy clubs.

What? Me worry?

Nah. I've got the microphone. It's ElectroVoice. I've got my 4-pack of Perrier. And I've got enough riot control cops here to rerun Kent State.

So I start shouting, "Do you want Honey? Do you want Honey? Do you want Honey?"

"WE WANT HONEY! WE WANT HONEY! WE WANT HONEY!"

Got 'em.

"FINE!!" I yell even louder. "THEN SHUT THE [recreational raunch deleted] UP!! SHUT UP!!"

Growling.

"SHUT UP!"

Muttering.

"Shut Up! Or no Honey! No Honey until everyone shuts the [term of low intelligence deleted] up! Shut up!"

I repeated the shut-up theme a few times.

I tilted my Stetson and lit a Camel to pristine silence.

"You guys are pretty warm," I told them. "I was supposed to warm you up. But I don't think you need it. So I'm gonna cool you down."

"[Obscenity deleted]!" my first shrimp of the night yelled at me.

"Hey! I'm sleeping with Honey, and you're not!" CRUNCH! The cops haul his tail outta there.

One down, 299 to go.

.   .   .   .   .

The police arrested 22 people, I crunched about 15, and Honey wowed 300-plus.

But afterward Honey was totally bummed. She decided her band needed a couple more warm-up dates. Boston's Orpheum Theater. 2,800-seats. She gets Boxer on it, between songs, before even finishing the gig.

(Boston's mayor eventually nixed that, because of this Worcester fiasco. The open-air City Hall Plaza was suggested as an alternative. Claude Boxer nixed that. And there you have it. *Newsweek's* lead story: HONEY BANNED IN BOSTON.)

Anyway, after the show, Honey and her bodyguard and I and a band member are riding up the Hotel elevator to our suites. Honey is slouching in the far corner. Her blond hair is a mess covering her face. She's in one of her moods. Don't touch me. Don't talk to me. Don't even look at me.

I was just riding the elevator—actually, feeling pretty good. Live comedy, after that first minute, is the most fun I can have without Honey on my lips. I had survived a lynch mob. Once I got them under control, it had been a blast.

Anyway, big silence in the elevator.

This woman gets on at the mezzanine. I wasn't really paying too much attention to her. Well, OK, I was looking at her stretch-pant-swathed little bottom. But I wasn't paying attention to her.

"Hey, didn't you open for Honey at Sir Morgan's Cove?" the woman suddenly blurts at me. Something feels wrong about the situation, but I don't know just what.

"Yeah," I tell her. Then I flash Honey a smile. The woman recognizes me, and doesn't recognize Honey: a first.

"You gonna party?" the woman asks me.

I shake my head. I realize that the female is older than I thought, maybe my age, and there's something about the voice that keeps jarring something in my memory.

But the woman slinks up to me, and asks, "Um, how 'bout if just you and me party?"

Well, Honey is giving me one of her bemused looks.

"Toni!" I suddenly shout. "Goddamn!"

Toni is disappointed in me. I'm not playing along. She's lost 40 pounds, she's gotten herself a nose job, done something wild to her hair, she's talking funky to disguise her voice, and she's snuck out here to Boston to freak me out, and she's doing her performance art trip, and I blow everything.

"Jimmy, Jimmy, Jimmy," Toni says, and gives me a big hug and a kiss anyway.

Honey is not bemused.

"Toni, I'd like you to meet the most famous woman in the elevator. Honey, I'd like you to meet my sister, Toni Bayan."

. . . . .

Go on tour, see the world? That's funny.

Climatically controlled celebrity.

Jet to stage to hotel suite to jet. Her tour hasn't officially started yet, but already Honey is hermetically sealed off from "Channel 1" by band members, lawyers, back-up singers, limousines, guards, techies, underlings, boyfriend.

How big is Honey's suite? We're lost. I mean, we actually don't know which room we're in. Rumor has it that there's an 18-hole golf course in here somewhere, but we haven't found it yet. There's no real danger. Phones are all over the place. When we want to leave, we'll pick up a phone, and a rescue party will come get us. I want to go exploring (I've counted four bathrooms, so far, different colors), but the ladies want to couch back and talk. About me.

"Tell her," Toni said. Sand trap!

"What?" Honey said. "What?"

"You're doing a good job," I said, with disgust. Well,

maybe not disgust. But I did wish she would shut up.

"Jimmy and I just have a special knack for pleasing our dear old Dad. Mom's a rock. But poor Dad. I majored in philosophy, and then dropped out of college just before graduation. Now I'm a boat bum. Divorced three times, no grandkids for Daddy. But Jimmy really one-upped me. We won't even go into you joining the Army, when you could have got disability."

"I notice you not going into it," I noticed.

"What?" Honey said. "Disability? What's wrong with you, Jimmy?"

"You," I pointed to my sister. "Shut up."

Toni smiled beauteously. Really, an incredible nose job, a little cute button. "Oh, nothing that two broken legs couldn't cure. How long were you in Vietnam again, Jimmy?"

"Nine hours."

My sister elaborated upon the full extent of my service to my country. "He got sideswiped by a jeep. An American jeep. A parked American truck. Jimmy in the middle. Knocked him right out. When he came to, he was back in the States, with a Purple Heart and two full casts on his legs."

"Change of subject," I pleaded.

The stuff women stuff into their purses. Toni pulled out an old, yellowing newsletter out of hers. This was not the change of subject I had in mind. Why couldn't I have been an only child?

"Orange County Board of Realtors Newsletter," Toni said.

Anyway, she starts reading. Quotes this big long thing. It's a review my father wrote. Basically, it says that my appearances on *Friday Night Live* are so dreadful that they have set my father's career back ten years and killed any chance he might have had to become a millionaire. And Toni is really getting into it, she's repeating the juicy parts.

The most famous fiancee in the world is encouraging her by laughing boisterously, and pointing at me; big jabs of mirth. Honey has ruined Dave The Axe's career, and I've ruined my old man's career. Honey thinks it's so cute.

Gradually, Toni becomes more serious. "You always strived so hard to get Daddy to notice you, didn't you, Jimmy? You even changed your name for him, didn't you? That was why you did it, wasn't it?"

I didn't say anything.

Honey decides out loud that if she had been born a man, that she would be me; which is about the silliest thing I've ever heard anyone say.

"Tell her," Toni says.

I didn't say anything.

"He sent Daddy a million dollars. A special Banker's check. It was a good one, too, 'cause Daddy cashed it. And it cleared. Oh, there was a little note with it. 'Here's your [f-word deleted] million dollars, Father.'" Toni was talking to Honey, but she was looking at me. "I always thought he made a mistake by cashing it. But I guess he had to call Jimmy's bluff. No bluff. So Daddy sent back his own special Banker's check four weeks later. A million dollars. With a little note. '[F-word deleted] you, Son.'"

Honey's gynecologist leaked the news of her pregnancy, Honey was slapped with three maternity suits, my contract for the following year at the Comedy Channel was not renewed, and I began receiving death threats. That's the chapter.

Honey in concert was something else. I'll say one thing for her: she really played the role. She became a projection of everyone's fantasies. The girl was theater.

Frustration is the high-octane aircraft fuel for rock. And Honey thrived on it.

Here I am. And you can't quite have me.

Then she would stick some part of herself in your face and wiggle it.

· · · · ·

"Tour with me, please," she pleaded with me. "Please? Jimmy, I don't want to be all alone."

All alone? With tens of thousands of kids screaming for her at every stop? Backstage Honey has guests: the most famous of the entertainers, and the most entertaining of the famous. Celebrities cancel their own concerts for the privilege of a few minutes backstage with Honey.

But I knew what she meant. And I couldn't go with her.

I caught a few of her shows, but I couldn't tour with her. I had a movie career I had to get moving, now that there was no place for me on TV anymore.

My boss at the Comedy Channel wouldn't even tell me why I was fired. He acted like he didn't know himself. In fact, I think he didn't like it, because I really was their best writer. All he knew was that the word came down to remove McCool. (As this book went to press, I discovered what I had already guessed: that [name deleted] had me fired because he was jealous of my relationship with Honey!)

. . . . .

One Honey show I was up for was JFK Stadium. We're talking 180,000 Honey freaks frying with excitement in the hard sun. And they're all out there rumbling for their goddess.

Pre-show, I throw this little black box at Honey. Same old underhand toss.

She catches it. "Not this shit again," she says.

Take-no-prisoners smile.

She opens the little box, and sucks in her breath.

It is such a sweet pleasure watching her.

This one is a ruby. It's mounted as part of a platinum pendant. Lots of little rubies around it. I mean, the thing is really beautiful.

Big?

Big. Carats up the ass.

"So let's set a date," I tell her.

She's still looking at the ruby. Do I see red in her eyes?

"For the kid," I tell her.

"Are you sure you wanna be Mr. Honey?"

"I don't want my daughter to be an illegitimate kid."

"Our son," Honey corrects me.

Outside, they're starting to chant. HONEY. HONEY. HONEY.

"No. I only know how to make daughters."

"I specifically selected for a son," she informs me.

It makes me smile, but actually, I wouldn't put it past her. Boy sperms are easily excitable. They swim faster and then they drop dead, while the Girl sperms just keep paddling on. What I mean is, you can sort them out. Sort of.

"Of course, we'll have to invite all your friends," I tell her.

"Oh, Christ, what a circus." She snaps shut the black box. "I don't know, Jimmy."

Outside: HONEY. HONEY. HONEY. HONEY. HONEY. You ever hear 180,000 kids chanting your fiancee's name? The word awesome doesn't even come close.

I tell her, "We'll have to invite Danny Sonnenfeld. Buck Stone. And of course, we can't forget Bruce Ranger."

Honey smiles, and looks at the ruby again. She comes over and kisses me. And then holds me.

Outside: HONEY. HONEY. HONEY.

Honey says, "And we have to invite Maggie. And Amanda. And we mustn't forget Mary Elizabeth."

GOD, I love this woman.

I close my eyes and hold her quiet warmth.
Outside, the chanting is becoming a roar.
HONEY. HONEY. HONEY. HONEY! HONEY!

. . . . .

Since Honey On Tour couldn't have me in the flesh, I sent my Juliet classy gifts. Strictly A-list stuff. Love offerings attractively wrapped with big silk ribbons and many-colored bows, hand-delivered to her in the farest away of faraway places with pomp and flourish. Just the way she likes it. Cherished reminders of our winsome affair, vintage masterpieces of romantic gesture.

A Croft pen and dildo set. Maybe she'll write me a letter postmarked Paris.

American-made Blank & Thatcher dildo floodlight attachment. For the places in Tokyo where the sun don't shine.

I also sent her practical essentials for the road. A 500-pound crate of M&Ms, with two five-foot wide serving trays.

Something to remind her of me. A sterling silver heart locket with a picture inside of my hat.

As a professional comedian I couldn't resist demonstrating my ability to reduce Honey to protracted howls of helpless glee whenever I wished. My old high school yearbook photograph.

George Thicke helped me set it up so that, no matter where she was performing, when her wireless microphone was handed to her just before she went on, there was always a single red rose from me wired to it.

For when she needed a cool cuddle: a 5-foot stuffed polar teddy bear.

A little brightly festooned and ribboned box, inside a black velvet-covered box, inside a red-striped wrapped box, inside a big blue polka-dotted box, inside a huge takes-three-guys-to-lift-it plain brown cardboard box. And inside all of that, a 10-inch high commissioned erotic sculpture: a horny couple doing the dirty deed on TV.

A moving message electric sign set up in her hotel suite with inside jokes and declarations of love that cleverly erased its memory (the evidence) the moment it was shut off.

Violets? Never!!

My homosexual spy within the Honey camp told me Bruce Ranger was backstage at her Philadelphia show. Oil of No Lay for the lady. I sent Bruce a wind-up Hop-Along Peter.

CHAPTER 24

It was your typical Southern California outdoor spring fever wedding. 60 guests: family and friends to witness the sacred union of the joyous couple. 5 helicopters, violating residential airspace and hovering above the Los Angeles hills with telescopic cameras to witness the sacred union of the joyous couple. 3 network news crews, 2 independent TV news crews, 1 live-satellite CNN link-up—so the world could witness the sacred union of the joyous couple. 29 photojournalists (in addition to the airborne variety), to desacralize and disseminate the union of the joyous couple. 40 Beverly Hills policemen, to control the rowdy would-be wedding-crashers, estimated at 10,500.

Have you ever been disseminated to every check-out counter in every supermarket in every State of the Union? I have. But for truly heavy-duty promulgation, that ain't diddley.

I mean, Honey and I played for the fourth-largest international television audience ever. (We learned about this statistical fact later, during our happy honeymoon.) Honey blamed it on me. She didn't mind being less popular than Neil Armstrong & Ed Aldrin placing the first footprints on the moon (back in '69), or even Bush's War Speech; but how embarrassing to be upstaged by Lady Di & "Ears" Charlie in another wedding, no less. Honey complained of being hitched to a low-life court jester, and lamented that she could pick a prince out of a hat and come up with better TV-Q. I immediately offered her my upturned Stetson, and rattled around some imaginary princes for her.

. . . . .

Since Dave The Axe couldn't go to the wedding, the wedding came to Dave The Axe. And there, in front of an estimated international mob of Nielsen-knows-how many hundred million TV viewers, down on an amphitheater stage upon which the two of us had once writhed sinfully and orgasmically, we solemnly said our sacred do's.

That's a white lie. Honey said, "Are you kidding?" A comedienne, this girl.

She corrected herself with an enthusiastic nod. And when it was my turn, I said, "I'll give it my best shot."

Bruce Ranger was there (was that Nasty bulge under his coat a .44 Magnum?). But what else could I do? The woman had gone and invited Maggie Tiel, and Dritchell, and the virgin Mary.

I responded in the manly fashion, and faxed invites to Stone and Sonnenfeld—both no-shows (Whew!)—and Nasty Sam.

Nasty Sam did not bring a date. Not funny.

Maggie Tiel brought our daughter Twilight to the wedding. Not funny.

Dritchell brought handsome young Black Super-Comedian Mega-Movie-Star Curtis Campbell. Not funny.

Mary Elizabeth brought her hymen. Not funny.

The Cool Crew was there. Black tuxedos. Outnumbered by the Honey Brigade. Black tuxedos. Outnumbered by Campbell's B-Boys. 2 pink tuxedos, 5 orange tuxedos, 6 green tuxedos, surrounding Curtis in his rainbow tux with short pants and white sox. There may be some humor here.

My Father didn't come to the wedding. Weren't homes selling, over there back of the Orange Curtain? Besides, our wedding was televised. He could tape the puppy. And it's important to remember that 50% of all videotaped programs are never watched.

My Grandmother was a *Hitler Madchen* in her youth—she couldn't come to the wedding, but she did send a representative. My Mother (and you can bet she gave me hell about my first marriage to a Jew) asked me, first thing upon arrival, "Jim, are you sure she's not Jewish? She looks so Jewish, and I've read that—"

"No, Mom, she's not Jewish. C'mon, let's go meet her. You'll like her. Honey's the sweetest witchy bitch slut dyke commie you'll ever meet. And she hates niggers; you'll have so much to talk about! Oh, hi, Campbell."

My cousins, sister, and close friends rated invites. Larry the butler put on sandals and a bola tie. Robbie Berger was Best Man.

At one point, pre-do, Bruce Ranger confronted me. You ever been confronted by Bruce Ranger?

The guy is taller than me, and heavier, and about twenty times more macho. He came up to me, growling, and he bent down and stuck his left eye four inches from my right eye, and snarled at me. "Do you feel lucky, punk?"

I didn't say anything.

"Do ya?" Ranger snarled.

I still didn't say anything. I just stood there. I didn't blink. I didn't move. I just looked back at him. I don't think there was any emotion on my face.

I couldn't put an emotion on my face, because I was so scared shitless, that my brain was short-circuited. My stomach was San Francisco after a 7.1.

Some close-up flashbulbs went off, and I realized someone was taking pictures of this.

Bruce growled again.

I can't explain it, but his second growl was pushing it too far. And I wasn't scared shitless anymore. It just seemed absurd. Bruce Ranger just seemed absurd. I mean, the guy really is older than Honey's father—I checked.

I smiled, easily, and I gave it to him in the eye, right back. "Yeah," I said. "I feel pretty lucky."

Bruce growled a third time, and walked away from me.

I visited one of Axe's bathrooms, and removed the tiny ball of shit from my underwear.

.   .   .   .   .

I was socializing (I think it's safe to call it that) with Maggie and lovely little Twilight, when Honey came over and lit the cigarette that was hanging out of my mouth.

"Hi, Twi!" Honey said, bending down to her, touching her hair and giving my little girl some one-on-one with the phenom.

Twilight was on tiptoes of excitement. Maggie was on her high horse, hands crossed, mouth zipped to a thin line.

"Honey," Maggie said, interrupting the little one-on-one. "You set back the feminist movement two years every time you do that."

Honey looked at Maggie, but she didn't say anything. It was such a long, silent stare, that I knew it was some kind of secret woman-to-woman message. Honey pinched my fanny and then glided off to do her blushing bride bit for some other guests.

"Ouch," I said.

Twilight and Maggie and I all stared after Honey; one with beautiful hero worship, one with beautiful scorn, and one with beautiful pain.

Maggie said something.

"Excuse me?" I asked.

"When she lights your cigarette! It's so nauseating."

"Maybe," I admitted. "But it does wonders for my fragile male ego. Maggie, can you imagine what a hit it is for me when the most famous girl in the world lights my cigarette for me?"

Maggie gave me that special look of hers that I best remember her by: withering contempt for me, the tall phallo-centric snot. "A woman over the age of twelve should not be called girl."

I opened my mouth to speak, but wisely shut it.

Maggie wasn't finished, anyway. She talked to me as though she were lecturing a small child. "Honey is a role model. A role model for millions of young women. She is a heroine. Honey is teaching the young women of today totally degrading ways of sucking up to men. Dammit, Jimmy, watching a Honey video on MTV is a consciousness-lowering session! I just don't understand her at all."

"She's trying to get me to quit smoking," I said.

Maggie made a noise of disgust that was almost a naughty word.

"I'm serious," I said seriously.

Maggie repeated her naughty noise.

Twilight looked miserable. Well, if I had three parents, and two of them said nasty things to each other and argued all the time, I'd look miserable too. I gave Twilight a wink of affection. I played with her bleached hair. I coaxed a half-smile out of her.

"Maggie, I am serious. She is trying to get me to quit. It's just the way she is. It's the way she does it. You know me, right? Three, four packs a day. Well, I'm down to less than a pack a day. Honey steals my goddamn lighters! She made me promise. No chain-smoking. When we're together, I can't light the cigarettes myself. Only she's allowed to do it. It's a joke that's gone stale. It was cute at first, but now it's just embarrassing. I don't want her to have to light my Camels anymore. It's starting to bug me. I'm smoking a lot today, 'cause I'm under a lot of pressure, but really, I'm almost down to half a pack a day."

The Axe hooked his arm around my neck and said, "How's it hangin', Shithead?"

"Down to the ground, Sir Shithead."

He laughed, and lurched off my neck, and toward the booze.

Maggie said, "Sharp guy. It took me five years to see you for what you are."

"Mom!" Twilight said.

It made me smile.

I love my little girl. She's all dressed up like a Honey wanna-be; she's been a Honey-in-training since she was eight. She is the sweetest, most wonderful little girl in the world. Smart as a whip, too. How much do I love my little girl?

After each of my live comedy shows, there are pairs of panties, thrown onstage by fans who've scratched their names and numbers in the crotch panels. Instead, Daddy is faithful to Honey. In each day's mail, we have the Mary Elizabeth letter, and perhaps a half dozen more young ladies of astonishingly sexy bodies fully revealed in porno-pose & porno-prose, who swear to me their unquenchable thirst for my seminal fluids. Instead, Daddy is faithful to Honey. Let's say I'm at LAX, waiting for a plane, and a female fox recognizes me; she probably won't ask me for an autograph, she'll offer me a dicky-dunk: I mean, I'm standing in line, and she gets behind me, starts gently touching me; I look around, it's a sexy chick, I think it's a mistake, I move a few inches forward; now she's gently touching me again, only it's more insistent now, it's more a rub, a stroke, than a touch, and it's all over; her leg is brushing mine, her arm is stroking mine, her hip is bumping at me; I look around at her face; she's licking her lips now; I say, "Hi," and she says, "Hiiiiiiiii, Cooooool," as she looks down at the growing bulge in my pants. Instead, Daddy is faithful to Honey. Or, say, I'm going to work at one of the FOX studios, and there's a sexy actress sitting in the reception area. Well, hell, the way she's dressed, a guy can't not look at her. So I look. She doesn't just look back, she starts caressing her thighs, rubbing her tummy, cupping her breasts through her clothes. If I walk fast, and think about my contract which is running out, I do not get a hard-on. Daddy is faithful to Honey.

It wouldn't surprise me a bit if some dome doctor told me that I fell in love with Honey so that my little girl Twilight could become the President of the Southern California chapter of the Honey Fan club. Twilight is one well-connected fan! Honey shipped two UPS trucks of Honey memorabilia and artifacts directly to Twilight McCool at the Tiel residence. Priceless stuff. Twilight gets to go on dates with Honey and me. Twilight has had her picture on a full-page spread with Honey and me in *US* magazine.

We are talking wanna-be heaven.

But I was in wanna-get-outta-here hell. I made temporary peace with Maggie, gave Twilight's head a pat, and went in search of my cigarette lighter.

I ask around. Mingle among the guests. Discreetly inquire. Dritchell is not offering her orifices up for stabs anymore. She's smiling. She's happy. She has just been crowned Pet Of The Year. Her hands are ALL OVER Curtis Campbell. That Black billion-dollar-box-office King Of Comedy is screwing my old girlfriend. And she likes it!

What does Curtis have to say about all this?

"Eeeh-eeh-eeh." I fight the impulse to put a Camel in my mouth by placing my self adjacent to my lighter and kissing my bride. The bride is fingering her gold crucifix. You could ward off vampires with this thing; it's the size of a steak knife.

.   .   .   .   .

What about Sexploitation Honey vs. Maidenly Mary? Mary Elizabeth proudly flaunted a pale-white silk dress of such untarnished purity that it brought a narrowing of Honey's eyes, and a Camel cigarette to my nervous lips. I think Ed Young coined the operative phrase here: "Chaste as morning dew." The girl was an insult to the bride. She was a tall Parthenos.

"Thank you for inviting me," Mary delicately said to me.

"I didn't," I told her. "She did." I indicated Honey.

Honey came to my rescue. She hitched up her wedding dress, pulled my gold lighter off her garter, and lit the cigarette in my mouth.

I needed that.

It may have been a woman-to-woman secret message, because Mary Elizabeth instantly turned her head and stumbled away from us. In tears.

CHAPTER 25

Where do you get purple silk sheets for a sixteen-foot-diameter circular bed? Hey, I just sleep here. But yes, Honey's Bel Air bed is Guinness Book material. Stone never slept in this bed. Sonnenfeld never slept in this bed. Bruce Ranger has never been here. Honey wouldn't even let me see it until after we were married.

I remember when I first carried her into her bedroom, and we whispered sweet love-talk to each other.

"Five months pregnant, and you weigh a ton!" I shouted. "Are you having twins? Quadruplets?"

"Jimmy, I have something caught between my teeth. After you put me down, I need to use your right arm for dental floss."

"Hey, *I'm* the comedian, around here. Christ! What the hell is that? It's too big for an orgy. And too small to sleep Southern California."

"I hope you like waterbeds."

OK, maybe I stopped walking kind of suddenly. But it is not true, as she said in two interviews, that I almost dropped her.

"You don't like waterbeds?" Honey asked.

"Waterbeds? I love waterbeds. I didn't know I was going to have to sleep in the Pacific Ocean."

I set her down on the padded edge of the biggest goddamn waterbed in the world. She pushed down with her hand, and got a ripple going that carried all across the vast surface, beyond the horizon, until the whole bed was gently whooshing up and down. This was not a waveless waterbed. "It's really reet, Jimmy; you can get this rhythm going . . . ." Honey pecked a kiss on my lips. "Thirds," she said, pointing. "Over there is for TV. Over there is for sleeping." Another Honey peck on my lips. "What do you think this third is for?" Honey peck. Honey eyes twinkling.

"Fleet maneuvers," I said.

.　.　.　.　.

If a single word could describe the married life of Cool McCool & Honey, it would be *miscarriage*.

Of economic justice: I signed a prenuptial agreement. We are not talking the Short Form. Her money is her money. My money (if any) becomes her money. There just is no justice. But this is not the miscarriage of economic justice.

Of movie careers: Pentagon released my *Ice-99* the same month Ursa Major released Honey's new picture with Television-hunk Stanley Greene, *Bullfrog*. (Stanley got second billing.) Absurd as it sounds, our careers were suddenly in direct competition with each other, as our two pictures scrambled for the summer consumer's limited spending money, in the face of theater tickets that topped ten bucks in places. Stanley Greene was paid a flat fee of $4 million to do the picture. Honey was paid a flat fee of $5.5 million to do the picture. I was paid in used cockroach exoskeletons. Well, as everyone knows, *Bullfrog* lost more money than *Ishtar*. The thing went into video rental while *Ice-99* was still breaking summer theater box office records. There just isn't any justice. It's even worse than that: Robbie got me my original mega-buck million dollar deal for the forthcoming *Ice Cubes* (!); but now they can't release *Ice Cubes* for at least another year, because they have to milk this one (wait until the fuss over Cool McCool from *Ice-99* dies down first). But this is not the miscarriage of movie careers.

Of nuptial bliss: Hell hath no fury like a Honey bombing at the box office. Here we have the most famous woman on the silver screen, a budget of $51 million, and Stanley Greene (whose *Vice Cop* TV show held the highest Nielsen ratings in its slot for five years); and we have a movie that just does not move. Naturally, it was all my fault. Her fans had deserted her, because the goddess had allowed a cockroach to crawl into her panties; and she liked it! Justice? But this is not the nuptial miscarriage.

.   .   .   .   .

The distance between Hollywood and Bel Air is ten million dollars, two savage guard dogs, six closed-circuit TV cameras, and two heavily-armed security guards. The roads between Hollywood and Bel Air are packed with pervs. Sunset, in particular. If the horny old men in Rolls Royces don't hit up on you, some famous speeder in a supercar might.

What I mean is, I wouldn't recommend it for a little eleven-year-old girl who hitchhiked because she didn't have cab fare.

But there was Twilight, at eleven p.m., at my front door. *Our* front door. OK, OK, *Honey's* front door.

Twilight was holding her little magnetic key, and petting the neck of Seven, one of Honey's normally savage Dobermans. Sheldon, one of the guards for Honey's estate, was carrying Twilight's luggage.

"My, my, Twi," Honey said. "Isn't this past your bedtime?"

"I ran away from home," Twilight said. "I can stay here, right?"

Honey said my name like a woman throwing up her hands helplessly into the air.

. . . . .

I called Maggie, and told her to cancel the APB. Then I drove Twilight home. I didn't let her stay the night. I didn't let her stay ten minutes.

Most men have a genetic flaw in their code: they turn to mush at the sight of a single female tear. But not me. There was nothing mushy about my white knuckles on the steering wheel.

So while Twilight cried herself into dehydration, I explained the facts of life to her.

Thou Shalt Not Run Away From Home. There was

nothing mushy about the hard-core truth coming out of my mouth.

Every story has a good guy and a bad guy. Maggie was the good guy. Cool was the bad guy. Maggie was the lonely loyal wife, waiting at home for her man. Cool was the cheating snake, the rambling man, having sex with a hundred women in fifty States. (I may have exaggerated a little, for effect. OK, OK, about forty-nine States worth of exaggeration.)

Twilight's rebuttal was a pint of salty liquid.

I was a sixty-second commercial for Alex Tiel, her new father. The story I told was very black-and-white, for eleven-year-old ears (that were behaving like eight-year-old ears). There were no shades of gray.

Of course, when I turned the terminally-tearful Twilight over to her lawful parents, this whole episode was my fault. How is she, the loving mother, supposed to have any parental authority over her child, when I, the shithead-snake, go and marry the object of her child's fixated hero worship?

Did Maggie have to cry while she was shouting these things at me?

To say that I felt lousy after all this is a gross under-statement. Because, never mind my macho lies, that flaw in my genetic code is alive and well and living in my DNA. After all those female tears, I was mush, I was pudding pop, I was painful Jello.

I drove two blocks, and had to pull the car over and park. I just sat there.

Mush.

My mind was swirling with awful memories in mushy, indistinct shades of gray. And in all those painful memories of Maggie and me, I couldn't find one good guy, one bad guy; we were all there in mushy gray.

When I was a struggling semi-failure, and Maggie had to support me, everything was wonderful. Even if we only had a day or two a week together, the love was so supportive and spectacular that it was enough to hold us together against anything. But when I started to click, and could finally say, "OK, now I'm going to take care of *you*," something went wrong. We started drifting further and further apart, emotionally, even though we were actually spending more time together. It got so that being with her or having sex with her just wasn't fun anymore, for either of us; so without either of us saying anything about it, we stopped having sex. But I was so excited that I was finally earning a living as a comedian, that it was all I could think about, and I suppose I thought that our relationship was *her* problem, that if it wasn't working, that it was *her* fault. One night, after one of my better shows in Dallas, an incredibly beautiful brunette tucked her hotel key into my inside jacket pocket. I tried to give it back to her, honest, but she wouldn't accept it, and quickly walked away from me, her hips smiling. I tried not to go there, honest, but the words "Hilton Hotel" just slipped out of my mouth to the taxi driver. She was married and wealthy and fun. Amend that: *FUN!* She made it clear that her calender would be open whenever I was in Dallas, all I had to do was call her secretary and make an appointment a few days in advance. Well, I started making a lot of special flights to Dallas . . . of course, it didn't take long for Maggie to find out everything and take Twilight and herself out of my life . . . and, of course, my fun, married, wealthy Dallas Lady's calender mysteriously became booked up years in advance, the day after I told her I thought I was falling in love with her . . . and then I met Amanda Dritchell.

Mush. Gray mush.

I started driving again. I made a wrong turn, got lost for a minute, and found myself down in Hollywood.

May I be forgiven for going down to the Improv, and doing a surprise Midnight show to make myself feel better?

May I be forgiven for then going out with wild Dickey Bets and fast-talking Wanda Witchel to Barney's for some beers and eight ball? That was before either of them had struck major-gold as comedians; but we all knew it was only a few ovations away, and it was fun to hang out again with some of the old gang.

But the theme is miscarriage. Am I there at Barney's, boozing it up and finding alternate uses for pool balls, because of my failure at fatherhood? No, I am here at Barney's to initiate a miscarriage of truth, so some fool-photog can snap our group pic, crop Dickey Bets out of the frame, sell it to the *National Toilet Enquirer*, where it winds up two weeks later front page with the banner headline: COOL McCOOL & MYSTERY BLOND CHEAT ON HONEY. Bets was insulted because he had been airbrushed out of the picture and the story. Witchel was insulted because they hadn't recognized who she was (this may have been an intentional editorial decision, because it allowed the follow-up story: MYSTERY BLOND IN HONEY LOVE TRIANGLE IDENTIFIED). Any insult to me miscarried. I was getting immune to this stuff.

Well, I had to leave my car in Barney's lot because I was so beery. When the taxi brought me back to Honey's mansion, there were all these flashing lights everywhere. Police. Fire engines. Ambulances.

The paramedics were there in force. The police wouldn't even let me into my own goddamn home at first! Well, *our* goddamn home. OK, OK, *her* goddamn home. And OK, maybe I was a little hysterical with fear and guilt.

And everybody already knew what I had yet to learn.

Honey miscarried. We are talking . . . expulsion of fetus from womb. My little would-have-been girl . . . well, OK, *our* little would-have-been *boy*.

Did Honey have to cry while she was telling me?

CHAPTER 26

So what do you give your loving wife, to take the place of a lost child?

Violets? I was sorely tempted.

No.

But what? There I was, on *The Georgio Show*, sitting down with the dude, and all I can think about is how lousy Honey feels, and how I've got to do something about it. My comedy routine was so bad that Georgio didn't hug me after. I got some laughs, but not one Bark. Usually, I get some Woof-Woofs from this crowd. Now, he's asking me all these questions, and I'm like brain-dead.

Georgio is sitting there, with his boundless enthusiasm and his smile-bypass smile, and we're talking about all this stuff; but I can see the secret terror in his eyes. I just am not funny. It isn't going anywhere. Viewers are switching to Kenny Johnson because of me. And Georgio is thinking, oh shit, I could get canceled before we make it to commercial because of this [ghetto patois deleted] asshole!

But Georgio is a genius, a real tightrope walker. I like him, and he likes me . . . I think. So he gets confrontational. He knows I can take it. He knows Larry Green can handle Robbie Berger's flak. I told him before the show that I want some hardballs. I'm tired of wimpy dialogue. In fact, I actually insulted Georgio a little, in front of his main squeeze, *cafe au lait* Pop Vocalist Candy Morrow: "What is this, the *I'm OK, You're OK Show?*"

"How does it feel to be Mr. Honey?" Georgio smoothly asks me.

I answer him, thinking: how does Honey feel, having suffered the most famous miscarriage in the world?

"Punched out any photographers, lately?" Georgio asks.

"Back off, Georgio. He got arrested, I didn't get arrested. I mean, the guy snuck into our house, and started taking pictures of our bathroom. Illegal entry. Trespass. There's blood all over the bathroom! Honey is a mess! They're trying to save her goddamn life, and this [Beeeeeeeeeeeeeeeeeeeep] sneaks in there and starts taking pictures! I mean, it's private property." I took two seconds to try and chill. In the studio audience, one lonely pair of hands applauded in a tentative way that stopped after four pats. "Sorry, man, I'm not trying to get you off the air. I like this show. I'm just a little upset about this."

Mr. Georgio started to say something, but I interrupted him. I don't often do this. He let me get away with it. I told you he likes me. "Look at it this way, Georgio. You're a man who values his privacy."

"You got that right!" Georgio said.

"Suppose you get married. And you do your manly thing, and your wife gets pregnant. And then in the middle of the night, at home, something goes wrong. And you 911 for an ambulance. Well, you like privacy, off the show, right? But now, suddenly, there's paramedics, and police, and police dogs, and flashing lights, and fire engines, and they're all there at your house, in the middle of the night. They're tramping all over your lawn, TV trucks are pulling up into your driveway, patching into their satellite relays, Associated Press is there in your flowerbed, the *National Flipping Enquirer* is there peeking in your windows, your wife is in the bathroom bleeding all over the place, the paramedics are afraid to move her . . . now keep in mind, this is your private property, you own the damn grounds—well, your wife does—and this jerk-reporter busts in a side window, sneaks into where the doctors are working on your wife, and starts taking pictures! What do you do? You grab the camera out of his hands! If he won't give you the camera, you goddamn take it! If he won't let you take it, you put your fist in his face! Defending house and home, right? Defending my wife!"

Georgio sits back, with his smile-bypass, and he slowly applauds, and he slowly nods. And his studio audience picks up on it. And I get a little solemn, respectful applause of admiration.

We break for commercial, and Georgio gives me a big reassuring double hand-clasp. I apologize. I tell him that my mind isn't really on the show. I tell him I'll leave now, if he wants. But Georgio is like, *Stop It!* And the studio audience (I can't figure it out) is emotionally behind me, in my corner. I'm not funny, but they LIKE me. It's a weird feeling for a comic. I mean, the hecklers are yelling, "Go for it, McCool!"

We come back, and we're talking more stuff.

Georgio gets into it some more. How my *Ice-99* is a surprise summer smash, while Honey's *Bullfrog* dived into the dumpster.

"Ooooo," the studio audience goes.

"I know," I say. "I feel so bad for Stanley Greene. First his *Vice Cop* goes off the air, and now his movies just go right out of the theater. Even the most famous actress in the world co-starring with Stanley can't save the guy's career."

"Ooooo," the studio audience goes.

We talk about the used cockroach exoskeletons I got paid for *Ice-99*. We show a clip of *Ice Cubes* that has the studio audience roaring with laughter.

I plug Robbie as the world's best agent. "He'd better be, because I'm not supposed to even have that clip of *Ice Cubes*, and Pentagon is going to be pissed as hell." I pause for two seconds, and then say quickly, in a smooth rush of words, "I'm moving off the Comedy Channel, Georgio, but negotiations are underway with Fox for a possible Cool McCool live comedy show similar to *Friday Night Live* and did you know that the female octopus has her vagina inside her nose?"

"Woof-Woof-Woof," the studio audience goes. These cats are barking at a white pup. Amazing, just amazing. And Georgio laughs so hard, he can't even talk for about fifteen seconds.

Georgio wants me to take him back to square one: "So, McCool, tell us now. We all know you're living at Honey's Bel Air mansion. What is it? Thirty-three rooms? Sixty-six rooms? How did a guy like you, ever get inside Honey's front door?"

Silence. And then, "Ooooo," from the studio audience.

I said, "The same way you got inside Candy Morrow's back door."

"Ooooo," the studio audience goes. Louder.

Mr. Georgio said, "Cool, I was told not to ask you about Honey. I was told that it's all anyone asks you, these days. Nobody wants to talk about you. They get you on their show, and then they pump you about Honey. Am I right?"

"Right."

"So, as a booking condition, I was told not to ask you about Honey. I was told not to even say the word *Honey*." Pause for laughter. "But I've gotta know. I hear these rumors. Is it true that when you first met Honey you were in Japan, and you dove down and went pearl diving?" Pause for applause. "Are we still on the air?" Georgio asked (big smile).

Isn't he great? I love him. "No. Scotland. We were in Scotland, Georgio. Let's see . . . Honey opened up her box lunch . . . I had Honey's binoculars around my neck . . . and I was washing this bird . . . there's a French Way you do it . . . fast is best, you know, *lickety-split* . . . in fact, I was about to talk to the canoe driver, when suddenly I sneezed into the basket . . . and—"

Georgio cut me off. "We have to break for commercial.

Be right back." Pause for audience Ooooo. "Are we still on the air?" Georgio asked (no smile).

Backstage, there was a minor disaster. I was never too clear on exactly what happened, but for some reason, Stevie Starr couldn't go on just yet. He's the guy who swallows stuff. Georgio jumps up, disappears for two minutes.

I sit there. Honey on the brain. There's a word for it: ruminate. The wife is hurting at home; what can I do? I want to bring down ET, and have him touch her tummy.

Georgio comes back, and says, "Let's do it some more."

We touch upon Honey's miscarriage. Georgio innocently asks how will that effect the maternity suits that were brought against Honey by men claiming fatherhood.

I say: I don't know. I didn't have to yell: Back off! Because the awkward silence that followed told me that he got the message.

We talk about Bruce Ranger.

Yes, it is true, I have just signed with Wide Range to do a supporting part in an upcoming Ranger western.

Georgio mentions the rumors that Bruce and Honey had a thing going for awhile. Georgio & audience drool for the straight dope.

I honestly answer that I honestly don't know, convincing everyone that I *do* know, and that they *did* have an affair.

I mention that Ranger & I are fairly friendly now, but that at my marriage, he pulled his Nasty Sam routine on me as a joke. I speak of the 7.1 stomach, the trip to the bathroom, and the removal of the tiny ball of shit. (The way I told it, everyone knew that I was only joking.)

I saw Larry cueing Georgio that his next guest is ready, and my instant reaction was: Thank GOD, I can FINALLY have a SMOKE!

And then the thought just came to me. "Georgio," I said. "Can I do something? It'll just take one minute."

"Quick: activate the ten-second delay!"

"Nothing like that," I said. "It's just that I got to thinking. What do you give someone who has everything? Well, you have to give them something that they would not be able to obtain, without you. So, what I'm going to do, right now, is quit smoking, on your show. I'm not going to smoke another cigarette . . . as long as I live. I swear it. In front of your whole audience. No more cigarettes. I quit."

I don't think anyone quite believed me.

"So that is my gift, to the lady who has everything— she knows who she is—I give her five more years of my love."

They still . . . didn't quite . . . believe me.

"Thank you, Georgio." I stood up. "Now that I've said it in front of so many people, I really have to quit."

Still! Still, they don't believe me! Not a peep from the audience. Not one hand clap. Georgio is waiting for the punch line: he thinks this is a comedy routine. Cool McCool, the smoking machine, stop smoking? The dude is just sitting there, confused, no smile-bypass smile. It's like, if I had been doing a comedy routine, I would have done it differently. And if I was seriously going to give up the cancer sticks, I would have done it differently, made more of a big deal out of it. But since Georgio's next guest was ready, and I was into overtime and improvising words on the spur, it just didn't emotionally happen.

In the small ungraceful silence, I saw a way to save it. I could have added in a certain tone of voice, "Oh shit. Now I have to stop. No really." But that would have cheapened it. So I just walked. If they can't handle a few serious words from a comedian, screw 'em.

Then there was a lone female shriek from the audience. Almost a sob. And a stab of recognition; I knew that voice. Cool McCool's #1 fan was there in Georgio's studio audience, and she was standing up in front of her seat, shrieking, "Do it, Cool! Oh, do it, Cool! Do it!" A videocamera found her, and she was there, on the TV monitors for a few seconds, one tear dripping down the right side of her face, but I didn't need to look at a monitor to recognize Mary Elizabeth McEnroe.

Even with a shill in the audience, this crowd still isn't emotionally with it.

"Wait a minute," Georgio says. "Are you really quitting smoking?"

"I just quit."

"Well, hey, I wish you luck with it." And there we go, with the big handshake that evolves into a big hug.

I said, "If your audience finds that hard to swallow, wait till they get a load of your next guest."

Smile-bypass smile.

CHAPTER 27

Perhaps I was not as supportive as I might have been to Honey. I really didn't get it. Miscarriage? This was not a catastrophe. This was a minor setback.

"So let's grow another one. And this time, we'll do it *my* way. What about right now?"

"Start without me."

This was the tough mega-woman who was beyond bitch. This was the perky high-energy point-woman for pop music. This was the lady with the vicious appetite for life.

Her doctors all swear to me that Honey is physically OK.

So why is she just lying there in her bed? A tiny, curled-up ball. The surface of the enormous waterbed, motionless. Every few moments, a moan of pain. The drapes are drawn against the day, the projection TV a gentle glow across Honey's bed, the VCR playing *Gone With The Wind* quietly.

"Is there anything I can do?"

"I don't know."

"Do you want me to hold you?"

"I don't care."

I swim over and hold her. Spoons.

"Does this feel good?"

Silence.

"Do you want a back-rub?"

"I don't know."

"Do you want to trombone?"

"I don't care."

I start to make love to her. But it's like, nobody's there. The sexiest woman in the world, and I can't get an erection.

"Would you like a nice long lick?"

"I don't care."

She really doesn't care. Her ears don't know I am licking them. Her nipples don't feel a thing. Her bellybutton just lies there. Innie. Her thighs are *Gone With The Wind.*

Honey is such a safe-sex nut, that I have never tasted her vagina before. She always stops me if my tongue ventures too close. She makes me spread out that clingy plastic food wrap stuff, and lick her through that.

This time she really doesn't care.

But it's like her vagina doesn't even know my tongue is there. Her clit can't get it up. She doesn't give me a real taste. No secretions, no nothing.

I give up on that. Hold her some more. Spoons. I think she likes it, but it's hard to tell.

"Do you want to talk?"

"If you want."

Silence.

"Do you want me to talk? Tell you a story, maybe?"

"If you want."

"I quit smoking."

Silence.

"I did it on Georgio's chatcom. I wanted to give you something to make you feel better. All I could think of is five more years of my love."

Silence.

"I mean, I figure if I quit now, which I have, I'll probably live about five more years."

Silence.

"Do you want me to shut up?"

"Yes."

. . . . .

Well, I couldn't just lie there in bed and do a John Lennon/Yoko Ono sleep-in for two weeks. Just lying in bed, this woman is making more money than I am. Not good for the male ego.

Bruce Ranger and I have started filming. The Fox network and I are trying to hassle out a contract. Robbie wants them to offer me the moon. So far, they've offered a toxic waste dump in Jersey. I'm thinking about it. The American Cancer Society is busting down Robbie's doors to get me to do commercials for them. Exxon has given them this huge grant (no comment). (OK, OK: comment. Some executive bumpkin saw me quit smoking on Georgio's show, and he thinks I'm the right guy to convince America that "tough guys don't smoke.") The ACS wants to pay me $2.5 million a year to save America from the scourge of cigarettes. Robbie wants me to do a brilliant set of anti-smoking commercials for them for free. I'm thinking about that too. But I can't think in bed, you understand?

One day, I come back to Bel Air, and she's gone. No Honey.

"Where'd she go, Sheldon?"

He gives me this silent smirk.

Sheldon makes $80,000 a year for doing things like walking around and looking tough (he's good at that), keeping autograph hounds off Honey's grounds (he's good at that), and keeping feeb-photographers in the neighborhood from taking Honey's picture (he's lousy at that). The man's job is to protect the home of the most famous woman. Period. He carries a gun. Sometime I'll take a paragraph to describe the way he twirls it around his finger.

"I'm talkin' to you, Pal. Where'd she go?"

"She went to the market, Cool."

"The supermarket? How many bodyguards did she take?"

"Uh, she just went alone, Cool."

"And you let her!? Are you crazy?"

"Hey, I don't have to take this shit from you."

"Hey, asshole. You like your job? You wanna keep it? I talked Honey into marrying me. You think I can't talk her into throwing your ass out on the pavement? Think again, Pal."

Well, he's wary now. "I've got a contract."

I just laugh. Big laugh. "You know what your contract is worth, Pal? Now, where did she go?"

"Uh . . ."

"Come on, asshole, where did she go? What supermarket?"

"Uh, she left yesterday, Mr. McCool."

I mean, I couldn't believe it. "You're on probation, Pal."

I call the Honey Hotline.

"Where is she?"

"Excuse me, sir, may I please ask who is calling?"

"Cut the crap! Where is she?!"

"Uh, Mr. McCool, we have her listed in our computer as being at her home in Bel Air."

"Cut the crap! She's not here. Where is she?"

"Mr. McCool, we don't know where Honey is, sir."

I take a deep breath. "You guys ALWAYS know where she is. Come on. The joke is getting old. Tell me where she is."

The female voice on the other end of the telephone is very small and very respectful and very upset. "I'm sorry, Mr. McCool, we just don't know."

"Thank you. I apologize. I'm upset."

Quickly, the female voice says, "I understand; it's a good thing what you did, Mr. McCool; it sets an example of courage for everyone."

"Huh?"

"Quitting smoking." And she goes into this long speech of admiration about how brave I am and about what a hero I am and how terrible I must feel going through nicotine withdrawal "cold turkey" like that and when I find Honey would I please call to tell them where she is because there's several important messages and she's tried to quit smoking several times herself but always (And like, the speech goes on and on and on and finally I just hang up).

I start calling Honey's friends.

"Hi. This is Cool McCool. Is Honey there?"

A guy who sometimes writes songs with Keith Richards says, "Yeah, butty. She's suckin' my [male part deleted]. Can't talk now, y'know?"

I try a real prince of a rockstar. The phone rings and rings and rings.

I try a major performance artist. I get this answering machine that plays this long cartoon snippet, and then goes Beep. "Hello, Laurie. This is Cool McCool. If you happen to see Honey, would you please tell her to call me? Thank you."

I try the princeling again.

Ring, ring, ring . . .

I try Bruce Ranger.

First ring, first goddamn ring.

I take a deep breath. "This is Cool. How ya doin'?"

"OK."

"Uh, is Honey there?"

Long Pause. "No."

Another long pause. I clear my throat. "I'll see ya."

She's there! I know it!

No she's not. Calm Down, McCool.

Calm Down. Poohbutt, *calm down*!

One more chance for the one born to the purple. I mean, you take all those rings, lay them end to end, and they'd reach the moon and back.

The rings stop. Heir presumptive answers: "Yes?"

"This is Cool McCool, is—"

"Cool McCool! Put the bitch on, I wanna talk to her. She's tryin' to scam me, I know it. You put Honey on, right now, man!"

"Oh, excuse me. Wrong prince."

I call the only female comedian funnier and nastier than I am.

An answering machine: "I can't talk now, 'cause Honey and I are tearing up the town with Donald Chapman. You can leave a message, but only for *Donald*. BEEP."

"This is Cool. Tell her I'm lonely. Tell her to call me. Tell her—"

The comedienne cuts in: "What's up, Poohbutt?"

"All right, Poohbitch, where is she?"

"How the [nasty deleted] should I know?"

"Well, if you trip over the female, tell her to call me."

I call the girl who just knocked Honey off Billboard's Number One spot.

"Hi. This is Cool McCool. I'm trying to find Honey." She just laughs.

I almost hang up (thinking that I pushed the wrong number), but she says, "Check your . . . no, no, call her number. Call Honey's number."

"They don't know where she is."

"No, no. Call her number. Her home number." She sounds breathless, as if I've interrupted her in the middle of exercising or sexercising or exerting her four-octave vocal range.

"I'm calling from her home number."

She laughs again. "Listen to her machine. There's a message on it for you. Call it from another line. You'll hear. I gotta go. See you, Cool. OH! Good luck kicking those killer death sticks!"

As I'm looking down at Honey's answering machine, I'm thinking that I wish to hell people would quit reminding me about cigarettes. Actually, I don't miss smoking. What I miss is playing with fire. But Honey had pretty much weaned me off that already. (Smart woman! She attacked the problem right at the cause.) OK, OK, I miss, a little bit, just having a smoldering white stick of macho hanging off the edge of my lip. But I've still got my Dingos. I've still got my Stetson. No prob.

Anyway, there's 26 messages on Honey's answering machine. But you need a special code to make them play back.

Call it from another line?

Anyway, I do.

So I call Honey's private Bel Air line, and I get exactly this:

"I'm Honey. If you're Cool, you'll call Colorado." BEEP.

Maybe Honey put a message on my telephone answering machine. Maybe Honey went there! Is that what 2 Weeks At #1 is trying to tell me?

I call my machine in Aspen. But when I beep the interrupt, nothing happens. The machine isn't working right. It won't play back my messages. I call Timothy's number in Aspen.

"Excuse me?" I mean, the guy sounds big, even over the phone.

"Hi, Tim. What's happening in Aspen?"

"Hi, Cool! Good to hear you." Pause. "Uh, we just had an earthquake. Just amazing. A new fault, nobody knew about. Four point one."

Four point one? That's an earthquake? I'm calling from California; I get a bigger rumble just talking to Bruce Ranger. "Amazing, Tim. Say, could you check my telephone answering machine, please? See if there's a message on it from Honey. Then, call me back, please." I told him Honey's private number.

Well, Honey did leave a message for me. She wants to play Hide 'N' Seek. Count to one hundred, and go to Eden Rock.

Timothy doesn't know where Eden Rock is. I don't know.

But the 800 loyal little dialers know. "Oh, she means the Hotel du Cap, Mr. McCool. It's at Antibes. She always stays there. Eden Roc is the topless beach." (The loyal 800 pronounce Eden Roc slightly different than Honey does.)

"Fine. Where is this place? East Coast? West Coast?"

There was this kind of pause on the telephone line.

"Uh, it's in France, sir." (The sir pronounced without a shred of respect.) "Antibes is near Juan-les-Pins, about midway between Cannes and Nice."

Hey, do I know how to mobilize the Cool Crew, or what? Phone call:

"Tim! Tell all the guys to get their passports. We're going to go check out the topless beaches on the Riviera. I'm picking up the tab. Let's Party!"

CHAPTER 28

I may not be the most famous personage on the planet, but at least I tell my people where I'm going to be. Unlike some people, I'm responsible. So I called Robbie and told him I was going across the pond to play hide-and-seek with Honey. (Sleeping on a sixteen-foot-diameter circular waterbed gives a person a new perspective on large bodies of water.)

"You're going across the [American lingo deleted] Atlantic?? To [Hollywood dialect deleted] around with that [hobo dysphemism deleted] bitch?? You're supposed to be shooting a [sexual perversion deleted] movie!! You've got a meeting tomorrow with those schtoonks from MTV!! And—"

"Goodbye, Robbie."

"Cool, WAIT! If you're serious about this . . . you'd better take Mrs. Agnes with you."

•   •   •   •   •

There are few people skinnier than Cool McCool. Mrs. Agnes is one of them. There are few people more fiendish than Robbie Berger. Mrs. Agnes is one of them. There are few people more intimidating than my sweet, gentle, giant Timothy. Mrs. Agnes is perhaps the only one.

She works for Berger . . . or vice versa.

At Kennedy, Mrs. Agnes scrapped my plans and took over. Imagine a scowling, gray-haired old lady who can put the fear of the Lord into you by moving her little finger. OK, now do it again, only meaner. Now add glops and glops of class. Aristocratic mean.

We flew across the pond in one of those French birds that flap their wings faster than the speed of sound. The giant and I, Mrs. Agnes and a male assistant, and three of the coolest Cool Dudes (the ones with passports).

100, 99, 98 . . . 3, 2, 1: Ready or not, Paris, here we come.

Some security doof from the DST met Mrs. Agnes, bowed to her as if she were rich royalty, and escorted the Cool Entourage through customs, Timothy and all.

Right outside, two small Mercedes limousines waited, doors open, just for us. Each car came complete with driver and burly bodyguard.

"Mrs. Agnes, may I nominate you for honorary lifetime membership in the Cool McCool Air Conditioning Club?"

She sniffed. "Not interested."

. . . . .

Debouched. That's about the limit of my French. We debouched, late afternoon, at the top of this narrow road full of crazy hairpin turns. (We got out of our limos, local PM, at the Hotel du Cap.)

Well, if I were the most famous woman in the world, I'd probably stay here too.

The French always treat me like shit. I do not mean hot shit. I do not mean Cool Shit. I mean, shit. They sneer at me.

And, as I inquired at the majestic desk about the whereabouts of Honey, there was much sneering. The essential message seemed to be, "Honey who? There is no ... Honey ... here." Christ, I know I'm jetlagged, but I'm not imagining it: they're looking down their goddamn noses at me. And they're working overtime to make damn sure I know it.

Mrs. Agnes shouldered me out of the way, and fired across the net (desk) a crisp serve in French. There followed a short, vicious volley of French verbs, back and forth. The only phrase of which I could follow, was: "Monsieur Honey."

Four minutes later, Timothy and I were alone, in front of the door to Honey's suite.

I had the key in my hand.

.   .   .   .   .

Four minutes after that, I was still standing there with the key in my hand. Timothy was standing behind me. We were both just quietly standing there in the elegant hallway. I knew the room inside would be fancy, because Mrs. Agnes told me the rate was approximately 1,700 U.S. dollars a night (she was doing the conversion in her head and apologized for any inaccuracy due to fluctuations in the exchange rate).

I hadn't knocked. I knew I wasn't going to knock. But I couldn't seem to get my arm to move to put the key in the slot and open the damn door. Timothy cleared his throat: sounded like a mine cave-in. My arm started to move. I opened the damn door, and walked inside. The smell of vomit.

· · · · ·

Jake, one of Honey's new bodyguards, was sprawled on the big bed.

"What do you think he's on?" Timothy asked me, as he lifted the guy's semi-comatose head up by his long, brown hair. Jake's eyes rolled around, he coughed, and moaned happily.

"Borrowed time," I said.

Jake was naked. The kingsize bed was messed up like five or six people had jumped up and down on it until one of them got dizzy and vomited. Jake had rolled over onto the vomit in his stupor.

On the dresser next to the bed were some drugs and associated implements. Three bags of (I assumed) different white powder. Ether. A glass pipe. Hypodermic syringe and a needle. Some other things. A tiny container of French bleach. Champagne. Empty glasses. And the illegal junk is right out in plain view for anyone who happens to glance in the bedroom.

"Tim," I said. "Can you lose this stuff, please?"

"You got it." Timothy handed me a Polaroid that he had extricated from the vomit. It was a picture of Honey and some other guy having tangled, riotous sex.

"That's a bidet, Tim. Try the other one."

Timothy started flushing drugs, while I walked slowly to the other bedside stand, which was littered with Polaroid pictures. All of them were of Honey having obscene sex with Jake or this other guy. About twenty pictures. Very amateur. Very graphic.

Honey did not look happy in any of the pictures. She looked desperate.

God, it killed me. With the smell of fresh vomit up my nose, I almost threw up, myself.

This was all my fault.

She needed me, and I hadn't been there.

.   .   .   .   .

Honey was easy to find on the beaches of Eden Roc: She was the one hiding her white boobs behind the *Hollywood Reporter*. This is one hell of a ritzy beach too, I mean, you've never seen so much gold in your life. The French . . . these guys crack me up . . . all around Honey, all over the rocks, are hundreds of bronzed bodies so heavily weighted down with gold jewelry that they don't dare go in the water, and they've all got this attitude like: Yes, over there is the most famous woman in the world, and I don't give a shit.

But I malign the French. One of the Frenchmen most certainly did give a shit. The other guy. Look at him, sitting there close, sharing Honey's towel. Look at him, on the other side of her, there, doing his little innocent act, slathering sunblock all over Honey's breasts with his busy fingers. *Moi?*

Honey knows I'm standing here, but she's pretending to ignore me. I mean, who the hell else could be standing here at Eden Roc in Dingos, Levis, Bugle Boy, and a Stetson?

The only gold Honey is wearing is her wedding ring.

Anything I say is going to be wrong. This frog-eater is tweaking Honey's nipples on these public rocks. There's only one way to keep this woman.

I get down close to her and blow in her left ear.

Are we talking romance? No. I'm blowing up a balloon. What an airhead you are, girl.

Behind her black-black sunglasses, I see her eyes shut, and her face grimace. Honey shrugs the other guy's hands off her boobs.

The guy shouts something at me. *"Foutez-vous le camp, ordure!"* I don't need a translator to know that he wants me to go away.

Behind him, one of the attendants starts climbing down toward us, joined by a big, burly bear of a man. They look like they mean business: eject McCool from Eden Roc. But I've got my Cool Crew behind me, and Mrs. Agnes is watching us from the terrace.

The bear and the attendant sort of stall when they see that Timothy is with me. Timothy may not have any gold on him, but by God he's got the biggest pair of swimtrunks on the Riviera. Just standing there, the guy is sunblock.

Honey hasn't turned her head toward me. She's still got her eyes closed, behind her blackest sunglasses. What does she think: if she keeps her eyes closed and ignores me, that I'll go away? Her hands holding the *Hollywood Reporter* go limp.

The other guy probably tells me to get lost again. *"Marie-couche-toi-la est bien roulee, oui?"* or something like that.

This French guy amazes me. He's got gold chains around his waist, around his neck, around his ankle. He's got a gold watch, gold bracelet, and a gold earring dangling from his *right* ear. He's got a goddamn toe ring on one of his feet! I know the standards for masculinity are evolving, but Back Off! If I didn't have pictures of this guy with his dick inside Honey, I'd ignore him as a harmless fairy.

"Hey, Witch, what is this guy," I ask Honey, "a display rack for Banks & Biddle?"

Then, while the French guy insults me and/or tells me to get lost again, I notice that Honey is holding her *Hollywood Reporter* upside down. This is the woman who reads, who *actually reads*, Camus, Kant, Plato, Pluto, all those guys. This is the woman who I bring my legal contracts to, when I want to know what the hell they mean.

Frenchy says, *"Elle baise bien. Elle est une sacrée baiseuse."* These French . . . all they know how to do is smirk!

Honey just moans.

I take off Honey's sunglasses. Blocking the sun's rays with one hand, I nudge open her left eyelid. She tries to fight me, but I get a glimpse of her eye. Almost no iris at all; the thing is all dilated pupil.

"Jimmy," Honey moans. She's squinting at me. Her word's slur together. "TakeMeHome."

I hauled Honey onto her feet. I started to pick her up in my arms and carry her, but Timothy wouldn't let me. Apologetically, gently, he gathered Honey in his arms and carried her over the Eden Roc rocks.

The Frog shouted, "*Il est con comme la lune!*"

Mrs. Agnes escorted Honey into the ladies' dressing room; when they came out, Agnes acted like a protective grandmother.

CHAPTER 29

Honey fell asleep faster than the speed of sound. Her head: plop, on my shoulder. Both her hands: holding my arm.

I drank faster than the speed of sound. Seconds. Thirds. Fourths. Doubles. Hit me again.

I sat there; stared at the back of the seat in front of us; drank.

Faster than the speed of sound, Honey woke up. She squeezed on my arm to get my attention. "Jimmy, I didn't do anything."

I turned and looked at her. Boy, was I drunk. (The Cool Crew kept filling me up with their bottomless flasks of Canadian Club.)

"Jimmy, I didn't do anything!"

She was wasted and weak, and a little strung-out. In the back of the bird, her soon-to-be-ex-bodyguard Jake was sitting up straight with this smirky smile on his face.

"Don't be a poohbutt, Jimmy. I had to boogie. I had to go somewhere. I had to do something. I needed two scoops of new! You weren't around, but I just had to GO!

So I went. I flowed with the feeling. But I didn't do anything, Jimmy."

Jesus, she was good.

"Jimmy, *take a major hike*, you don't think I went to bed with that French weasel, do you? Jimmy, at least, give me credit for better taste!"

Christ, she was the best.

I had them in a flat, little black box, inside my coat, close to my heart. All the Polaroids. Timothy and I had searched Honey's hotel suite. Benson, an Ice Dude if ever there was one, had ripped off (with a little inside info from Mrs. Agnes) a set of eight pics from Frenchy's clothes in the men's changing room at Eden Roc. There was a very good chance, I thought, that we got them all. And I had them all there in the little black box, for Honey.

I was supposed to toss them to her. Underhand toss. The gift more valuable than diamonds: Her privacy.

But Reality is always throwing you curve balls, and you can't always set up the Cool moves just right.

So I pulled the little black box out of my inside coat pocket and handed it to her.

It brought a hush to her. She held it, touched it, ran her fingers along the edge of it. "Gosh," Honey said, in a husky voice, "I don't know if I deserve a guy like you." There was a genuine lump in her throat. "Thank you for trusting me, Jimmy."

It takes an exceptional joke to make a professional comedian laugh. Even if the pro comic is drunk, you have to tell it just right, or he won't laugh.

But Honey told it just right.

It was even funnier when she opened the little black box and saw the Polaroid on top: of Frenchy's wang in both her little hands and his come dripping out of her painted lips.

. . . . .

At Kennedy, Honey bought a ticket to Los Angeles, and signed autographs.

I told her I was going to stay in New York for awhile.

Honey cancelled her ticket, and signed more autographs.

So I bought a ticket to Denver.

Two tickets, please, Honey said, and posed for some photographs.

Fine, I told her, you and Timothy.

I walked away, apologizing to the confused Cool Crew for cutting short their topless Riviera trip.

Honey gave a short interviewette, and then ran to me, grabbed hold of me, and shoved me down into a chair. I tried to stand up. She wouldn't let me. She sat on my lap. She faced me, hot thighs on Cool thighs, her legs spread wide.

"Talk to me!" Honey shouted at me.

"I'm drunk. Go away."

"You bastard." Honey slumped a little and banged her head into my head, where she stayed, forehead on my forehead. Her fingers brushed through my hair, like she was trying to get at my brain. "Tell me I don't want you," she said. I was so drunk, I didn't know what that particular combination of words meant.

A photographer was snapping off pictures of Honey sitting on my lap.

I stood up. Rather than get dumped on the Kennedy carpeting, she hung on and then stood up too.

"I'm drunk," I told her again. "Go away."

"What are you going to do?" Honey asked quietly.

"I don't know," I answered truthfully. I added, even more truthfully, "But the first two foxy women who throw themselves at me, get me."

CHAPTER 30

Honey met me in the downstairs lobby of the Maxwell Building in New York, and escorted me up the elevator to her office.

We didn't have a whole lot to say to each other.

"Hi, Cool."

"Hi, Honey."

Four words, and a hand motion for me to please follow her, were the extent of our conversation.

Click, click, click, went her high-heels. Ka-thump, ka-thump, ka-thump, went my cowboy boots.

In the elevator our communication continued.

I observed Honey. Her sleek nylon legs. Her shiny-black high-heels. Her businesslike black pinstripe ladies' suit, and unbusinesslike push-up bra (I can see black-lacy wisps of it) pushing up her mammary development a third over the top of her double-breasted coat because she's not wearing a shirt. Her tangled freshly-peroxed blond hair, cut seriously-short & seriously-sexy. OK, she gets the message: I can't help but look longingly at her.

Honey observed the elevator lights. I get that message too: We're not here to fix our marriage; we're here to finalize her divorce.

We debouched from the elevator. Behind our backs the elevator doors sneer.

Honey leads.

I follow.

Nothing new in that.

The Japanese take good care of Honey. She has full use of the Maxwell Records corporate jet, a New York furnished apartment with corporate limousine standing by.

Everyone who passes us in the building, everyone we see, either studiously ignores her or merely nods respectfully to her. She has trained everyone here not to acknowledge her as the recording artist whose records pay all their salaries.

Honey showed me her office. Outside is the perfect secretary. Male.

There's a brass nameplate screwed onto her door: HONEY.

It's a corner office, with four windows, trees, a lowered conversation pit, a floating granite-top desk, a private bathroom, a de Kooning, a Picasso.

"I never use it," Honey says.

We go straight from there to the conference room.

A gold-plated Thermos, coffee cup and saucer for Honey. A gold-plated Thermos and *et cetera* for Cool. A yellow pad for Honey. A pad for Cool. A box of sharpened #2 pencils for Honey. Ditto #2s for Cool.

The table is a rectangular giant, with maybe twenty

chairs around it. The two place-settings are, unexpect-
edly, in the center of the long edges, opposite each
other. At least we won't have to shout.

"Please sit where you like," Honey says. She closes the
door. She walks around and closes the other door. It's
just us two.

Well, if I really sat where I liked, it would be on the
edge of the table, with my arms crossed, and a snide
French sneer all over my face. But I just want to get this
over with, so I sit down in front of one of the place-
settings, and slouch.

Honey sits across from me. Back straight. Palms
clasped in front of her. One of the side spotlights catches
her gold wedding ring just right and blinds me for a second so that I have to adjust my slouch to the opposite
side of my chair.

Honey sets the tone of the meeting with her first word.

She looks me straight on, and says, "Love means
always having to tell the truth."

Short silence.

"I've been lame, Cool. Major naughty. I've told you five
lies. Very big lies."

"Cut the crap. Let's get on with the divorce."

She smiles . . . sort of. "I could use a juicy divorce,
right now, to get me out of this career slump, but [f-word
deleted] that." She smiles again . . . sort-of-plus. "It would
even help me if I snuck out a few of those Polaroids to
the right entertainment reporters. But I don't want to.
I want us to be lovers again. If it costs me a few million,
[f-word deleted] it. If it costs me fifty million, [f-word

deleted] it. If people don't like me loving you, [f-word deleted] them."

Silence-plus.

"I'm in love with you, Cool."

"Tell me another one, Witch." I adjust my slouch for maximum comfort. Adjust the trim on my Stetson.

Honey brings out a white sheet of paper from a pocket of her suit, and unfolds it.

She places it in front of her. She runs her fingers over it to flatten it out.

"I lied about Bruce," Honey says. "I'd been seeing him for a few weeks, and we were getting pretty serious, before I met you. That night in Aspen, when I left you and your party . . . well, I was telling him goodbye. It was sort of a goodbye-[f-word deleted]. I lied about that. But, Cool, I had to. I owed him something. We had an understanding. And I couldn't very well tell you about it, or I'd ruin everything between you and me, before you and me even got started!"

The hell with the slouch. I stood up, frustrated.

"Cool, please listen to me."

"You don't want a divorce?"

"I want us to talk. I want us to be lovers again."

"Do we have to do this here?"

Honey sigh of frustration. "No, we don't. But if we go somewhere else, I know you, we won't talk. We'll trombone. Or we'll game-talk. Or we'll argue. Or something else will happen. But we won't *talk* talk."

"I can't talk to you in a goddamn conference room!"

"But—" Honey noise of frustration. Then she laughed

a little. "But that's what conference rooms are for!"

I paced along my side. "I wasn't built for the corporate world. I can't function in a conference room. Let's go somewhere else."

Honey watched me. "You can't? Or you won't?"

I walked around on her side. Nothing new in that.

I pulled out the chair on her left, and sat there, and held her hand.

She let me, for a few seconds, and then pulled her hand back, with a pert little laugh. "Cool," she warned me. "I *know* you. I want to talk. I don't want to trombone on this table. What are you so afraid of?"

I tried to find words, but there didn't seem to be any.

"Cool, sometimes you make me want to *scream*! Go back over there, where you belong."

"I'm trying to be close to you, like you say you want, and you tell me to go away!"

Honey noise of frustration. "Cool . . . of all the guys I've known, you're the toughest nut to crack. I—"

"I've only got one working ball left, and now you want to break that one too?"

"Cool, I can't get through to you. You don't communicate. Instead you *make funny*."

"You married a comedian, what do you expect?"

Honey shouted: "Stop taking your work from the office home with you!!"

I had a fast, razor-sharp reply for her that I'd brought home from the office. I left it locked in the briefcase.

"Cool, Cool, Cool—I understand your actions. There's a softness, a caring about you that is so sweet and special.

I've never felt it with anyone else. But you hide it. You won't put it into words. Cool, I know you love me, you tell me that nonverbally all the time. Why can't you say the words? Why can't you share your feelings with me? What are you afraid of?"

Pause.

"Honey, you're torturing me."

"Why?"

"I don't know."

"Then let me tell you some more of the lies I've told you. In Philly—"

"Honey. Stop. Please."

"Cool. What are you afraid of?"

I tried to talk, but there just wasn't anything in me. I just wanted to get out of the damn conference room. This was the wrong place to talk love-stuff or to try to salvage a relationship. I needed to use my major tool of debate.

Honey sounded wistful, and pained. "Cool . . . you're so sweet, but you make me feel so lonely. You're with me, but you're not with me. You won't even listen to me."

I grabbed her hand. Grabbed it. I wanted to shout: I'm here, damn it, I'm here! I held her hand fierce and tight, with both my hands. She was hurting inside; and it hurt me to feel her hurting. "Honey . . . you're the princess . . . and I guess I'm afraid . . . because . . ." I smiled sadly, and bit my lip. "No matter what you say, I'll believe you . . . I guess I'm afraid to listen to you, because no matter what crazy lies you tell . . . I'll believe every word."

"There won't be any more lies." Conference-length pause. "I think that's what I needed to hear from you, Cool."

Love pause & finger squeeze. "I needed to hear something genuine from behind your Berlin Wall."

I gave Honey her hand back. "I need a cigarette," I said.

Honey got up, and started for the door.

"Stop," I said. "A joke."

But Honey continues walking. She walks all the way around the table, over to the other side, takes a long reach across to snatch back her notes, and sits down in my chair over there. "Stay there!" Honey says.

Do I stay put? Nah. I pick up her coffee Thermos, carry it around to her, pour her a cup of coffee.

Then, I sit down next to her there. "I don't need a smoke. What I need is a trombone on this table. Whadda ya say?"

I'm not sure it makes sense, but there was affectionate anger on Honey's face. "Cool, you're insane, intimidating, fearless, exasperating, invigorating, uncontrollable, you're an AMBUSH, and you're *nice*!" Somehow, the way she said "nice," it sounded like the worst of put-downs. "Oh, I don't know what you are."

"I'm a good lay, and that's all I'll ever be to you. Remember? You said so, yourself. A good lay, and good publicity. And c'mon, let's trombone on the table, right now."

She was silent for a long time, thinking Honeyed-thoughts. I was watching her think Honeyed-thoughts.

Honey said slowly, "I want my cake. And I want to eat it all. And I want it to be brightly lit with flaming candles, days after the party is over, intact, with all the pretty frosting untouched. I want my cake in the Hall of Fame. I want my cake to be shared with everyone. And

I want the real you to come popping out of the cake and see through to the real me and promise the real me forever on a platinum platter." Honey's voice was solemn, and her eyes looked not quite at mine; or perhaps so deeply into my eyes, that she saw into something that I myself would not see in a mirror. She continued speaking. "And I suppose I want a protective, chauvinistic stud to throw the cake in the face of anyone who doesn't treat me like a queen. I want you to write frosting love-sonnets to me on my cake, decorated with candy hearts. And I want to feed you bites of the cake, and have you lick my fingers clean and kiss them."

"Before or after we trombone on this table?"

Honey shakes her head and then consults her notes. "Bruce came to one of my shows in Philly. Right before you and I were married. We had a little private party after my show." Pause. "That was a goodbye-already-[f-word deleted]." Pause. "Actually, it wasn't a trombone. We didn't go all the way. But we did fool around." Pause. She seemed calm & collected; but then she screamed: "Tell me what you're thinking!"

I waited. She waited.

"Cool! Say something!" She was shouting.

"What am I supposed to say?"

"Say what you feel!"

"You're so sexy when you shout."

Now she's about to leap out of her chair and claw my eyes out. "Cool! I cheated on you! How does that make you feel? Talk to me! How does it make you feel?"

"I don't think I have any feelings left. They're shredded."

Honey called me a naughty name. It's about the naughtiest name a woman can call a man.

"Drink your coffee before it gets cold," I told her.

Honey grabbed her coffee and threw it in my face.

It wasn't all that hot. And there wasn't all that much of it, because she spilled most of it before she got it aimed right. Actually, more of it went onto the table than went onto my face and Stetson.

"Decaffeinated," I said, with disgust. It was a dangerous thing to say, because Honey was murderously angry.

Her wild anger turns into a moan of heartbreaking anguish.

She whisks up her notes, and zooms around the table and sits opposite me. "Stay there, Cool. If you won't talk to me . . . all right. If you won't, you won't. If you can't, you can't. But LISTEN. Stay there, and LISTEN. Take it like a man."

CHAPTER 31

I wiped the coffee off my face like a man.

Honey said, "Sometimes I have to do things, to find out how I feel. Sometimes I have to travel, to find out where home is. I have to go places, to find out where I miss, where I wish I was. Sometimes I have to be with someone, sleep with them, to find out how I feel about someone else. I was a little chippy, to find out how I felt about you. I didn't like what I found out. I couldn't feel a thing, unless I thought about you, during. I couldn't feel anything. I couldn't [f-word deleted]. I couldn't [f-word deleted] unless I was fantasizing about you, Cool. I hate being in love, but what can I do, here I am. It makes me feel too vulnerable. LISTEN!"

Honest, all I did was squirm in my chair.

Honey said, "When I lied to you on the Concord, I did it because I was afraid. Also, I really didn't know what happened. I thought I might have . . . there were funny, little blurred moments, but . . . . Have you ever done horse?"

"No."

"Horse is really dangerous, because it feels so good, but if you only do it a couple times a year you won't get hooked."

That was the second craziest thing I'd ever heard. Was she saying it to make herself believe it? You don't shoot heroin and not get hooked. And yet, Honey wasn't a junkie, her body was in good condition, she didn't have needle marks all over her arms. But the idea of someone using heroin recreationally, just a few times a year, was pretty hard for me to swallow. (Writes the guy who spent some of the Sixties playing Russian Roulette with his mind, swallowing tabs of LSD. Lesson 31? *Don't Do Drugs!*)

Honey said, "Sometimes I can't remember much afterward. Francoise gave me too much. I went into a nod. Cool, I never intended to cheat on you while in France. It just happened. I don't know whether I led him and Jake on, or whether they took advantage of me. But, yes, I should have been more honest to you about it. I didn't because I was afraid. I lied on automatic pilot. Because—"

"Hey," I interrupted. "Can I say something?"

"Yes."

"Why are you telling me all this? I—"

"Cool—"

"Can I talk, please?" She let me. "I just don't get it. I mean, I'm not going anywhere. I don't want to hear all this. It's like information overload. It sounds like you're trying to negotiate some new level of intimacy between us. But you're doing it all wrong. Every word you say pushes me further away from you. I don't want to know the names of every guy you've slept with. Just swear to me that you won't cheat anymore, and make me believe it, and we'll go on from there. Your turn to talk."

Now that it was her turn to talk, she didn't. We entered another conference-length period of silence. Finally, she continued. "I've told you most of what I needed to tell you. But there is one thing more." Pause. "It's a secret." Pause. "I don't want to read about this in a magazine someday." Pause. "It's a *secret* secret."

"Honey, this isn't necessary. You don't need to strip-mine your soul for me. Your hills and valleys are pretty just the way they are. I like living here. I'm not going anywhere unless you evict me."

"No," she said, "I have to tell you this, because you may wish to leave me. I have to give you the option."

"You've been faking your orgasms. I know all about it. Bruce told me."

Well, what do you know . . . *she* got up and walked around the table, and sat down on *my* side.

Immediately, I apologized. "I'm sorry. I'll stop being an asshole. Forgive me."

"Jimmy . . . excuse me, *Cool* . . . and that's another thing. I apologize for calling you Jimmy all the time. I know you like to be called Cool. I wouldn't like it if you called me Ivy all the time. I'm sure calling you Jimmy was part of me trying to keep you in your place."

"I like it when you call me Jimmy!"

"No you don't. I won't call you Jimmy anymore. I promise."

Perhaps the most disturbing thing about this whole

scene is that she no longer wants to call me Jimmy.

"Jimmy . . ." She stopped, and we both laughed. A little. "Cool, I have to tell you something, but I'm afraid. I love you. But I don't even know if we're friends. It's like we're both playing for an audience. You entertain me. I entertain you. I don't know how you feel about me, I don't know what you like about me, or don't like. You don't share your work with me, I don't hear about your problems or your triumphs—when we're with each other we fall into a game of entertaining each other. Cool, why are you with me?"

"I'm Taurus, you're Capricorn. Perfect fit."

Honey look: *talk* talk to me, damn you, or I'll get mad again.

I got out of my chair, got behind her chair, and started giving Honey a neck-rub. "Honey, I don't know a better answer. I'm Taurus, you're Capricorn. How the hell should I know WHY? I'm here, and you're here. And we both like it. I think you're getting too intellectual. You've been reading too many of those nutty philosophers. You're hittin' me with all this heavy stuff. But I come from a different world. When I want to relax, I watch comedy on TV, or listen to a Lenny Bruce album. Ask me specific questions, and I'll give you specific answers. I don't talk about my work because I don't want to bore you. You're the brightest star in the galaxy, why should I bother you with all my shit? It's not like I'm hiding things from you."

Her neck jumped up out of my fingers. "Cool," she said, "sit down." Honey was standing. I was standing.

"No trombone?" I asked.

"Cool, sit down," Honey ordered.

I sat down. Honey started giving *me* a neck-rub. She plopped my hat down on the table. Quietly, she said, "I need something else from behind your Berlin Wall. The Commies knocked theirs down, why can't you knock yours down?" Glasnost pause. "Have you . . . cheated on me?" Honey's fingernails: like hammer & chisel on Checkpoint Charlie.

"No."

"Not at all? Not ever? Mary Elizabeth?"

Jesus, now I was embarrassed. I made do with a negative head shake. No, no, no; while Honey's fingers worked me over.

"What about the two foxes?"

Christ, now I was *really* embarrassed. "Not yet. Nobody's thrown themself at me, yet. The promise stands, however. I'm falling a little behind in the adultery department, and I need to catch up. The next two foxes to throw themselves at me, get me."

It was a brave thing to say, while both of Honey's hands were wrapped around my neck. The fingers stopped their gentle ministrations, and then continued.

Gently.

"Cool, there have to be things that you're hiding from me. Please tell me some of them. I have a secret to tell you. I need a secret from you, first. I need a *secret* secret. I want to share my life with you. Share has to be two-way, Cool."

Maybe it was the tremor in her fingers as they touched

my neck. Samson's fingers toying with a pillar. Or the hurt I could hear in the tone of her voice. Trumpets of Jericho.

"OK," I said. "I hate waterbeds."

"You're impossible," she snapped.

"Impossible, *and* insane, intimidating, fearless, exasperating, invigorating, uncontrollable, an ambush, and nice."

"Jesus, Cool, I spill my insides to you, and that's all you've got? You hate waterbeds?" Honey got down on her knees behind my chair, and hugged me with both arms. Crossing her arms in front of me, she said, "Give me your hands," and we clasped hands. "We out-number you, you know. Comes the day, there's gonna be a vote. And we'll get rid of you. Oh, we'll keep a few of you around, as pets. In zoos. But testosterone will be illegal. All the little boy babies will have their little balls surgically removed at birth."

I shuddered.

"Cool, I want an equal, nurturing, noncompetitive love relationship with you. And I'll have it, damn you."

That was even more frightening.

Silence. Long, lean & mean.

Other than the fact that I'm terminally in love with her, passionately, insanely in love with her, there isn't that much on this side of the Iron Curtain that's of interest. I can't really think of all that much that I'm hiding. A couple of things, maybe . . . neither of which, I dare to mention. How can I tell her how hurt I am that she doesn't like to French Kiss? She doesn't trust my saliva. She doesn't trust my semen. She wants to share souls, but share saliva? Does she let me kiss her nipples as regular foreplay? Are

You Kidding?? It involves my saliva and her mucous membranes. Christ, I've been to *her* goddamn doctor, and she doesn't believe the test results: she thinks I'm infested with STDs! I mean, Honey treats me like she thinks I slip out to the gay bar every weekend for a gang-bang buttpoke in the back room. Nurturing? Back off! Noncompetitive? Equal? But there's nothing I can say. She's the most famous fox on the fruited plains. And who am I? She's out shooting up horse—and I only counted one needle for three people. She's the one out screwing the guy with the earring dangling off his right ear. But just let me stick my tongue in her mouth, and she'll turn away from me.

"Knees," I said. I know what she's going to say: All you give me are knees and waterbeds? But this is really a deepdown secret, and she'll have to settle for it. "And *I* don't want to read about *this* in a goddamn magazine. My knees are all screwed up. My right knee almost always hurts. It's the muscles and stuff in the back of my knees, actually. When I do something macho like pick you up and carry you around, it hurts like hell for a few days. And the reason I always push you away, when you try to cuddle and lay your head on my chest . . . I know you like to fall asleep that way, but when I'm on my back . . . I can never get the bend in them just right. They hurt. Especially my right knee. It's just something about laying on my back. I can't get my legs in a position that's comfortable."

"The pillow for your feet," Honey said.

"Yeah. When I sleep on my stomach, I have to have that pillow under my feet, because even with the pressure on the front of my legs, if they're straight, they hurt too

much. My right knee is so [f-word deleted] up that I
almost have to sleep on my left side to completely be comfortable. It's why I can't handle a missionary [f-word
deleted] on the floor. On a bed, OK, I can deal. It's why
I don't like to swim, or run, or dance. I dance for twenty
minutes, and my knees start hurting, and they hurt for
three or four days. And if you tell anyone, I'll cut you into
little pieces, and throw the little bloody bits in the
Aspen snow."

Honey snuggled against me thankfully.

"And don't give me shit about it," I warned her. "If I
want to pick you up and flop you over my shoulder, and
haul you around like a macho caveman, I will, damn it.
And I don't want you going, 'Oh, Jimmy, don't, you'll hurt
your knees.'"

. . . . .

Big long silence.

Well, Honey uncuddles me. Maybe she's pissed at me
because she thinks all I'm telling her are dweeb-secrets.
Honey sits down in the chair next to me. Pours us both
coffee. Drinks her coffee, hiding behind the cup, holding it with two Honey hands, for awhile. She scooches
her chair closer to mine. Why is it that hot steam coming off a cup of coffee reminds me of cigarettes?

I try to reach to touch some part of Honey, but she won't
let me. She wants me to face forward. I can slouch all I
want, but I can't look at her. She doesn't want me to look
at her.

Honey starts talking. It's a long story. It's B-movie stuff. Tells like a projected TV series. Her mouth is inches from my left ear. Honey is not putting her heart into this monologue. Her voice is real quiet, as if she's afraid someone is listening at the door. The sentences are jerky, halting, and her speech rhythms are off. Honey has a speech coach and a voice coach, but they didn't help her with this. She keeps moving her hand, as if she wants to put it on my arm. She keeps pulling her hand back, not touching me.

When I turn my head to look at her, she shuts up and points for me to look straight ahead. After a few such unsuccessful points, she takes my head in her hands and turns it physically.

How does the Honey-story start? It starts: "I haven't lied to you. I've always tested HIV-negative."

It ends: "So, you see, I have lied to you. I have AIDS."

There's twenty or thirty minutes of stuff in the middle. Stuff that wasn't in Doubleday's *My Diary*. Stuff not in the Pocket Books *Honey*, or mentioned in Harper & Row's *Honey Biography*, or even hinted at during *Rolling Stone's* six-part series of "Honey Revelations."

Since all of them couldn't suss it out, I won't rat it here.

The expurgated version would read something like this. Wherever Honey is, if she's reading this now, I feel that she would authorize this version. It conveys the essential emotional truth without betraying Honey's confidence. Let's just say that when Honey was in her early teens, she fell in love and had lots of high-risk sex with a notorious womanizing actor (he also manized upon occasion), who shall remain anonymous, and who shall remain dead, since he died of an AIDS-related disease in the early Eighties, about three years after their love affair ended. OK, Honey?

At three ELISAs and three Western Blots a year, for more than a decade, Honey has to be the most authoritatively HIV-negative woman in the history of AIDS tests. Never mind the negative test results, Honey knows she has AIDS. Never mind that all this high-risk sex occurred eleven and twelve years ago, never mind that Honey has been tested negative practically yesterday for human immunodeficiency virus antibodies, Honey says she can feel AIDS churning around inside her, just waiting to drag her down into illness and death.

I was hurt. I was really hurt. Honey has conned me, really conned me. She really is the best at it. She's dragged out of me, my lowest, deepest hidden, secretest secret. My fall-apart fragile wimp-out knees. While my friends go skiing on the slopes, I have to lie about having to stay indoors to work on my new routine. My ladyfriends learn quickly not to take me to discos. "Fine, you want to dance? Go dance. I'm going to see if 36-24-36 in the black leather miniskirt and sequins has a sense of humor." What does Honey think? That I pop ten aspirin a day to lower my cholesterol count? My knees hurt, damn it! Not even my sister knows how bad my knees are. I tell the love of my life, in a moment of weakness, and what secret do I get in return? This silly, neurotic fear. And she's really obsessed with this. Honey needs psychiatric help, she doesn't need more sex tests.

Finally, Honey's voice falls silent. It's OK for me to look at her now. But she's now afraid to look at me. Her hands are afraid to touch me.

And in a flash I'm suddenly charmed, as I realize what her safe-sex compulsion is all about: she's deathly afraid that *she's* going to give *me* something. A hundred ugly little sexual memories of affronts and aspersions to my person blossom with beautiful new meaning: in her foolish way she has been trying to protect me.

Honey's hands are trembling like a Mary Elizabeth. Honey's lips are nervously biting. The most famous face in New York City is contorting.

If I don't do something blazingly affectionate, she's going to cry. If she cries, I won't be able to handle it. I've been with her long enough to know what she needs.

Unqualified acceptance.

Well, there was only one thing a real man could do.

Unprotected [phrase deleted by Attorneys Francis, Lake, Green & Weber] on the conference table.

"Oh, Jimmy, don't!" Honey screeched. "You'll hurt your knees!"

CHAPTER 32

CIGARETTES SUCK.

The most successful anti-smoking campaign in the history of anti-smoking campaigns.

CIGARETTES SUCK.

Talk to kids in a language they can understand.

CIGARETTES SUCK.

Use bottom-up peer-pressure, not top-down authority nonsense. We all know that cigarettes kill people, but direct arguments about the danger always go up in smoke. The danger is the excitement, the appeal, the feeling of freedom from authority. The toughness associated with cigarettes has a seductive charm stronger than self-interest.

The key was harnessing the peer-pressure.

First, we renamed the doers of the deadly deed. A smoker was a sucker. "What a sucker!" "Oh, I didn't know you were a sucker." "I know, Tommy really sucks."

Second, we made sucking uncool. "Sucking is so *stoopid*." "Hello, cancer-breath." "Hey, pollution face!" "I'm gonna tell the EPA!"

Third, we renamed cigarettes. Slang is social ID, and words are weapons. A cigarette was a tampon. "He looks so tough with a tampon in his mouth."

Fourth, we put an assumption in the smoky air that all suckers were in the process of quitting. "Are you still sucking on virgin tampons?"

The TV commercials had to mostly go on cable, but what the hell, cable was where the kid's eyes were anyway.

Late night network TV carried a softer-edged commercial of mine: "It's Cool to quit. No Shit!"

Honey lit up an anti-sucking song, smoked a video for it, and put it out on her *Night Love* album. The song, exhaled as a single, blew to #4 on the Top-40 smokeless ashtray. *Night Love* was Honey's sleeper CD: eventually her second-biggest seller; at first, you couldn't pay kids to play it.

.   .   .   .   .

And so the relationship of Mr. & Mrs. Honey entered into a new phase. A kinder, gentler marriage.

I wish to point out two macho tokens of resistance.

1) I never gave Honey any violets.

2) I knocked her up again. My tool of debate engaged in forceful unprotected & unwrapped rhetoric, dispelling Honey's sexual fears and fertilizing Honey's famous womb.

We talked intimately and tenderly to each other; before, during, and after sex. And in place of sex.

We French-kissed like crazy.

I skywrote COOL LOVES HONEY all across the Southern California skies. When I looked up, I did not cringe in embarrassment.

A prominent billboard on Sunset, that Honey had to drive by on her way home and back had a picture of my Stetson and me, and proclaimed: "Thank you, Honey, for helping me to quit smoking. Thank you, for five more years of life. I give these years to you." In my hands, together, offering, are the words: five more years of love.

CHAPTER 33

You ever go window shopping with the most famous woman on Rodeo Drive?

I was there the day Honey bought out the Chanel Boutique.

Honey charges things like $400,000 sports cars and $900,000 speedboats and torn $10 1940s dresses.

Honey can't go into a Mall or a supermarket, even with bodyguards, but the University of Rodeo Drive alumni are usually pretty cool. Since Honey is having a career slump, her suave Rodeo Drive enthusiasts have a special Southern California laidback way of snubbing her. They audibly ooh and ahh, and shy up to her . . . and ask for *my* autograph. Honey is having so much fun *getting to know me* that she pretends not to be hurt.

One of Honey's boys is up the sidewalk with the credit cards. Another of her boys is hanging ten on the sidewalk, downscale, with wads of cash. Honey's long black limousine follows us on the street: Brigade backup.

How, you may wonder, does a loving wife get a no-nonsense hard-driving macho-man husband like myself to kick back and coast?

"Gosh, Cool, my undies are so *ratty*! I'm goin' out for new lingerie. Wanna come along and preview coming attractions?"

So there we are on Rodeo Drive, noodling along, holding hands, laughing & lollygagging, *window shopping* for godsake.

Honey mentions that she wants the two of us to do a picture together. It's a recurring theme in our new era of liberty, equality, and sorority. You know; Get To Know Thy Mate: WORK TOGETHER. And Honey is really gushing with enthusiasm about this.

Well, real men are never threatened by all this "equality stuff" that the feminists and the female supremacists spout. Nah.

. . . . .

I gave her fingers a special little love squeeze. "Sure, Honey. We can do a film together. But I get first billing."

Honey's eyes narrowed. "The movie's credits will be listed on the screen alphabetically," Honey said, diplomatically.

McCool's eyes narrowed. "I don't know," I told her. "Robbie wants me to co-star with a big box-office draw, not some nowhere actress whose last picture couldn't even—OUCH!"

"A thousand and one nights, Cool," Honey said. "The story of Scheherazade. You get to be the Sultan. I get to be the daughter of the Grand Vizier of the Indies. It'll really be reet. Have you ever read *The Arabian Nights*? It's killer!"

"No," I said, hobbling along like a cripple after the impact of Honey's nylon-armored kneecap against my right tinkertoy knee.

"We'll do it as a comedy," Honey said. "To set the theme, we open with a scientific close-up of Mr. and Ms. Praying Mantis. I saw one in high school once—it was awesome! Did you know that Mr. Mantis does it dead? Soon as they start tromboning, big Ms. Mantis bites off his head. Then, boy, he really starts tromboning. The more of him she eats, the harder he trombones. Her mouth eats all of him. Except his penis. Her vagina eats that."

"A comedy. Right."

"See, the Sultan is ticked off at women, 'cause he caught his wife cheating on him."

"Yeah, I could identify with that guy—OUCH!"

"He's depleting the kingdom of young ladies. He marries them, and then Chop-Chop! Off with their head. Credits. (Alphabetically.) Scan to white wedding and cake and stuff, then black-out on the honeymoon noises—grunting, bedsqueaking—we hit 'em with both barrels. Then, right at the moment of passion . . . Whhhhooooicht! And this female head comes rolling out of the darkness, with this, well, surprised, expression on her face."

Honey made a chopping hand-motion to her own neck, and pantomimed a grotesque death.

"I have a guillotine in my bedroom?"

"Yeah, you're really gamed into bondage and naughty stuff. Ohhhhhhh . . ." Honey's eyes softened as she spotted a perfect pearl bracelet walking out of Cartier on the wrist of an older lady. As the bracelet got into a waiting Rolls-Royce Corniche, Honey continued, with a spurt of bright enthusiasm: "Pubococcygeals!"

"You do, and you'll clean it up," I warned her.

Honey grabbed my chin in her hand, and shook it. "Focus, Cool. The bride dies, she goes into posthumous multiple orgasms; contractions like crazy; Kegals all over the place; start to focus, Cool, this is important."

. . . . .

Anyway, we go into Cartier's. Slimes like me in Dingos (tiny scuff on right toe) and Stetsons (worn too jaunty) get thrown out of snotty French ice shops like this one. Unless the cowboy boots are playing follow-the-leader with the most famous pair of high heels in the Western World.

Inside, Sheri is walking like an Egyptian, between two glittering display cases, apparently trying to find something for her latest Boy Toy that will update the sundial. [Name deleted] is draping an ice dreamscape around the neck of girlfriend Johnny. This is arguably the coolest ice shop on the West Coast, but the entrance of The Goddess & The Cockroach kicks muted elegance in the butt.

Sheri stalls like an Egyptian. [Initials deleted] drops the ice. A Cartier clerk gasps (whether at the diamond avalanche or at Honey & Ice Man, is not clear). Lookie-Lou mini-mamas beside the gold, and Beverly Hills bimbo-bitches near the precious stones are all zapping

Deity & Insect with an absolute global shitstorm of unholy eyeservice.

Honey is loudly saying the most obscenely ridiculous thing I have ever heard her say, but I almost miss it because of the way everyone is gaping at us. This is why Honey married me. It's really too bad that she's looking so intently up at my face and talking so insistently that she doesn't notice.

We just walk in the store, and everyone acts like they just got splashed with urine-filled exploding water-balloons. Pregnant Goddess & Scuttling Cockroach, and everyone just knows that she has been spreading her legs and inserting that icky cockroach right up inside her . . . without a condom!

Honey's two boys follow us inside, and stand quietly, as unobtrusively as it is possible for Hulk-sized men to stand. Honey's voice is so clear and shrill, that I'm sure while the glass door was open it carried as far as Nebraska.

Nobody in Cartier is speaking, except Honey.

Nobody in Cartier is moving, except The Honey and The Coolest. I mean, I have to move, I'm holding her hand.

This balding, authoritarian jeweler behind the glass case closest to us, probably some French guy imported to run the shop, is bending so far forward toward us that he has to hang on Honey's every word to keep from falling on his face.

The sight of the perfect pearl bracelet deflected Honey into this shop. But she is so urgently trying to communicate to me this movie idea of hers that she's now forgotten why we are in here. She's forgotten even where we are. She's so infected with this idea and the excitement of the thought of the two of us working together on it, that she isn't even aware that anyone else besides me is listening to her. That's the way Honey is when an idea gets ahold of her. Call it single-mindedness, call it selective blindness, whatever, it's why she's the best.

Honey is not whispering. She's so animated she's almost singing. "See, the French Legionnaires used to [f-word deleted] chickens. This was, like, an elitist thing. Officers only! Or maybe they would butt-[f-word deleted] the chicken . . . I dunno, I'll have to check, I've got it written down in one of my old diaries. Anyway, they'd shove their [term for male member deleted] up inside this *bird* . . . it might have been a goose . . . and they'd butt-[f-word deleted] it and butt-[f-word deleted] it until they were just about to [teen slang for orgasm], and then they'd cut off its head with a knife! It was really a big thing with the French Legionnaire officers. The dying spasms of a chicken . . . yes, I think it was a chicken, were considered incomparable. They thought it was better than a woman! *Eat it up!* Better than a woman! The French thought that butt-[f-word deleted] a dead chicken was better than laying a horny woman! Kinda says a lot for pubococcygeal contractions, doesn't it? Oh! Hi, Johnny! Hi, um . . . um . . . *Sheri*! Hi, Sheri. What's up?"

While the famous ladies globbed together to gossip, I discreetly measured Honey's neck-size and then inquired of one of the Cartier gentlemen, "Do you have any diamond-incrusted guillotines for the bedroom, with a blade that can deal with a neck, oh, about this size?"

CHAPTER 34

Anyway, post-Cartier, we get in Honey's limo, ride for awhile, and then debouch. I'm really starting to like that word.

More window shopping. Honey talks better walking, so we're walking.

She's talking.

"See, you're such a naughty Sultan that you've been killing off all the young, nubile maidens, just to get those yummy vaginal contractions."

"Yummy."

"That's where me, the sweet, virginal Scheherazade comes along. I switch everything around."

"Sweet. Virginal."

"You could show a tiny bit more enthusiasm, Cool. Do you have to be so critical?"

"Who's being critical? I—"

"Cool, you dis me all the time!"

"Honey, I think posthumous vaginal contractions are great. I've already ordered a guillotine for your waterbed."

Slowly, she smiled . . . mischievously. "You're so

sweet," Honey said, and then pecked me with a fond kiss. "I have to tell you now. I got you a chicken farm for Christmas. And a big, sharp *knife!*"

Honest to Jack Benny, this is one of the few women who can make me laugh. If it's possible to laugh, and yet almost burst into tears of sheer joy at the depth of my affection for her, that was me at that moment. (So banish me to the Valley of Cliché; I'm McCool, not Shakespeare.)

"OK, I'll be good," I told her. "Listen, Honey." We stopped walking. Honey's bodyguard ahead of us stopped walking. Honey's bodyguard in back, stopped. The slow-rolling limo stopped. Fans following us across Rodeo Drive milled aimlessly, and waved (To get Honey's attention? To get Honey to walk some more?). "You don't need to sell me on anything. If you want me to do a picture with you, I will. OK? Now here's what I want. I want your next picture to *kick butt.* Your last picture didn't do so good. I want your next picture to go right into the heart of America and surgically rearrange the way we pump blood. I want your next picture to do major box-office. I'm just not sure I'm the best co-star to help you bring it off."

"Cool, I know you are! You're hot! We'll be a terrific team. *Ice-99* is killer!"

"Honey . . . Even so . . . I'm just not sure America is ready for necrophilia and anal sex with chickens."

"Pick up a newspaper. Any newspaper. Anywhere."

"That's not what I mean."

"I know what you mean," Honey snapped. "Double-standard bimbo-bullshit."

"That's not what I mean."

"Is So!"

"Honey—"

"Stop right now! I'm an artist, the same as you. I'm an actor, the same as you. You think you can do anything, because you're a man. Well, I can do anything. Because I'm a woman. You think you can play any role, because you don't have the weight of *obscene* fame chaining you to some obsolete image that doesn't mean anything anymore, but that people just won't give up." Some teens across the street started screaming her name: I mean, right on cue. It gets a single-syllable laugh out of her—and a new determination. "Well, I can play any role, too, Cool. People don't see me anymore. They just see my image. Well, I'll MAKE Them See Me! Cool, if I don't break through the goddess stereotype, I'll smother."

"OK, it is what I mean. Just 'cause I mean it, that doesn't make it wrong. The Beatles took their audience with them. They grew and matured, and changed; and they brought their audience right along with them. You lost your audience on your last flick."

Honey made a sound of pain. "Not you too." She turned away from me, and watched traffic. It was a warm, sunny day, but she clutched her shoulders.

I put my arm around her. "We're loitering. Come on. Let's walk."

We walk.

I try to encourage her. "Tell me more about this picture that we're going to make together."

"Cool . . . can we just not talk for awhile?"

"Sure."

Well, as soon as I agree to that, Honey immediately says, *"The Beatles?* My God! Look what happened to the Beatles. You would wish that off on me!? You would curse me with that!? McCartney! I can not listen to ANY-THING that man sings. It's like his brain just SHUT OFF as soon as the Beatles broke up. He puts me to sleep. Elevator McCartney! I refuse to say bad things about George, because he's my fav Beatle. But what about Starr? Hopeless alcoholic. He would have died, and beat John to it, if not for Barbara Bach and almost ten years of her love, and she had to go down into the bottle to pull him out of it!"

Honey was saying some bad things about John Lennon, but I wasn't hearing them, because I was simultaneously saying, "Bullshit, bullshit, bullshit, with a capital BULL, and a big pile of SHIT. Bullshit, bullshit, bullshit. My turn to talk, shut up, shut up, shut up." I put my hand over the most famous mouth in the world, and made it be still. In the process of this, we both stopped walking, and both stopped talking.

"You may be Honey," I told her, "but that doesn't mean you're woman enough to insult John Lennon."

We walked some more, not talking.

I didn't talk, because I didn't have anything to say.

Honey didn't talk, because I still had my hand over her mouth. After awhile it was funny, and she silently giggled.

Somebody shouted something obscene from across The Drive.

After another awhile, I gave Honey her mouth back, unfettered by foreign fingers.

"You will not insult John Lennon," I told her again. "John Lennon was the deepest, most sophisticated comedian who ever lived. End of sentence. When he married Yoko Ono, I laughed so hard I got a *nosebleed*." Pause. "*That's funny*. Now, please continue about our picture. What do Sultans do on weekends? When I'm not beheading virgin chickens, or searching nearby farms for pleasingly plump farmer's daughters, what do I do for fun?"

Honey shook her hair in the breeze, and grumbled. "Oh, you're so Eighties. Mostly, you just kill people and have group sex."

"Standard crack-smoking party animal. OK. What about you? What's so special about Scheherazade?"

"I teach you fun things like fellatio and erotic fairy tales." Honey is dragging her feet, doing little toe things on the sidewalk.

"What are you trying for, an X-Rating?"

"No, we can hold to an R."

"Do you have to play a prostitute? Or courtesan, or whatever."

"But that's Hollywood, Cool. If you're a woman, the only roles in blockbuster A-pictures are girlfriends or moms or hookers. That's it, unless you want to do a small-budget sensitive picture and release it during woman season. The four good high-concept movie parts for women so far this year are all prostitutes! It's not a top-down sexist conspiracy; it's worse, it's bottom-up box office numbers, and foreign receipts that make it that way."

"Yeah, Honey, but look how much the parts for women in movies have improved. The Lady used to be terrorized by an evil meanie, she would faint, and then be saved by a man. Now, Lady Doc waltzes out of open-heart surgery, she's terrorized by an evil meanie, then she cuts him a few good ones with her scalpel before she faints and is saved by a man."

Honey is shuffling her feet; she gives me a sad smile. "I don't want to walk anymore."

So she whistles up her limo, and that's that. The little people are riding up front: three huge, burly men. The Royal One & The-Rug-Beneath-Her-Feet are in the backseat, behind the roll-up window.

Honey is silent and sad. I can't figure out her violent mood swing. Something I said? Something I didn't say?

"What do you want for Christmas?" Honey suddenly asked me. The non sequitur from hell.

I reached my hand over and patted her six-month pregnant tummy.

Honey moaned, and . . . I think the idiom applies here . . . she threw her arms around me. And she hugged me tight, tight, tight. "Don't ever leave me," she said, almost choking with emotion. "Don't you ever leave me."

My right hand wandered over toward the intercom switch. "Jerry, could you pull over, please? I need to get out here."

While the limo eased to a silent stop, Honey kissed the hell out of me. That idiom applies too. There was considerable exchange of saliva. My finger lifted off the intercom switch, but somehow I never got around to opening up the door.

Well, sure, I could go for a little automotive nookie in the backseat with the spousal unit. I was erect and a half.

Honey was in one of her moods. She didn't want to trombone. She wanted to piccolo.

Now, Honey is the consummate cockroachsucker. With or without a condom, she can have my sperm swimming in formation, doing the breaststroke, back flips . . . I mean, she makes fellatio an out-of-body experience.

But, I don't know, it was just something about the three steroid-swallowing necks in the front seat, facing forward. This was the limo without a privacy screen, or a curtain. It probably should have excited me. I can't explain it, but it wouldn't have bothered me a bit if people saw me and Honey screwing, but I did not want people to see Honey with my penis in her mouth. I mean, she was Honey . . . hell, I don't know what I mean.

We all have our sexual quirks, right?

"Cool, stop. I'm a fat cow. Just let me do you."

"You're Honey with a bump. Get it over here."

I tried to pull Honey over me. She tried to stay curled into a ball next to me. Well, she had the advantage: She had teeth.

Honey started giggling. She took my penis out of her mouth, held it, and talked to it: "Cool, will you stop trying to protect my reputation!" She shook my penis. "Oh, you're impossible!" I was half erect, and losing it fast.

We compromised on sexual positions. We both got out of the limo and walked some more.

Well, we're noodling along, but now, for some idiot reason, I'm so horny I can hardly walk.

Honey is walking, so she's talking. "Scheherazade was a pre-feminist female, see, this was before MTV, and she's no mud duck either, but soon's she scopes out your yummy palace, with all your Benzos and Beemers parked out front, she's not about to do a ghost after a one-nighter. Course, soon's she sees you, she's moist, verging on damp, this girl."

"What are Benzos?"

"Mercedes Benz!"

"Oh."

"Anyway, Scheherazade is like, 'Oh, Mr. Sultan, sir, I'm so lonely and afraid, and this is my first time, you know, gosh, could you please invite my sister to, you know, sort of, keep me company? She's prettier than me, honest, and she won't say a peep.' How'd ya'like THAT, Cool? While you're devirginizing me, there's my pretty sister in your bed too, holding my hand." She looked at me curiously.

"Cool, are you listening to me?"

"Yes. So, do you have a treatment on this yet?" Maybe Honey's mood swing was contagious, because my skin started tingling, and I felt really strange myself.

"We're already in pre-production."

"Who's directing?"

"I'm trying to get James Stalling, but he won't talk to me. Do you think you could talk to him?"

"What makes you think he'll talk to me?"

"*Ice-99.*"

Some kind of police action, unrelated to Honey in Beverly Hills, was going on down the block.

It was hard to see what was happening, because afternoon sunlight was blazing off two car windows into my eyes. One police officer was stopping traffic. Another was walking toward us, stopping at each car on the street to speak with each driver. Honey wasn't looking down there, she was looking at me.

"Humm. What are you going to call this movie?"

"Scheherazade Surprise!" Honey said.

I watched the police officer. The car he was standing next to burst into flames.

I heard Honey's voice. "Cool, are you all right?"

The police officer walked up to the next car. He was holding some kind of gun in his hands. It was dripping fire, like a flame thrower. He pointed it at the driver in that car. He torched that car. Fire splattered out onto the sidewalk. The driver and the policeman continued to talk calmly to each other . . . but the driver was burning up. I closed my eyes, but nothing happened: I could still see the cars on fire, the police officer with his flame thrower, he walked to the next car, and that one exploded into flame. I was breathing very fast, and each breath seemed to suck the universe smaller with each inhale. I opened my eyes, but nothing happened: It made little difference whether my eyes were open or closed. "Blue," I tried to tell Honey. "I need to look at blue. Just blue. Find me some blue. I'm having an LSD flashback. I need to look at blue, it calms me. Please, this is a bad one." But my mouth was gone; it did not exist; and my knees were talking the words, like backwards Japanese. The sidewalk was quicksand, trying to swallow me, I was sinking into it.

I turned to look at Honey, but she wasn't there. I could feel a warm, friendly snake coil around inside my shirt, slithering against my skin. It was huge, like a boa constrictor, with a gigantic mouth that was taking a warm soft bite out of my neck.

Then things *really* got crazy.

CHAPTER 35

Honey says I hit her in her right eye with my elbow, pushed her to the ground, and then started taking off my clothes. This behavior did not endear me to the Honey Brigade. Or the nearby policemen.

So there I was, the coolest dude alive, naked on Rodeo Drive, screaming crazed animal noises, and urinating on the second most expensive real estate in California.

Honey knew what was going on, even if nobody else did (myself included). When I ran inside the Chanel Boutique, Honey ran after me. Honey's boys ran after her. And the two cops had to follow, naturally.

Well, Honey is a professional singer with a commanding voice and a natural instinct for grabbing everyone's attention and upstaging even a naked guy yelling like an escaped lunatic. "I Want To Buy Everything In The Store!!" Honey shouted. "I Want To Buy It NOW!! And I Want Everything Delivered To My Home Tomorrow Morning By Nine A.M.!! Put It On My American Express!! Since There's Nothing Left For Anyone Else, Get Everyone Out Of The Store, And Leave Us Alone!!"

Honey shoved her bodyguard with the credit cards in the direction of the counter.

And so, while I fought a wrestling match with a scarf rack (and lost), the Chanel management cleared the store of customers, and the nice policemen brought Honey my clothes.

My flashbacks never last very long, but this was the longest and worst one ever. When it faded out, I found myself all tangled up with a scarf rack and a pile of dresses. I was so tense I was shaking. The tension quickly drained out of me, and I was so exhausted I could barely sit up. My knees were killing me. In my struggles, somehow I had managed to squirm up half-way inside a blue silk party dress, which was now ripped and shredded.

Honey was kneeling down with me, putting her arms around me, quietly saying, "It's all right, Cool. It's all right."

Behind her, I could see two cops eyeing me dubiously. I realized I was naked. (Well, if you had thousands of huge antlike things crawling all over you, you'd damn well get them off you, too!)

In a virile two-fisted way, I covered myself with the dress.

Was I embarrassed? Was I apprehensive?

Very. I mean, what did I do? Are the cops going to haul me off to jail? Did I break things? Christ, I was almost wearing a dress!

I gave Honey my confident take-no-prisoners smile. "Didn't know I was a cross-dresser, did ya!"

Oh, shit. The two cops started walking toward me. They had their pads and their pens out. Probably detailing all my felonies and misdemeanors before they haul me away with their handcuffs.

The gruff police sergeant said, "Honey, I think you're just the greatest. Could I please have your autograph for my son?"

Honey signed autographs for both the nice policemen.

And then the [crude Cool-talk deleted] policemen arrested me.

CHAPTER 36

Fox held my time-slot over for the *Cool McCool Show* until I got out of jail. Robbie didn't get me the moon. But he got me *Mir* & two Space Shuttles the first year, and Star Wars the second year. Depending on ratings, I might get the dark side of the moon the third year.

Either way you look at it.

Attorneys Francis, Lake, Green & Weber were unable to avoid conviction. Exposing myself in public was not that serious. Disturbing the shopping within the Chanel Boutique might have added, at worst, a hundred hours of community service to my punishment. But against the charge of urinating on Rodeo Drive, my lawyers were helpless to avoid a short jail sentence.

The actual criminal charges filed against me were armed assault, resisting arrest, and destruction of property.

In my view, however, my worst offense was naked urination upon a holy shopping shrine. It was the word of three serious Beverly Hills Lawmen against one misbehaving stand-up joker. I was accused of pulling a *Rocks 1*, of uncooperative and violent behavior there in the police station. I have absolutely no memory of attacking three policemen, escaping from the holding area, or of the shootout where I allegedly destroyed a detective's telephone with gunfire.

I can think of three possible ways to explain events.

1) Perhaps I dropped so much acid during the Sixties that it shredded my brain. Maybe I really did go crazy, for a few minutes, there at the Beverly Hills Police Station, and afterward blanked on it, just forgot everything.

2) Perhaps when I admitted to the arresting officers that I suspected that my unacceptable shopping behavior at Chanel was caused by an LSD flashback . . . well, perhaps they began to view me as a dangerous goon in the same category as a PCP user or a crackhead, someone who would be best kept off the street. Perhaps they trumped up the charges against me to protect society.

3) Perhaps the Malibu PD teletype had been communicating with the Bev. Hills PD teletype on the subject of a certain beach house. Possibly my name figured prominently in the report. And perhaps it was decided that in the interest of beach house safety, additional trips back in time by the USS Enterprise should be discouraged.

Francis, Lake, Green & Weber unanimously recommended that we avoid useless delaying actions, appeals, etc., and suggested that I just quickly get it over with. I don't blame my legal advisers for what happened. I wanted to be out in time to be with Honey when my daughter was born.

. . . . .

The first *Cool McCool Show* was almost my last show. It was never broadcast. It is not available on videocassette.

The only people who saw the first *Cool McCool Show* were those in the studio audience.

Backstage, the coolest crew of comedians the Nineties had to offer were all The Show Must Go On and Neither Sleet Nor Snow Nor Rain Nor . . . and they were asking not what their Cool could do for them, but rather what they could do for their Cool. It made my eyes moist, thinking how strongly they were all behind me. Or maybe it was something else making my eyes moist.

Out front were my tools: my ElectroVoice and two 4-packs of Perrier on a convenient little stand.

It was something about the way I walked from behind the curtain out to the microphone.

The studio audience quieted, but did not applaud.

I removed the microphone from its stand, and left the Perrier in its place. I could hear them breathing, that's how still and hushed the auditorium was. 1,600 people breathing. 1,601 people thinking the same thought: Honey.

"Your tickets will be refunded," I said.

They were uncomfortable. I was uncomfortable. There are times when people are just not in a mood to laugh. I put the mike back on the stand. I should have turned my back on the audience and walked off stage. I planned to do exactly that.

Instead, I twisted off the top of a Perrier, and took a swig.

"Zsa Zsa gets her pick of interior decoration to do her twenty minutes of hard time, and half hour of community disservice. What does Cool McCool get? Los Angeles County Jail. Throw the book at celebrities? Noooooooo. Now, normally, if you have some bucks, and the legal system slaps your wrist for naughty behavior, you can arrange for a private cell; but not if you're suddenly the most famous convict in America, and the legal authorities decide to prove to Hollywood that rich cockroaches get treated the same as poor people."

Swig.

"My jail cell was prison-room pink. I mean, I could vomit and come up with a better color. It was a two-man cell. My three cellmates were a 7-11 robber, a Cessna hijacker and an attempted cop-killer. I'm there for pissing on the sidewalk. Cross-section of America, right there."

I shook my head and took a swallow of Perrier.

"I was a little worried that I wouldn't be able to get aspirin while in prison." Pause. "I get nasty headaches sometimes, and I'm used to taking a lot of aspirin for 'em." I sort of laughed. "First day, first [f-word deleted] day, one of the guys offered me two free tabs of Window Pane, and told me he could get Sunshine, Brown Dots, Zen, Strawberry Fields, whatever I wanted. This guy says he's heard all about me, knows I used to do a lot of acid, and wants to be my friend. I thanked him, but told him that I really preferred crack. So he showed me his bag of brown rocks, and he assembles his pipe. The crack pipe was made out of a Bic pen, part of a stapler, a penny, and a melted Styrofoam coffee cup. I admitted that I was only joking, but that I could really use a pack of Camels. And so to the American Cancer Society, I formally apologize. Almost the whole time I was behind bars I smoked tobacco. Everybody got a big laugh out of watching Cool-on-TV tearing up cancer sticks, while Cool-behind-bars chain-smoked them. I apologize. I have once again quit."

A dry, sad pause. About ten seconds.

Swig. Actually, I needed two swigs and a gulp at this point.

"I know the rumor-rag stories say that prison life revealed me as a wimp. One story said that I was reduced to tears and that I cowered in the corner of my cell. Not true. Another story said that prison life turned me into a bed-wetter. Not true. The guys there at LA County were real friendly. But I don't want to give the impression that all the men at LA County were well-behaved. The first night, one of the guys tried to crawl into my bunk with me. The second day there, I was raped."

Swig. I opened my mouth to talk. Didn't.

Swig. I tried to talk again.

Swig.

"I'm not ready to talk about the unpleasant specifics of forced anal sex, from the receiving end of things. I'm also not ready to talk about the unpleasant specifics of my third, fourth, and fifth days at Los Angeles County Jail. Everybody. And I do mean everybody. From the warden on down. Every prisoner. The 7-11 robber, the Cessna hi-jacker, the would-be cop-killer, everyone at LA County knew that I had been raped. And everyone knew who did it. We are talking a massive loss of self-esteem. A catastrophic loss of face. I became the lowest form of animal life. What happened to this horny homo rapist with the dirtied dick? Nothing! The son of a bitch is strutting around like King Fag at the eyeball palace."

Swig and a half.

"Well, I don't know if prison life corrects anything that's wrong with men, but it sure as hell corrects heterosexuality. I had to fight to protect the sanctity of my asshole. You would not believe the number of men who wanted to [f-word deleted] the one who [f-word deleted] Honey. Take a toothbrush. File down the tip, heat it with matches to harden it up, and you get a sharp, usable cutting weapon. Melt down Styrofoam coffee cups and you get . . . well, let's just say that there are lots of things you can use for weapons. Desperation is the mother of invention."

New bottle of Perrier.

"There were killers who wanted me for their babe, and they promised to keep me perfectly safe. But, I'm sorry, that just wasn't Cool."

I contemplated very carefully my next few words. I raised the bottle to my lips, but did not drink. I lowered the bottle.

"On my sixth day at LA County, someone threw hot cooking oil in the face of the guy who raped me."

Big swig. I needed that.

"It hard-boiled his eyes. Blinded him. And as unbelievable as it sounds to the guys who knew him, the hot oil made him uglier."

Swig.

"Now, you have to understand, this blind-rapist had

been there at LA County Jail for a long time. He had a lot of enemies. He was a huge, repulsive [underworld unmentionable deleted]. I'm sure a lot of guys had been meaning to clobber the sonofabitch. But within ten minutes of his hot-oil douche (I think that's a fair statement alluding to the looks of his face), everyone in the prison, from the warden on down, knew that I was the guy who did it. Never mind that I've got the perfect alibi, everyone KNOWS that I did it."

Swig. And I put on my face the most honest, trustworthy expression that I own.

"I didn't do it. I don't know who did it. But everyone else knows that I did it. So instantly, I'm BMIP, Mr. Macho, and everyone *stands back*, and *steps out of my way*. And what, you may ask, happened to the guy who EVERY-ONE KNOWS blinded the [vulgar rape word-play deleted]? Nothing! I'm the skinniest macho-man in Los Angeles County Jail. Guys offer themselves to me; will I please protect them? They will [the gamut of passive fellation, active irrumation, and absurd anilingus deleted] for hours just to be my babe, so other guys will leave them alone. I mean, Back Off!"

Swig.

"Besides, I'm only going to be there two more weeks. Honey wanted to give me her Get Out Of Jail Free card, so one day she came to visit me. Against orders. I told her, never, uh-uh, no way, don't you dare come to see me. I figured I could deal with letters and phone calls, but I didn't want to look at Honey and have bars between us. Actually, the steroids were very considerate. (That's what we call the guards: steroids. It's because their muscles are phony, while ours are real and hard-earned with the weights.) Anyway, they gave Honey and me a room to ourselves, with only one steroid observing us from a distance. During a few seconds when he turned his head and wasn't watching us, the most famous pregnant woman in the world took a little baggie out of her blouse, quickly reached way down, and smeared the gooey, smelly fluid on the prison floor."

Swig.

"Inside joke."

Swig. Nobody's laughing. But nobody's bored. Everyone is silent. Rapt attention for the first, and almost the last, *Cool McCool Show*.

"Anyway, they put me on a prison bus. Los Angeles County Jail is too good for me. Where are they taking me? Sacramento County. Why? I don't know. The steroids are real friendly. We're having a great time. It's just me. A whole goddamn prison bus and it's just me and the three guards. We're kicking back, watching videos on the bus. Stone: *Rocks 7*. Douglas: *Black Rain 2*. Well, this place we're going to is in Northern California. So we stop halfway for some food. And the guys are real considerate. I talk them into pizza. Screw Burger King, I want some PIZZA! They let me out of the bus to walk around for awhile. I get back in the bus, and something has changed. They've been talking on their radio. 'Sit down, convict!' one of the guards yells at me. I sit down. And he unsnaps his gun and pulls it out, and he and another guy come over to me. The other guy's got some kind of black cloth in his hands. He snarls: 'If you bite me, faggot, I'll blow your brains out.' 'Why would I bite you?' I ask. But they're not interested in conversation. The black cloth is a black bag. They put it over my head so I can't see anything. Then they handcuff my wrists and my ankles to this bar right near the floor. Not a comfortable position for a bus ride." New Perrier. "OK, so maybe pizza was not such a good idea."

CHAPTER 37

I can see that Herschel, my producer, never went On-Air with this, but he's got all the cameramen taping like crazy.

"I know the name of the institution where they took me. But I'm not going to say. We'll call it Prison X. Say I'm paranoid, if you want. I didn't see too much of Prison X. When they took off the black bag over my head, I was inside a green interrogation room. It was a weird green. I could never decide whether the lights were incandescent or fluorescent, but they bathed the room in an eerie green that was like . . . it was almost like being underwater. Oh, you'll love the way they walked me out of the bus. They left my hands handcuffed. And they left my ankles handcuffed, or ankle-cuffed, however you want to say it. And these are, like, *handcuffs* on my ankles, so all I can make are little three-inch steps. The guard in front of me had some kind of a hook on a stick that he was pulling me along with, when he wasn't poking me in the stomach with it. And they put a rope around my waist, and one guy was pulling me from behind, so if I started to lose my balance he would yank me backward. I had to jump down the steps of the bus, and I can't see anything, they've still got the bag over my head. But . . . it didn't really worry me. I mean, I've been through frat-initiations, and some mild hazing in the Army, and I figured this is just something they do to all the incoming prisoners at Prison X. What do I know? Judge Keble at my trial made such a big thing about how he was going to treat me just like any other citizen, and completely disregard the fact that I was the most famous husband in America. So: equal treatment; I can handle it."

Swig and a half.

"Well, when they take off both my cuffs, and the black hood, I'm in the green room, and everyone's wearing surgical gloves. What, me worry? These guys are great conversationalists, too. 'STRIP, FAGGOT!' So I take off my clothes, and they sit me down in this cold chair, in this cold room, and I have to hold my ID in my hand. The whole time I'm in the room, they make me hold the ID in my hand. I mean, if they forget who I am, they can look, right? Let's face it, prison guards are not MBAs. Well, this new guy comes in, and he's got this Doctor's Bag with him and a female assistant. And this guy gets serious. Surgical gloves. Face mask. Goggles. [F-word deleted] goggles for his eyes. 'I didn't do it,' I swear. 'I didn't do it. I haven't got any hot oil on me. And I promise: I won't throw my ID in your face.' 'Skinny butt-[f-word deleted], isn't he?' the Doctor-type says."

Swig. I did not like remembering the green room.

"He gets out this hypodermic. And some other things. First, I thought he was going to shoot me up with something. But he wants a blood sample. Well, I tell him that they've already got samples back in LA, can't they just FAX the reports up here? He shoves the needle up my arm and sucks out about half my blood." Perrier suck. "And as he was sucking out the blood, I figured it out. It's scut-face corn-holer with the seeing-eye dog. C. Everett Koop was right: Yes, you can get AIDS by pissing on the sidewalk; if you're a celebrity, and the judge is running for reelection and throws the book and the made-for-TV-movie at you, and you wind up at Los Angeles County Jail with horny-homos manufactured by the Southern California penal system who rape you up the ass without a condom. Well, it takes three of them to do it, but they haul me over the chair, and hold me, and the Medical mother-[f-word deleted] rapes me up the ass with his fingers. I don't know what he was doing up my ass, but Jesus Christ, it hurt! It hurt my ass, it hurt my balls, but most of all, it hurt the tip of my penis. Imagine the worst pain you can think of: That's it. My dick is leaking semen or something, and he gets a sample of that. Well, I figure, now I've felt everything. Wrong. It gets worse. When he's finished, he daintily wipes my anus with toilet paper. I'm naked, bent over this chair that's bolted into the floor; one guy wearing surgical gloves is holding both my wrists; one guy with gloves is holding my right leg; another guy with gloves is clamped onto my left leg; this woman is standing back watching, but she's wearing surgical gloves too, just in case; and this Doctor Son-of-a-bitch is daintily wiping my butt with toilet paper." I shook my head. "I cannot express the depths of my outrage."

So I drank some more Perrier.

"Well, even proctologists eventually run out of fun things to do in the anal region. They let go of me, and sit me back in the chair. So, I figure, now I'm initiated into Prison X. Now, I've felt everything. Wrong. *New York Post* November 3. The one that broke the HONEY HAS AIDS story. Big picture of Honey on the cover."

Pause.

"They wouldn't let me read it." Pause. "Not that I would have wanted to read it." Pause. "They shoved the front page in my face, and started . . . verbally abusing me."

Perrier.

"I didn't believe it. The *New York Post* isn't information, it's kitty litter. But God . . . it gutted me. That they would do that to Honey; print such total bullshit about my woman, and throw it out into the world, display it on the newsstands, and the checkout counters . . . it killed me. I needed to go to her, comfort her, hold her, and then go out and fire-bomb the editorial headquarters of the *New York Post*. Instead, I'm naked, in some cold green prison room, holding my prison ID in my right hand, and I'm guarded by idiots wearing surgical gloves who believe every [convicts' jargon deleted] word of it. I can see it in their eyes: It's all my fault; the cockroach has given their Goddess AIDS. And these guys are not happy about it."

End of Perrier.

Why am I saying all this? I don't know. Except for one woman near the front over on the left who is sniffling, everyone in the studio audience is a dead hush. They're hardly breathing. I don't need to up the house lights to recognize that single, lonely sniffle. That subdued whimpering is the sound of Mary Elizabeth McEnroe.

I continue. "I figure I was in the green room about 30 hours, while they insulted me. I guess they were afraid I would spit AIDS-germs on them, so they taped my mouth shut, and spit on me. After a long, long while, the first three guys have about yelled and spit themselves out, so they turn the insulting over to the second shift. So two other guys with surgical gloves insult me. They didn't spit at all. I liked the second shift. Then a third shift with gloves comes in. These two guys don't spit, either, and one of the guys is really quite erudite. This guy can really verbally abuse. I'm impressed. I'm also thirsty. After a long, long, long while, the three original assholes with gloves come back. I try to tell them I'm thirsty. Big mistake. They start spitting again. I can have all the spit I can drink. In retaliation, I pissed on the leg of one of the guys."

Beginning of Perrier.

"I think he would have killed me, if he hadn't been so scared of getting AIDS. I've never seen a guy strip off his pants so fast. It took two pairs of surgical gloves to hold the guy back. While he frantically doused his legs with rubbing alcohol, and they were arguing over whether to kill me, maim me for life, or merely beat the shit out of me, I finished emptying my bladder. I aimed my penis upward, pissing a perfect long-range high-pressure arc up into the green air, which splashed down at the feet of the struggling guards, who cursed and scurried out of firing range. I wiggled my penis back and forth, creating really neat patterns in the air. Jail life was beginning to spoil me, so I just waited afterward for someone to come over to me with toilet paper and daintily wipe the few drops from the tip of my penis." This got a few titters. But just a few. I wasn't playing for laughs.

I looked at the Perrier, but I wasn't really thirsty.

I wanted to scream: Shut the [f-word deleted] up, Elizabeth! Security! Will you grab that weeping woman and get her the hell out of here!

"They don't use rubber hoses anymore. You know what they use? You'll *never* guess. Twenty questions, and you'll never guess. Phone books. *They beat me up with phone books!* I didn't know what to think, when they each grab a big thick phone book with both hands, and started coming at me. You wouldn't think getting hit with a phone book could hurt very much. Wrong. These guys are pros, not like those LAPD amateurs. No marks, no broken bones; just the pain. Afterward, they dress me and they put me in the hole. Solitary. Armed 7-11 robbers, and Cessna hi-jackers, and would-be cop-killers are kicking back in their pink jail cell, going out on weekend furloughs to screw their wives and girlfriends, and other mens' wives and girlfriends; they're smoking crack and dropping acid and having a really great time . . . and I get solitary confinement. The other guys in the Prison X hole are crammed two, and sometimes three to a cage. But not me. Cool McCool gets put on first-class ice. Solitary solitary. Do you know what it's like for a professional comedian to have no audience? They really know how to torture a guy. On the little walk to my new cage—actually, they were mostly dragging me—I lifted what I thought was a knife out of one of the guard's pockets. Big disappointment. It's a felt pen. I palm it and keep it anyway."

Swig. Now I was thirsty.

"Solitary confinement is like being locked in a bathroom. 'Been there. Done that. What's next?' And this bathroom is the size of a closet. It's like, about three feet wide, seven feet long, and six feet tall. I can't even stand up straight. There is nothing to do. Nothing. And these guys are so cute. There's one light. They turn it on and off about every hour. One hour on. One hour off. When it's off, it's absolute blackness. When it's on, it's this dingy yellow. In each of the corners of the ceiling, someone has drawn a female crotch with legs. Cute. Well, I made playing cards out of cigarette wrappers, and played every solitaire game I could think of or invent. NG. I need people. I need an audience. So I draw an audience on one of the walls. Hundreds and hundreds of people, laughing at my wonderful humor, some of them standing up, applauding me. This felt pen is great. It's some kind of laundry marker that supposedly will mark on anything. Does a great job on painted steel. Now that I've got an audience for my jokes, I work on my routine."

Swig, swish & swallow.

"Solitary confinement cuisine is pretty flat. Lunch is delivered in a brown paper bag. Maybe tuna sandwich, an orange, a brownie, carton of milk. Unfortunately it has to fit through a slit that is one inch high, so the [prison jargon for homosexual guard deleted] outside stomps on the bag to flatten it out, pours the milk inside it, and shoves it through the slit in the steel door. Yummy. So on another wall, I draw an open refrigerator, and stock it up with all the goodies. Beer. Steak. Fresh fruit. Ice cream. TV-dinners. I draw a TV to watch, while I'm eating the TV-dinners, and I draw a microwave to heat them up with, and a stereo to play some tunes. I draw a cable-TV hook-up, so I can see myself in reruns, and finally I draw a telephone so I can call Honey and comfort her and tell her that they're all assholes and who cares what they think anyway; then I whisper some sweet love-stuff to Honey over the phone."

Swig.

"While I was in the hole, there was a murder. [All particulars of the brutal, racist killing deleted by publisher.]"

Perrier time. The audience was audibly troubled by my vicious chronicle.

"Things are pretty quiet in the hole after that. But I can't sleep. It's the damn light. It drives me nuts. No matter how I turn my head, the light is in my face. I toss and turn for forty-five minutes or so, just barely fall half-way asleep, and suddenly I jump up, wide awake in total blackness. I fall back asleep, and then this blinding light wakes me up. When the light goes on, it wakes me up. When the light goes off, it wakes me up too, I don't know why."

Swig.

"So this light has got to go. It's mounted into the ceiling behind this clear, indestructible plastic, held in place by six hex-key aircraft screws. My matches don't do a thing to the plastic. Well, the only metal I've got in the cell is my zipper tab and the clip on the felt pen. But there's nothing else to do in solitary, so I go to work on the aircraft screws. By using up all my matches, I melt the one-way plastic inserts, so they will turn, and by scraping on them for hours and hours, I get enough of a groove in them to turn them backwards and get inside at the light bulb. I unscrew it, and settle back to get a good night's sleep. In the morning (Local Hole Time), my spirits are up, and I want to have some fun. So I screw the light back in, wait for it to come on, and then I unscrew the bulb and short the circuit out with the clip from the pen. Then I put everything back, except a circular strip of metal, which I hide. Never waste a piece of metal in prison."

Swig.

"Well, after awhile I hear all this yelling. There's a damn riot going on in the hole. Yelling, banging. They want their lights. So I start yelling too. 'I want my blinking light!' The lights for all the cells in the hole are on the same circuit breaker, so when I shorted out mine, they all went out. After awhile my light comes back on. So I short it out again. It comes on . . . I short it out. I do it about ten or twelve times. Then the power stays off. I put the cover back. And there goes the riot again. They want their lights. So I'm yelling too. 'I want my blinking light!' After a few hours, two guards and an electrician open up my cell. They've each got flashlights. They're joking to themselves until they see that I've drawn pictures all over my walls. Apparently, crotches in the corners are OK, but refrigerators and telephones are definitely OUT! The big, fat [prison homosexual lingo for fag-guard watchqueen deleted] gets so mad his face turns red. He picks me up, and throws me outside into the hallway, and yells various obscenities at me. The thin guard behind him thinks it's kind of funny, and the electrician thinks it's really funny. But the one big guard is pissed to the max. He goes in my cage and grabs the marker off the top of my sleeping space."

I stopped for a drink of Perrier. Thank Charlie McCarthy for Perrier.

"I never bothered to hide the marker because I knew that as soon as they saw the walls they'd demand it, and I knew that the first place they would look for it would be up my ass. The hell with that. So now the big, fat guard is shining the light and shaking the marker in my face and yelling at me and spitting at me, and slapping me around a little. While this is going on, an interesting thing happens. The other guard and the electrician leave to check another cell first. And they never came back to my cell. They Never Checked My Light. Well, this big, fat [f-word deleted], he shoves me back in the cell, and before he leaves, he tells me, 'Oh, yeah, I forgot to tell you, McCool. You're a daddy! Honey pushed out a pup. You're the father of a five-pound, one-ounce dead baby boy.' And then he laughs so hard he about shits in his pants, and locks me up again in the dark."

CHAPTER 38

A heckler said something inappropriate, and for the first time in my career I did not counterattack. I did not have to. The people around him said, "Shushhh!"

I continued. "I got a good night's sleep in the unblinking darkness. I didn't believe the guard. I knew it was all mind-[f-word deleted]. The next day, they take me out of my cell, and park me out by one of the guard stations, handcuffed to a bar. The guard there wants my autograph. I give it to him, hoping that he won't spit on me. Nobody is wearing surgical gloves anymore. He tells me that I'm HIV-negative. And that's all he tells me. Meanwhile, there's all this activity going on. All these guys hauling heavy equipment back and forth. Two trusties go by with paint and rollers to repair the damage to my cell. OK, so while I was out handcuffed to the bar, I hear these two jack-hammers start up. They're making a hell of a lot of noise, all these outside construction people going back and forth, extra guards watching them, carrying out huge chunks of concrete in wheelbarrows."

Swig and a half.

"This guard won't tell me shit. But at the shift-change, the thin guard takes over this station, and he's friendly. He changes my handcuffs and loosens them so they're more comfortable. And we talk. He says he's sorry, but it's part of his job to turn the lights to my cell on and off every hour. I commend him for his timely dedication to duty, and ask him about all the construction bullshit that's going on all around us. He says the electrical wiring is shorting out underground, that the pipes are so old that the electrician can't pull the wires out and put in new ones. So they have to dig the pipes out and put down fresh wiring. Well, I'm sorry, I know comedians aren't supposed to laugh at jokes, but damn, this was about the funniest thing I'd ever heard. They were tearing the [f-word deleted] prison down, just because I had shorted out my electric light with the clip off a laundry pen."

Two swigs and a half.

"Well, the guard thinks I'm crazy because I'm laughing so much. I really can't stop laughing. I laugh and laugh. The guard takes a folded newspaper clipping out of his shirt pocket, unfolds it, and says, 'I'm really sorry, Mr. McCool.' He wants me to look at the newspaper clipping. So I do. It's from today's *Sacramento Bee*."

I dropped the damn Perrier bottle. It clunked on the stage, rolled around, foaming out the top. I went over, bent down and picked it up and set it on the stand.

"The newspaper clipping said that Honey was in New Cedars Hospital. She had given birth prematurely. The male baby had lived less than three hours."

A long pause, with only the sound of female sniffling

coming from one Cool McCool fan.

"For the first time, since I'd been in prison, I was afraid." I tried to find words to explain the depths of my fear, but there weren't any words. "I asked if I could call Honey. The guard said no. I asked why. I don't remember my exact words, because I was so upset—as I remember, I was even stuttering—but I said something about the unreasonableness of my punishment, and I demanded to know why I was being treated this way. The guard said that he was instructed not to convey this information to me. I asked him if showing me this newspaper clip was part of his instructions. He said yes, it was. Well, then my fear went away. I think I couldn't afford to believe it. Anyone with a Macintosh and a laser printer could knock out phony newspaper clips on both sides of aged paper. So I didn't believe it. It was mind-[f-word deleted]. They won't allow any outside communication, because they know that if I talk to Honey, I'll find out that she's home in Bel Air, growing our soon-to-be baby girl, and thinking up long lists of boy's names. So these guys are just playing with my mind. Does it bother me? Nah. I'm playing with their electrical plumbing."

I opened a new Perrier and drank it right down like carbonated water.

"Everybody makes mistakes. My mistake was taking the circular strip of metal out of the light receptacle. It was stupid for several reasons. I might have killed someone with it. Cut it into fourths, sharpen up the edges, and support it by a make-shift handle, and it would be perfect for cutting throats. I'm here for pissing on the sidewalk; all

I need is to murder someone, right? Actually, my violent fantasies mostly concerned cutting off the fingertips of the head-waiter of Prison X Catering Service. But also, it was stupid of me to remove the metal strip. I can get it any-time. I don't need it under my cot. Leave it where it is. If I think of a use for it, I can get it in three minutes."

I've cancelled the show, and it's already turning into a two four-pack routine.

"Well, the construction work stops. Big silence in max-imum security. I figure it's quitting time. Then the fat-fag peek-freak screw comes charging up the bars in the hallway, madder than . . . well, madder than a guard who's just been pissed on. The guard who was in charge of me sort of liked me, so there was no actual physical violence to my person. Fifteen minutes later, the suits showed up. The electrician is there, the trusties who were painting my cell are there, and everybody is yelling, and passing the buck Big-Time. They've found the circular metal band from inside the light receptacle, they've found the metal clip that I shorted out the circuit with. They've found me out. The [criminal colloquialism for warden deleted] is there. He just listens to everyone shouting and dis-claiming responsibility as he looks at me. He's got this sweet, dangerous smile on his face. It's the same smile one of my old girlfriends gave me just before she clob-bered me in the left testicle. Some other suits are there. Lawyers? Jailers? Prison Officials? I don't know. Then, I swear to Joe E. Lewis, the [same criminal colloquialism for warden deleted] winks at me. He [f-word deleted] winks at me. He tells them to put me on the bus.

Professional killers, they like; it's amateur electricians they can't stand."

Swig.

"The hole at Prison X is too good for me. No more First Class treatment for McCool. So I'm going for another bus ride. Well, I'm used to bus rides; no sweat. They put the handcuffs on my ankles, and on my wrists, and they put the black bag over my head; I hop on the bus, and they handcuff my arms and legs to the same little bar down near the floor of the bus."

Swig.

"I'll be doing physical therapy for three or four more months, just to get 98% of full-mobility back, after that damn bus ride. Because the bus ride was my destination. I don't know how long I was on the bus. About a week. The longest week I've ever spent in my life. Sometimes there were other prisoners on the bus with me. Sometimes I seemed to be the only prisoner on the bus. I even had to take a piss and a crap while handcuffed and blind-folded and legcuffed. There was no dinnertime. I had to tilt my head up and drink through the black bag. I'm seri-ous. They never took the bag off my head, until they stopped to give me a shower. It seemed I was stinking up the bus. I don't know, for sure, where we stopped, but I think it was a truckstop in Tucumcari, because it remind-ed me of a place in New Mexico where I nearly froze my buns off during the early Seventies while hitchhiking. They had to take the bag off my head because they had to prove to the angry truckdrivers that I really was Cool McCool, the Goddess-[f-word deleted] who had given

Honey AIDS, knocked her up with a stillborn piece of AIDS-shit, and gotten America's heroine so depressed that she killed herself. These truckdrivers in a tantrum, who are giving me the cold water splash with the buckets, are so poetic about it too. These are some well-informed truckers. They have even read *Entertainment Weekly* magazine. They know that Honey drives a V-16 Cizeta-Moroder. And they tell me this total bullshit about how my wife has front-ended her Cizeta at 190-miles-an-hour against an eighteen-wheeler hauling steel rebarb. They're so cute with the made-up gritty details, too, like how her car's average height after the collision was eight inches. And these guys are really convincingly angry as they drench me with the cold water, and whop me up-side the head with the tin buckets. I mean, this is state-of-the-art mind-[f-word deleted]. Where did the prison system get these guys? Central Casting? I want these guys for my next Cool McCool movie. I really have to admire the length to which they are willing to go to jerk me around and [f-word deleted] up my mind."

Mary Elizabeth wasn't the only member of the audience audibly in tears. I was silent. I had run out of words. I wanted to tell them how I had dealt with the truckers from "Hollywood," about the rest of the bus ride, about how they had finally released me; about the press conference where the prison suits had sat there, all lined up, and suggested that I please tell the reporters how I had been treated appropriately and humanely; and how I had been so numb with shock and weak from lack of food that I had been unable to even respond, as I discovered from the reporters' respectful questions that the most famous woman in my heart was dead. That's a lie. The only woman in my heart.

CHAPTER 39

If DiMaggio can lay down flowers forever, for his lady, can't I do it too?

Violets.

Fresh.

Three times a week.

Just the way she likes it.

Forever.

. . . . .

As you know, all her biographies have been at pains to point out that there is no evidence that Honey ever tested HIV-Positive. A small fire at the office of Honey's gynecologist destroyed Honey's complete medical history. At the laboratory which routinely worked up Honey's medical tests, a sewage overflow obliterated the computer disks and hard copies of Honey's coded test results. Removable hard-disk back-up files, stored in the lab's special fire-proof (but not water-proof) bottom file cabinet, also were damaged and proved unretrievable.

Honey's Doctor, now, and in the foreseeable future, refuses to disclose privileged information. Laura Boyer and Geoffrey Neely, reporters (I use the word advisedly) for the *New York Post*, have decided (in a prepared statement) that in light of the strange complete disappearance of their journalistic documentation (both the originals, somehow misplaced at the editorial offices, and the copies apparently lost during a burglary at the Law Offices of Ellin & Berube) and because of the impending lawsuit filed against them for slander and defamation, well, they have decided that they must have been mistaken: Boyer & Neely officially stated that their November 3rd story on superstar Honey is false; they retracted the accusation that Honey tested HIV-positive. Disclaimer Time In Hollywood: All I know about any of this is what I read in the papers.

I don't believe that Honey committed suicide. She was depressed because of her second miscarriage and the HIV- & AIDS-Headlines, but I think she was just going for one of her late-night speeding trips. I can't explain how she got over onto the wrong side of the I-5 freeway, but perhaps she was trying to evade the police chase that developed.

. . . . .

That's almost the whole of my story, but there is a tiny bit more. Sort of an epilogue.

I never shed a tear over the death of Honey—or at least it seemed like never. I was burnt out inside, unable to work.

Totally alone. There is a sweetness to melancholy that almost seduced me into suicide so I could join her in death.

One month went by without a tear.

A second month went by without a tear.

I began to work again. I discovered that I could function on automatic pilot. I was dead inside, but I could still blow audiences away.

Cool McCool's #1 fan became more persistent in her attempts to get to me. Mary Elizabeth stormed my stage during live performance. She smashed some glass and artwork in the reception area of the Fox studios where I was taping my *Cool McCool Show*. She was arrested breaking into my home in Aspen, armed with a Smith & Wesson. I had to send Timothy down to bail her out of jail and get the charges dropped. I mean, I wouldn't wish that on anyone.

I allowed myself a weekly pilgrimage to Forest Lawn, and I allowed myself a twenty-minute visit, as I solemnly placed another antique cigarette lighter upon Honey's immodest gravestone. There were never any tears.

I never cried until about two and a half months after I got out of jail, when I saw a perfect pearl bracelet on the wrist of a dignified lady, and I thought: I've got to get one of those for Honey . . . and all at once, it hit me.

I was a river, I was gone, I was destroyed.

The same evening that I wept, I visited Honey a final time, and gave her a final lighter. It was a cold evening, and the wind was blowing. The wind blew more tears from my eyes. One by one, slowly, and without water, I began to swallow the reds. I had been drinking. My melancholy thoughts ached so sweetly, with such wonderful pain. My eyelids began to droop. My arms and legs felt so heavy.

I swallowed another red.

And another.

How many barbiturates would it take to bury me next to Honey?

I guess I was so lost in my own thoughts and pain that I didn't hear her, until she was right behind me. Out of the corner of my vision, she walked around and faced me.

It wasn't just my blurry, sleepy vision: Mary Elizabeth looked like hell. Her hair was greasy, her face was pale with a dark smudge across her right cheek, her dress was wrinkled and messy. But what looked like hell, most of all, was the revolver she pointed at my chest.

"I was for you," she said, aiming the revolver at me, holding it with both hands. She was trembling. She was aiming all over the place. Five feet away from me, and her aim was all over the cemetery.

I was going to step toward her, gently take her gun hand, and hold it pointed straight against my chest. I had something terminally witty in mind, something about signing my heart, but my thoughts couldn't seem to come together, and I was so tired, I had to slowly get down on my knees, and then I sat.

Mary Elizabeth continued to point the revolver all over Forest Lawn, occasionally at me, as she trembled, and shouted at me, over and over, as if it were my fault: "I'm not a virgin anymore! I'm not a virgin anymore! I'm not a virgin anymore!"

Sitting up took too much energy, so I lay my head

down on a soft pillow of wind and leaves, closed my eyes, and waited for gunshots.

In a moment I would be with Honey.

But the girl wasn't shooting. Mary Elizabeth was suddenly tickling my face with her hair, and shouting my name, and shaking me, pulling the sleeping pills from my fingers. The last thing I remember, was her shrill scream, as she bounded up and ran away.

And the way the scream continued, down into my sleep.

.   .   .   .   .

Actor-Comedian Cool McCool lives with his wife, Mary Elizabeth, and their son and daughter, Jason and Ivy, in Aspen, Colorado & Beverly Hills, California.